Lincolnshire
COUNTY COUNCIL

discover libraries

This book should be returned on or before the due date.

NEI 01/19

To renew or order library books please telephone 01522 782010
or visit https://lincolnshire.spydus.co.uk
You will require a Personal Identification Number.
Ask any member of staff for this.

The above does not apply to Reader's Group Collection Stock.

D1425164

05252031

Acknowledgements

I wish to thank Dave and Jenni for constant encouragement, help with editing and for their belief in me as an author.

I should also like to thank Jim Palmer, editor of 'Writer's Muse' magazine and Calum Kerr, editor of CK Publishing, for their encouragement and support and for setting me on the path to publication

RED STILETTO

Sheila Adams

BB

First published in 2009 by Bredbury Books
Stockport, Cheshire

Typesetting by Dave Uttley.
Cover design by Sheila Adams and Dave Uttley

Printed and bound in Great Britain by Deanprint Ltd,
Stockport, Cheshire

ISBN 978-0-9564183-0-2

www. bredburybooks.co.uk

For Dave, Jenni and David with much love

1

I'd been violently sick after I'd stumbled across the body, a red stiletto protruding from its eye. In shock, I rang Steve's mobile, rather than ring 999. When I'd finished telling him what had happened in the small country park in the shadow of the Humber Bridge, Inspector Steve Rose's first question was, 'Is that stiletto as in knife or as in shoe, Rach?'

'Shoe. Size six I'd guess.'

'Well, I hope you haven't contaminated the crime scene. What the hell are you doing up there on your own anyway?'

'I'm not on my own. Mum's with me. Or at least she's in Dad's car in the car park.'

'What?'

'My car burst into flames yesterday and Dad won't let me take his car out on my own.'

'But your mum can't drive.'

'Yeah, well. Dad's doing her head in with his broken arm, cluttering up the place and being a rotten patient. He let her come out so she can make sure his car doesn't go up in flames as well.'

'I'm not even going to ask about the car,

sweetheart. When are you going to quit that job?'

'Don't go there now, please. I've just been sick.' I wasn't going to get drawn into our long-running dispute over my job as a private investigator. Steve's been on at me ever since he re-appeared in my life, telling me to pack it in and do something else. Police inspectors don't have much time for private investigators at the best of times, and having one for a girlfriend is practically a hanging offence. He's not the only one. Mum and Dad aren't exactly keen either, though Dad restricts himself to the occasional muttered remark along the lines of 'not what I supported you through university for'. Mum, on the other hand, was going to have a field day if she thought this body had anything to do with my work. She was always reading out job adverts to me, or else reports of dreadful crimes that I might somehow become involved in through my work.

'You still haven't told me why you're up there anyway.'

'Client confidentiality. I can't say.'

'Rach, this isn't one of your normal cases. This is a dead body we're talking about. Sod the confidentiality.'

'Alright, but don't shout at me. I came to meet a bloke called Terry Rogers. He was going to give me some information about the whereabouts of Lucy Turner. She's a missing person case I've just got. Look, I'll tell you the rest tonight if you want to come round, but I'm almost out of credit.'

'OK then. You know you'll have to hang on there until the scene of crime crew arrive and you've

2

filled them in.'

'I know. Oh, Steve, one more thing, can you ring my dad too, and tell him we'll be late, please?'

'Course, I've got nothing else to do.'

'Very funny. Look, I'm sorry for being a nuisance, but I'd be really grateful.'

'Well, I'll see about that tonight then. Bye, love.'

The country park was almost on the banks of the river. A chill wind was blowing down the estuary off the North Sea, and the Humber Bridge loomed high above. It was a bleak place as the pale spring sunlight faded, and I shuddered as I remembered people who'd jumped to their deaths. Everyone had been so proud of the bridge when it was first built. Mum told me they'd talked about building one across the Humber as far back as she could remember. No-one ever really expected it to get built, because it was too difficult to put a tower in the tidal river and it wouldn't actually go anywhere of any importance. Eventually though, engineering whiz-kids solved the problems and motorways linked the bridge, and Hull, to the rest of civilisation.

It was starting to rain by the time the police car swept into the car park. I gave a statement to a DI Jordan, suggesting Terry Rogers as the probable victim. As he knew I was Steve's girlfriend, the Detective Inspector didn't keep me hanging around as a possible suspect, so I was soon free to drive Mum home. By the time we left, the place was heaving, and not just with police and forensic people. Why the police hadn't blocked off the entrance road to the country park, God only knows. It looked like half of Hull had come out especially to try to get an eyeful. I thought of the £2.70 toll. The bridge operators must be raking it in. On our way in, Mum had held up the queue for ages, scrabbling round for change, complaining that she'd had to give all hers to the milkman. As tempers had frayed behind, I'd slipped low in my seat and pretended she wasn't with me.

Mum and I made a detour on the way home to my favourite bakers to stock up on fresh cream chocolate éclairs. I could still see the victim's face in my head but the cakes went some way towards curing the shock. We ate the cakes with a cup of tea while Dad quizzed me over the gruesome details. As she listened, Mum paled and I swear she would have run out of the room, if she hadn't planned on popping round to tell her best friend next door when I'd left. Good job she hadn't actually seen the body. She'd stayed in the car when I got out to meet Terry, complaining about the cold wind outside.

I managed to escape before Gran called in for her usual visit on the way home from bingo, otherwise she'd have had me driving her back to the crime scene for a look. I think that out of all my close relatives and friends, Gran understands the most why I enjoy being a private detective. I like to think I've inherited her thirst for excitement, though hopefully not her craziness. I swear she gets worse as she gets older. She doesn't seem to care what anyone thinks of her. Caked-on black mascara and scarlet lipstick clash with her tight grey perm and her typical outfits include shiny bright-coloured tracksuit trousers with demure cardigans and fake pearls, or plain knee length tweed skirts with garish sequined and embroidered tops.

Steve came round to my flat that night as promised. For once he wasn't late, probably because he was concerned and wanted the whole story. As a result, I'd not had to resort to scouring the cupboards and eating anything that came to hand to stave off hunger pangs. Well, I did have one or two chocolate chip cookies, but they don't count, particularly when you're counting on a bit of exercise with your boyfriend to use up the extra calories.

Steve's often late, or rings at the last minute to say he can't come round. It goes with the job, but I never really get used to it, and I can't say it's a barrel of laughs having a police inspector for a boyfriend. Maybe it'd more accurate to call him my lover and best friend. There are weeks when I hardly see him, so boyfriend is perhaps overstating the relationship, and we don't get many romantic evenings out. We were both at Hull University. He was a Law student and I did English, but we both took a Psychology module and that's how we met. We were boyfriend / girlfriend and it was quite serious till he decided to join the police force. He went off to do his training and never came back. About a year ago I ran into him outside Mum and Dad's house. He'd been promoted to Inspector under the fast track scheme and posted to Hull. He'd come to ask me if I'd like to see the latest Bond film, as if we'd never been apart.

Despite my firm resolve to make him grovel his way back into my life, particularly after the way he'd obviously assumed I'd be unattached, we ended up having passionate sex that first night and I remembered what I'd been missing. Sex of any sort actually, but sex with him in particular.

It didn't seem to surprise anyone when we took up with each other again. Things have changed in that we're older and wiser (well, he's certainly got more serious) and neither of us are sure we want to commit to the living-together, marriage or whatever thing - we've got used to living independent lives. My mum likes Steve and invites him round for tea whenever she sees him. Gran's more blunt about it. 'Rachel's not getting any younger, Steve. She'll make a lovely mother, but she needs to get on with it soon. And I'd like to see her married to someone responsible like a policeman. She needs looking after, always getting into scrapes.'

He'd like to think he does look after me, but as I said to Mum, he'd actually have to be around more to do it properly, and I manage fine on my own. Also, my job annoys him because he thinks it's dangerous. He thinks it's alright for him to run off and chase criminals, but he's not happy when it's me. In truth my job is usually mundane – following spouses and the like. Anyway, because we're both stubborn and like to pretend we're independent, we keep separate flats. Well, at least I think I pretend, but I'm not sure about Steve.

After we'd eaten, Steve settled himself on

the settee and I stretched out, my head in his lap, and brought him up to date on my latest run of minor domestic calamities – the shower had leaked through the ceiling into the flat below, I'd got a virus on my computer and the toilet seat had broken. I thought it best to alert him before he lifted the seat and it fell back down. The thought of it made even me wince, so I definitely didn't want him finding out the hard way. Neither did he. He actually said that if I got a new one he'd fix it, instead of letting me have a go myself. Once the domestic stuff was out of the way, Steve turned more serious.

'Now, about your corpse.'

'He's not mine. I don't want him.'

'Do you want to hear what I've found out for you?'

'Yeah, sorry. What were you going to say?'

'Well, you didn't hear this from me, but the stiletto was probably inserted after death. Could have been to mislead us into thinking his attacker was female. Apart from that and the signs of torture…'

'Torture!' All colour drained from my face.

'As I was going to say, the initial thoughts of the pathologist are that, despite his age, he probably had a heart attack, because there were no other injuries, apart from the torture.'

'I don't think I want to hear this.'

'The victim's little finger had been cut off.'

'Yuck.'

'It would require some force, indicating a man, so the stiletto is probably just a red herring. Anyway, you said earlier you went to meet a bloke called Terry Rogers, and that's why you thought he must be the victim, although you've never met him before. What did you want to see him about? One of your cases? If so, it sounds like you're mixed up in something dangerous.'

'I'm looking for a missing girl, Lucy Turner. Terry was her ex-boyfriend and I thought he might be able to help, that's all. I'm sure it's nothing to do with his death.'

'You thought he might be able to help? Isn't he your client, then?'

'No, that's her current boyfriend, Craig Dobson. He's worried about Lucy because she disappeared almost a week ago and she's been very depressed. He knew Lucy split up with Terry not long ago but didn't know anything about him but his name. He couldn't find a number because Terry's ex-directory and so he thought I'd have more luck, as a private detective.'

'How did you get an ex-directory number then?'

'Er…' I didn't want Steve to know I had a contact who did things that weren't always strictly legitimate. 'Well, I got in touch with the girls where she used to work.' It was true I'd been in touch with the girls, but what I didn't say was, they didn't give me Terry's number.

'This Craig not think to try that?'

'They wouldn't talk to him. One of the girls who worked behind the bar with Lucy was Terry's sister and they thought Lucy should have stuck with him rather than taking up with Craig.'

'So how come you didn't just pass Terry's number to Craig?'

'Terry said he wouldn't have anything to do with Lucy's new boyfriend, and I wasn't to pass on his number. He said he'd meet me instead. He suggested the country park near the Humber Bridge because he worked outside Hull, near the foreshore at Hessle, and he often went and ate his lunch in the park. I thought I'd be safe meeting a stranger there because it's a public place.'

'That freezing deserted park a public place, then, sweetheart?'

'Stop teasing. It's usually full of happy families – and I did have Mum with me.'

'Oh yeah. What did happen to the car?'

'Don't ask me. I was driving it along Holderness Road when suddenly there was smoke coming from under the bonnet and then these tiny flames appeared at the edge, so I got out to take a look. Then it burst into flames.'

'Calamity just seems to follow you around. Anyway, I guess now the trail's gone cold, you can tell Craig you can't find her.'

'I'm not giving up yet. She might be in trouble.'

'You might be the one in trouble if you don't give up on this case, Rach. I don't like the fact that her ex-boyfriend ended up dead, when he was supposed to be meeting you. I've not heard of Craig Dobson, but I'll ask around, see if he has a record.'

'Mmm.'

'And I'll ask Mike Jordan to put out an alert

for your Lucy. You let it drop now, Rach. Leave it to the professionals. Seriously love, I mean it. There's nothing you can do that Humberside's finest can't.'

'Don't you be too sure of that. You are staying tonight, aren't you?'

The next day I felt suitably relaxed and torture seemed a million miles away. I'd been thinking though. Terry might have been tortured for several reasons, but there was just a long shot that it was to find Lucy. If he'd given away where she was, then Lucy was right in the shit, and it was up to me to find her and put her somewhere safe, while the cops put the bad blokes behind bars. I wanted to find out Lucy's mother's address and phone number from Craig. He'd told me Lucy wasn't from Hull and that's why I'd concentrated on the local contacts first. Even though Craig said she'd not gone home to her mum, I wanted to check for myself and if she wasn't there, see if her mum had any other ideas.

Later, much later, of course, this line of thought would seem incredibly stupid, but hey, that's me, dive in first and make it up as I go along. It was a good job Steve wasn't hot-wired into my brain as well as my body.

I pulled on jeans, a long-sleeved red t-shirt, thick jacket and ankle boots and opened the door to that distinctive smell in the air that I've known since childhood. Mum always says it's the fish docks. I'm not sure whether it is, because it doesn't really smell of fish. It's only around occasionally but it's not really very pleasant - well to be honest, it stinks - but somehow it belongs so clearly to Hull that it makes you feel at home. Steve says it makes him feel like throwing up, but he's not Hull born and bred.

Dad hadn't let me have the car again. He said it was to keep me safe at home, but Mum told me he was afraid I'd end up with a dead body in it and bloodstains on his immaculate upholstery. Anyway, this isn't Hollywood; I didn't have a succession of mates ready to lend me their cars, so I rang the insurers and insisted they give me a courtesy car till the cheque came through. After much discussion, they finally relented and said I could have one of those little Ford KAs. Sometimes I'm amazed at how hard I can sound. I'm soft as butter really.

I parked in the multi-storey car park and walked to the amusement arcade in Paragon Square. Even early in the day it was filled with the weirdest selection of people you could imagine – a bit like the creepy bar full of aliens in Star Wars. Most of them looked alien to me, anyway. When I'd last spoken to Craig, he said I could always get a message to him at the arcade, as his mobile had just been nicked and he was hardly ever home. I suppose I should have worried that I'd only got this strange contact for him, but he'd seemed genuinely worried about Lucy. I'd somehow forgotten to tell Steve or DI Jordan about the arcade. It must've slipped my memory.

The brassy blonde at the counter was bored. She was filing her nails among the already unappetising selection of rock-hard scones and those individual packets of biscuits that are always broken. I got a mug of tea. It was as brown as varnish and slopped all down the sides of the mug. I tried to add sugar with one of those thin bits of plastic that don't even remotely resemble a spoon. I hoped that might make me fit in with the crowd of head-scarved, gnarled-faced women who clutched their wheeled shopping-trollies close to their seats, unless there was a chance of taking someone's ankle off. I admit that women like these only live in Hull. You may not believe it, but I've actually travelled out of the East Riding on occasion and I know that headscarves and boxy shopping trollies died out about twenty years ago in the rest of the country. I don't know why I still live here. But it's got a character of its own and it's hard to break free. Ask anyone. People who are born here tend not to move away. Of course, it's also where my family live, and now Steve's here too, and there are miles of sandy beaches just down the road. You have to admit the coast's beautiful, where it's not collapsing into the sea.

Anyway, despite looking somewhat different to her usual customers, I managed to get the blonde to talk to me about the regulars. It seemed like Craig was always in there, fixing up some deal or other. I got the picture. Craig rapidly went from worried boyfriend to evil drug-baron in my mind – possibly with overtones of pimp to escaped Lucy. Craig usually hung out with a Dean Hornby, who owned a pub on Anlaby Road; the Steam Packet – packet as in boat, not container for drugs, that is.

The Steam Packet was just opening when I

12

got there and parked in the car park. It had obviously escaped any attempt to drag it even into the second half of the twentieth century, let alone the twenty-first. The air was thick with dust and the remnants of years of smoke, any pictures or photos were so dirty as to be unrecognisable, the carpet, such as it was, stuck to my shoes and the tables were scratched and burnt with cigarettes. And of course it stank of beer spills, urine, sick and more besides.

I bought a J2O. I can't drink and drive. Apart from Steve killing me for breaking the law if I did, I quite literally can't drink and drive. I can't drink and much else either – one glass of wine and I'm wobbly; two and I'm anybody's, which is another reason Steve would kill me, in case he wasn't with me at the time.

I asked the barman if Dean was there. He said he'd be in later, so I hung around. I didn't have any other cases on the go, and all I wanted was a contact number for Craig. I was sure he must have got a new mobile by then; people can't get by without them for long these days, can they? I'd followed my instincts so far, but I wasn't going to meet Craig again till Steve'd checked him out.

I just wanted to ring him and ask for Lucy's mum's number so I could check for myself that she was fine. I texted a few people, ignored a call from Steve, and was busily writing a shopping list, when the barman shouted across that Dean was in the back, and did I want to go through? I figured with the barman around and the few customers who'd turned up, it'd be safe enough, so I went up the dimly lit passage, through the open door at the end, and came face to face with Craig. I turned back but it was too late …

2

When I came to, my head throbbed and my hair felt sticky and tight, like there was a bloody great lump. I couldn't feel it because my hands were tied behind my back. I was in a cellar. It smelt damp and the marks on the wall suggested it was frequently flooded. I guessed it was somewhere near the river. It was gloomy but there was an open window grille, high on the wall. As my eyes scanned round the room, I heard a moan. Stretched out on the floor was a girl.

'Lucy?'

'Yeah. Who are you?'

'I'm Rachel.'

I filled her in on the details and my stupidity in not seeing Craig for what he was. As I was talking, the penny dropped. I'd told Craig where and when I was meeting Terry. How could I have been so gullible? He must have tortured Terry and got to Lucy. It got me wondering if there was more to my car bursting into flames than just the usual run of disasters that regularly befall me. What if Craig had tampered with my car so I'd be late to my meeting with Terry? I'd borrowed Dad's car but it was really short notice. Maybe Craig was just hedging his bets, expecting Terry to turn up early to check the place out, but trying to make me late as well. He might even have intended that I was in the car when it caught fire. After all, once he had the information from me, I was no longer of use to him, and it would have looked like an accident if I'd died in the car; just an electrical fault.

Things didn't look at all good. If he'd killed once, what were our chances? And it was all my fault. And the cavalry couldn't come because I'd not answered his call, or mentioned the arcade, and no-one would find my car cos it wasn't mine and it was all just too awful to contemplate, so I stopped right there and asked Lucy what had happened to her.

She'd been going out with Craig for a couple of weeks, she told me. He seemed like a nice bloke – he was a plausible liar, after all. Then she'd realised his business deals involved drugs, and she'd just about decided to dump him, when one night there'd been a fight outside Dean's pub and Craig had pulled a knife and stabbed a bloke. Lucy had simply run. She'd been too scared to go to the police. She'd just tried to disappear for a while.

'I feel awful that I led him to you.' The apology sounded inadequate even to my ears.

'If not you, it'd have been someone else. Poor Terry. He really was a lovely bloke. He helped me even though I'd finished with him. I was staying in his flat when some heavies burst in and grabbed hold of me, bundling me out and into a van. They came yesterday, about an hour after Terry went out to meet you.'

'Craig tortured him and must've rung through the address to them.'

'Well I don't blame Terry.'

'You don't need to. He probably didn't even tell Craig where you were. It seems Terry had a heart attack, so Craig probably got his address from something in his pockets. His wallet had gone and there was nothing on his body to identify him. They must've gone round to his flat to look for a lead on you and struck lucky when they found you there.'

'You know, he was only going to tell you he didn't know anything, but he wanted to tell you to keep well away from Craig. He decided to meet you so he could be sure you were taking him seriously. Being too kind got him killed. Anyway, are you OK?' Lucy was trying to sound quite matter of fact, but she didn't fool me. Her voice was shaky.

'Think so, apart from a rotten head and a load of bruises I can't see. What about you?' I kept up the pretence that this sort of thing happened to us every day.

'Same here.'

'Lucy, have you tried shouting for help?'

'Yeah, but there's no-one around for miles. When I was carried in here, I could see it's one of those old warehouses by the River Hull, near where Scott Street Bridge used to be. No-one with any sense comes round here anymore.'

'Have you got anything on you to help us get out of this duct tape?'

'He took my bag away when he snatched me from Terry's flat.'

'I've got a couple of hairgrips. Do you think you could pull one out with your teeth and pass it to me?'

'What good would that do, Rachel? We need a knife for the tape. We're not trying to pick a lock.'

'I'm always losing stuff. When I can't find scissors to cut sellotape, I punch a load of holes in a row and rip along them like perforations. I know duct tape's strong, but let's at least try.'

'OK. Where are the grips?'

'Buried in this lion's mane somewhere.'

I love my long hair, but it is a bit unruly. Just for once I wasn't cursing the fact it was difficult to keep in line. The first grip dropped onto the cellar floor in a pile of dirt, but eventually Lucy got the other grip from my hair and put it between my fingers. I started stabbing at her duct tape. It took ages but the alternative of waiting for night to fall and maybe being taken to an isolated bit of cliff and pushed off, was much worse.

Eventually, using a combination of my teeth and Lucy pulling her tied hands apart, we managed to break the tape along the perforations I'd made. Lucy found the other grip and we worked together to free me as well. By the time we'd finished, a couple of hours or more must have passed and it was getting dark.

'Damn, this old door must be locked. It won't budge.'

'Is there no way we can get it open?' Lucy

sounded exhausted.

'Shh!' I'd heard a car brake sharply and its engine die. I started shaking and offered up a prayer. 'Please God, let me out of here and I'll never keep secrets from Steve again. I'll even give up chocolate and cream cakes.'

I could hear two voices, one of them clearly Craig's. 'I'm not touching them. Let's just torch the place. They'll never get out.'

Lucy and I gasped. We were locked in a cellar and were going to be burnt to a crisp. I thought fondly of Steve and the pile of shirts I'd offered to iron for him. Well actually I thought of the other things on Steve's 'to do' list first, and that cute little top I'd bought yesterday and not had chance to wear for him yet. How the mind wanders when you're under stress.

After several long moments, we heard a crackling sound above us. There was probably plenty of flammable rubbish left in the warehouse. The car doors slammed and it raced away, tyres squealing. We ran to the window grille and screamed blue murder. There was already a strong smell of acrid smoke. At least freeing our hands had given us a chance to get out of this mess. I whipped off my red t-shirt and poked it as far as I could through the gaps in the grille, wiggling it about to try to catch someone's attention. We were nearly hoarse when we heard shouting.

'It's going to be OK, Lucy. Someone's seen us!'

'But the smoke's getting in now'. Lucy

started sobbing.

'You get down low, away from it. They'll ring for help and there'll be a fire engine here in a few minutes. Thank God for mobile phones.'

I conjured up strong sexy firemen in my imagination, breaking down the cellar door and catching an eyeful of me in my bra, but missed the realisation of my fantasy as I must have blacked out with the effects of smoke. I woke up in hospital. Through half-opened eyes I could see Steve sitting by my bed reading a copy of Cosmopolitan, but I couldn't tell if he was concerned or angry. Then I noticed the box of cream cakes on the locker and I knew it was going to be alright.

I moaned as sexily as I could, and opened my eyes fully, prepared for one moment at least to promise to give up my job, to give him my body (again), in fact anything he wanted, if only he'd feed me the cream cakes and hold me tight.

'What the hell did you think you were doing, Rach?' Steve was most definitely not smiling. I'd have to play my cards right for the cream cakes.

'How's Lucy?'

'Don't change the subject. She's in a better state than you, but she's in protective custody. Craig's gone on the run. If only you'd called us in, before walking your way into trouble. Enquiries had already started but you kept the important leads to yourself. If it'd been up to me, I'd have used you as bait. I told you to leave things to us. You nearly got yourself killed.'

'Yeah, but I saved Lucy. You might not

20

have got there in time. By the way, who do I have to thank for calling the fire brigade?'

'A couple of blokes on their way home from the pub saw something red being waved around out of a cellar window. When they got nearer they heard you shouting, smelt smoke and then saw flames inside the warehouse. They rang 999.'

'Good job I was there then, to raise the alarm.'

Steve ignored me. 'God knows what your mum'll say when she finds out.'

'You mean you haven't told her yet?'

'I didn't fancy a tongue-lashing from her. Mind you, at least she'll not let up on you till you pack in the detective agency, so it'll be worth telling her, just for that.'

I didn't comment. I distracted Steve from discussing my job the only way I knew how. 'So if Lucy's got protective custody, does that mean I get it too? In which case, maybe you ought to move in for a few days.'

At that, he smiled for the first time since I'd opened my eyes, pulled me close and said, 'I think that can be arranged'.

Steve may have hated me working as a private detective, but I loved the freedom, and there wasn't anything else I'd had any success at. My degree's in English Lit. The department in Hull's really good, but I misled myself into thinking I'd make a good teacher. The kids rioted and set fire to the waste-paper bin when I was on teaching practice and I didn't fancy spending most of my life panicking at the thought of going to work. I signed on and was sent to a variety of jobs, before being taken on by the Department of Works and Pensions.

Unfortunately I got stuck in the front office, and the clients, as we were told to call them, were worse than the schoolkids I'd run from a couple of years earlier. I tried to get into publishing, but no-one liked the look of my CV and there weren't many jobs to apply for anyway. So I temp'd in offices, doing clerical work all over Hull in the hope I'd find my niche at one of the places I was sent.

By the time my friend Julie asked me if I fancied helping her out in her one-woman detective agency, I was crying out for a change, so thought I'd give it a go. I'd got used to never having a regular income so there was nothing new in that. I took over the business, if you can call it that, when Julie emigrated to New Zealand with her boyfriend. The lure of sunshine and wide-open spaces was too strong for them to resist. I liked the freedom of not having a boss to answer to, so I cleared her ongoing cases, and then people kept ringing and, well, it's just become sort of permanent.

I mainly get suspected infidelity cases. As a woman I'm less likely to be taken for a stalker, and I find people open up to me and let slip all sorts of information, which is useful when talking to neighbours, work colleagues or friends. I've even been asked to follow bridegrooms on their stag night, but if a woman can't trust her man at that stage in their relationship, then that should ring alarm bells without the need for a private detective, so I say just that and turn them down.

In the hospital I'd thought I'd go after Craig when I got out but it was just a knee-jerk reaction to the danger he'd put me in; a need to be in charge of the situation. In reality I knew tracking him down was just too dangerous and not my job. I'd never been involved in anything remotely frightening until this last case. So, after I got out of hospital I really tried not to annoy Steve too much. I was also a bit shaken to tell you the truth, so I even quit the usual run-of-the-mill cases and went back to temping in offices for a couple of months.

At one place I was talking to the HR Manager – that's a Personnel Manager for those of us not into office abbreviations - as I was leaving, and she was really interested in the fact that I'd done private detective work.

'My uncle's having trouble with a pilferer. Money keeps going missing from handbags, that sort of thing. He keeps burying his head in the sand and thinking it'll stop or he'll see someone doing it, but he's too busy to do anything really. I wonder if I could give him your name? Maybe he could give you some temp work in his office now you've finished here, and you could try and track the pilferer for him? He doesn't think it's worth the effort of involving the police.'

I agreed. It seemed an easy and non-dangerous way back into the job. I figured my experience temping would help and also hoped it'd make me a bit more money for a change. I told the manager of Philips Tools and Pipe Fittings that I'd need to be paid an hourly rate like a normal temp for the work I did, but then there'd be my fee and travel expenses on top.

Steve wasn't too happy at first, to put it mildly. He said he'd only moved in with me because he believed I'd promised to give up being a private detective. As if. We had a few words on the subject, and he moved out. It wasn't like we'd broken up or anything, though I did feel the need to ring my mate Sarah and indulge in some retail therapy. She left baby Josh with her mum and we behaved like students again, giggling in changing-rooms and trying on clothes we didn't mean to buy, just for the sheer hell of it. Both of us were short of cash, but even though we only actually bought a cheap necklace each, we were out for ages and really enjoyed ourselves. Being on my own again meant I could wander round in my dressing-gown and slippers eating choccie without feeling like I ought to do something to my hair, so I should have been happy at having my independence back, but some days I had my doubts.

At least it wasn't just my job that made Steve move out. He'd been working all hours on a nasty murder case. The body of a young woman had been found at the bottom of cliffs to the south of Hornsea and although he was tight-lipped about the details, it was clear she was subjected to some kind of unpleasant ordeal before she was killed. I think that affected Steve's judgement as to what was a safe job for me, as well as meaning he was at work more often than not anyway, and his flat is practically on the doorstep of Hull Central police station.

Anyway, he turned up one night a week or so later with one of those enormous bars of chocolate that they only used to sell at Christmas. I'd missed him like hell, but I didn't think I should make it obvious. Nice idea. Keep the man on his toes. Unfortunately I couldn't follow through with that plan, and blurted out, 'Don't I get a hug any more?'

'Sorry, love. Just tired and hungry.' He gave me one of those close all-body hugs I'd been waking up dreaming of. 'That better?' he asked with a smile.

'Yeah, thanks. I didn't mean to moan, but I haven't seen you for over a week.'

'Well, I've brought your favourite chocolate to make up for it. Have you any wine in? We could have a drink and you can tell me what you've been up to. Have you caught your petty thief yet?'

I wasn't about to tell him I couldn't be bothered cooking for myself since he moved out and I got by on any old thing, so I just said, 'Don't you remember me saying they didn't want me till after the Bank Holiday? I've been kicking my heels round at Mum's a bit but I'm bored to death. Sarah's with her other half at weekends and Easter's like a double weekend. I'm even up to date with paperwork and ironing. Another day of this and I'd have been suicidal, but I start tomorrow, thank God. What have you been doing since we last spoke?'

'There was a stabbing down Hessle Road. Not fatal and the attacker got collared. Thank God there were no other new cases today, because CID's so understaffed with the murder case. I'm still working full-time on it. I've spent the day going over all the statements from people who last saw the victim. She's been identified now as Susan Hardy, an au-pair living with the Taylor family in Cottingham. I've been backwards and forwards checking over the facts again and trying to establish a time line. It seems she just disappeared into thin air after going out one afternoon. She'd asked Mrs Taylor for a few days off.

Someone must have seen the killer with her in broad daylight. It's not as if she went missing in the middle of Hull. Cottingham's a quiet well-to-do suburb. The Taylors didn't report Susan missing at first and her parents live abroad. But I just can't fall for the boss's theory that it was her employer, Peter Taylor, who did it. He seems a really genuine bloke and there's not a shred of evidence linking him to the killing, and no motive either. The boss reckons he was having an affair with Susan, but no-one I've spoken to, thinks the Taylors have anything but a rock-solid marriage. Susan just happens to have been a pretty blonde. Oh and Taylor's a photographer.'

'You mean the boss has him down as taking kinky photos?'

'He's just a wedding and baby photographer. Nothing arty, just straight recording of events. The potential link is, and you're not to mention this to a soul, there were photos found under Susan's body.

26

Photos of her chained up, wearing nothing but the flimsiest of tarty underwear, stuff that most definitely didn't belong to her. The boss has had me checking out Taylor's equipment and his suppliers. Despite the fact that nothing matches with the photos at the scene, he's like a dog with a bone. He's convinced he's got his man and won't start looking elsewhere and I'm getting frustrated it's not going anywhere. The photos were just too sick to tie in to Mr Taylor, I'm sure of it.'

'Why didn't they report her missing straightaway?'

'She said she was spending the weekend with a friend. She didn't say who it was, but they assumed it was a girl.'

'So you think it was someone she knew who killed her?'

'If she knew him, she didn't confide in anyone else and it must have been someone she'd just met. She'd only recently started going out a bit more socially. And that's the worst thing - knowing that the murderer might strike again if he just picked her up and groomed her because he had a fancy for degrading and killing a young woman. By all accounts Susan was a quiet old-fashioned sort of a girl. It's a nasty case, Rach. She was obviously kept like a prisoner until she was killed and she must have been very frightened. Then the bastard strangled her and left her body like a sack of rubbish on an exposed beach, where it could have been kids that found it.'

'Oh, love. This case has really got to you,

hasn't it?'

'Maybe because she looked a bit like you, only younger. I'd have worked long hours anyway, but I've not been able to tear myself away. I've been trying to find anything that might point to where she was actually murdered. It's highly unlikely she was killed on the beach. We've put out appeals but nothing's turning up. She seems to have vanished into thin air from the time she left the Taylors' house to when her body was found.'

'Steve, you know what? You really need a holiday.'

3

'A holiday?' Steve smiled sadly. 'No chance, Rach. Sorry.'

'Well you always say, "wait till this big case is over", and this time I'll hold you to it. Promise me please.'

'I'll try. But big cases don't just come along with nice two week gaps between them, sweetheart.'

'If there's only a couple of days' gap, we'll be away and they can't drag you back. At least not if you leave your mobile', I couldn't help but add.

'I still doubt I'll be able to get two weeks off. And what about you? You can't just skip out in the middle of a case.'

'I'd manage somehow. We can't miss out again this year, Steve. Anyway, I'm definitely not going to be out-done by Gran. Even she's having a holiday this year.'

'And where's she going then? Which place is going to suffer the invasion of the mad grandma?'

'You'll never guess! She's going with some of her cronies from bingo.'

'Las Vegas? Torremolinos? Blackpool?'

Steve grabbed me by the waist.

'You're tickling.'

'I have ways of making people talk…'Steve whispered in my ear.

'Mmm. I'd really like to find out what they are, but tea's ready', I giggled.

'Ok. Let's eat. I can live without knowing.'

'Iceland', I produced my trump card.

'I knew you'd not be able to keep it to yourself. Surely you have to be kidding me though. She wears two jumpers, a cardigan and thick stockings in Hull, for God's sake and it never gets much below freezing here!' Steve laughed. 'Anyway, why Iceland?'

'She said…' I was almost doubled up laughing now. 'She said, "because it's there".'

'You what?'

'She must have heard people say it and thought it sounded good. Afterwards though, I heard her tell Mum that Granddad's trawler used to go there. She doesn't seem to realize he went fishing in the waters off Iceland and never set foot on shore in all those years.'

'Maybe she thinks he had a mistress there and she's hoping to track her down and exact retribution?' joked Steve.

'Don't be daft. She was happy as Larry that he was away so much and if he'd had a mistress she'd have said good luck to him and more fool the woman. Happiest day of her life when he eventually ran off with Ada Jenkins from the chippy. Just think of all the blokes she's had hanging round her ever since. I'm actually surprised she's not going away with that bloke with a good head of hair. Though he does have a bit of a limp.'

'Which one's that? Albert?' asked Steve.

'No. He was the one with a few ginger strands combed over the top. Hardly ever took his cap off. I don't know this one's name. She goes through them so quick, I can't keep up.'

'She's crackers, your gran. All your family are a bit crazy, but you're as mad as she is. Maybe that's why I love you.'

'Do you want to eat this pizza now, or shall we have it later?' I teased, turning the kettle off with one hand while the fingers of my other hand intertwined with Steve's.

'Eat quickly and have it later', laughed Steve as he moved out of reach of the inevitable strike from the oven-gloves.

'I might have known food would win out. OK, but just so you know, I'll be turning your mobile off and demanding your full attention.'

I turned up for work on the Monday morning, the week after Easter, at Phillips Tools. The Managing Director had rung me and told me everyone was back in that week. He hadn't wanted me wasting my time working when the thief might be off. First thing in the morning I dressed in an uncustomary suit, blouse and heels, with my hair pulled back in a ponytail. I managed to find a scrunchie instead of a rubber band, to complete the working girl image. I drove up to the small industrial estate and parked my new Fiesta as far away from the skips and piles of metal as possible. I'd only had it a week or so and I intended to look after it. Well, a girl can hope. I know I'm accident-prone.

Amazingly I was on time, and walked in the door a couple of minutes before 8.30. I almost walked straight back out to check that I wasn't in the Tardis. The office looked like it was in a time-warp, decorated and equipped in 1950's style. Striking the only jarring note were the computers, but they looked like they didn't belong. It was no good looking for a reception desk. I was straight in the office. A gormless scruffy-looking bloke, aged around 45 looked up from his copy of 'The Sun'.

'Y'alright?'

'I'm Rachel. I've been sent by the agency', I managed to say. I was vaguely aware of other people sitting at rough-looking wooden desks or leaning against ancient olive-green filing cabinets. One thing was for sure, I was way over-dressed. I should have come in an old tweed skirt and jumper if I'd wanted to fit in.

A woman in her 30s came up and said, 'Hello, I'm Cath. You'd better come with me.'

She led me down the office to a desk, switched on the computer and gestured to a pile of scribbled sheets, which turned out to be orders taken down from customers over the phone by 'the lads'. My job was to enter them on the computer. Fine, if I had a degree in handwriting deciphering or ancient Sanskrit, I thought as I looked them through. Somehow, with the help of Cath when she wasn't filing her nails, I made it through to lunchtime, when I was set free from the splinters on the old wooden chair that had snagged my suit, as Cath told me I could go to the kitchen to make a brew. She said she was going out for lunch and disappeared. There was a kettle and nothing else. I had no teabags, no mug and there was no sign of any spare ones, but a girl who introduced herself as Sue offered me hers as she'd bought a can of coke from the shop.

'I'm right off coffee, now I'm expecting', she beamed. I think she was proud of her pregnancy. She looked about sixteen, and the photo she proudly showed me of her Darren put him at fifteen, tops, in my estimation.

I noted the lack of wedding ring and cautiously asked, 'have you got everything for the baby yet?'

'Mum's got most things from her catalogue. We'll be living with her at first. She's thrilled to bits.'

Somehow I doubted it, but you can never tell. Maybe it was the height of her ambitions for her daughter. I turned to Charlene and Donna, Sue's friends. 'What do you all do here then?'

'I do the typing for Mr Phillips', said Donna.

'And I do the sales letters', said Charlene.

'And Sue?'

'I input the invoices for Geoff.'

'So who's the older lady?' I gestured down the office at a grey-haired lady who was staring into space.

'That's Gloria. She's got Alzheimers', said

Donna.

I waited for further explanations, but none came. They turned back to discussing the previous Friday night's episode of 'Eastenders'.

'And the men?' I persisted.

'Geoff's the bookkeeper, accountant or whatever. The only other blokes who work in the office are Harry and Pete who take the orders, Mr Phillips, and Mr Phillips senior. He doesn't come in very often now. He's semi-retired. Then there's the lads in the workshop. A bit macho, but they're not a bad bunch. You might get to meet some of them.'

Half a day and my money was on Gloria. It beat me why Mr Phillips had seen the need to employ a private detective to catch his pilferer, but I wasn't complaining. I was getting paid for it. When I got back to my desk, Gloria hadn't touched my bag. Maybe it would have been too obvious as she was the only one in the office, but I had hoped to wrap it up quickly before I had to sacrifice another pair of tights and strain my eyes even more deciphering the orders. I left my handbag under the desk when I wandered out to the car, keeping a close eye on it through the window, but neither Gloria nor anyone else went near it.

Later in the afternoon, I got up to go to the loo, then nipped back through the door half a minute later to catch anyone loitering by my desk, but didn't get anywhere either. It looked like I would have to go back the next day with some marked notes in my bag and leave it untouched all day to give the pilferer plenty of time to take them. I was exhausted by the time 5.30pm came. Mr Phillips believed in extracting a full eight hours' work from his employees. I was only surprised he didn't expect the lunch hour to be worked as well. He called me into his office as the others were rushing for the door on the dot of 5.30.

'Poor you. You'll never get away', said Donna sympathetically.

'Have you got the thief?' He wasted no time with pleasantries.

'Well, no, not yet, but I was wondering if Gloria might be taking it without realising.'

'Mum? What do you mean? She's my mother, it can't be her. I've searched her bag of course, but she's totally lost it. Mum wouldn't know what to do with money if she had any.'

It seemed that Gloria was Mrs Phillips senior. She came into the office to feel wanted two days a week, and the other three days she went to a day care centre. At weekends Mr Phillips senior cared for her. They couldn't bear to put her in a home. My growing animosity towards Mr Phillips and his old-fashioned ways shrank considerably as I realised the family were old-fashioned in their attitude to looking after their loved ones as well.

I explained my plan to leave the marked notes in my bag the next day, but told Mr Phillips that it might take several days for the thief to get an opportunity to take the bait. Give him his due, he didn't moan at the extra cost, but said he'd try and call employees into his office in ones or twos, to leave less in the office at one time. He seemed to understand that it wasn't easy to manufacture an opportunity for the thief.

I drove to Mum's for tea as it was late and I was tired. I knew she still cooked for at least one extra person. As I drove I mulled over the possibilities for chief suspect number two. Dad's arm was better and he'd taken Mum to Hornsea Freeport so she was keen to show me her bargains. Gran just wanted to know where Steve was.

'Such a nice lad! And a copper too. You won't do better, Rachel. It's time you snapped him up.' She offered to lend me some rouge so I wouldn't look 'so washed out' and told me for the umpteenth time that I'd have him eating out of my hand if only I made him proper food like Yorkshire pudding, instead of 'that foreign stuff'. She'd be horrified if she knew that I didn't even cook him lasagne, but warmed up frozen pizza more often than not when Steve was coming to eat.

I got back to my flat at about ten to eight. I left their house as the familiar opening bars of Coronation Street's music started up, and drove almost straight home apart from stopping at the off licence for a bar of chocolate. I know I'd had a full dinner, but my feet were killing me in heels and I planned a soak in the bath followed by a glass of wine and some choccie when I emerged.

As I walked up the last couple of stairs I noticed red smudges round the letterbox. I unlocked the door, pushed it open and trod in something sticky. I reached for the light and found myself standing in red paint. It was all over the carpet and my post, giving a whole new meaning to the phrase 'red letters'. There was red paint splashed down the inside of the door beneath the letterbox and therefore it was reasonable to assume someone had poured it through from the outside. I took off my shoes where they were, leapt across the puddle of paint and tiptoed through the flat. Everything else seemed fine. It was hardly an accident so someone must have had it in for me. I wondered who or why. I tried to remember if I'd told off any kids lately, but it looked a bit extreme, spending money on paint to get their own back. Before I spoke to Steve, I thought I'd better see if there were any witnesses. I went downstairs to see Les. He was a nice old bloke, if a bit on the nosy side.

'Hi Les. How're you doing?'

'Alright, I suppose. You're late in tonight.'

'Went to my mum's for tea', I said, knowing this would please him. 'Have you seen anyone hanging around the stairwell, Les? Anyone knock at your door today?'

'No, but I saw a small thin bloke with one of those baseball caps pulled down low over his face. He came in the block but he went up past my door. He was carrying a B&Q carrier bag. I didn't get a good look at him, but I got his number-plate as he was a stranger.'

Not kids then. Thank heavens for Les. He's a one-man Neighbourhood Watch scheme. I got the number from him and made up some story about being left the wrong parcel as I didn't want to alarm him, and went back upstairs to attempt a clean up. It was late when I'd finished, so I made do with a shower and collapsed in bed. Tomorrow I'd get on to the number-plate. I'd been mulling it over in my mind, trying to decide if it had to be Craig, or if it could be another of my clients. It wouldn't hurt to find out the car owner's name before I spoke to Steve. He'd have me giving up my job again if it wasn't Craig. If I did confirm it was Craig, then I could tell Steve what had happened, omitting the fact that I'd got the plate identified and knew who it belonged to (I didn't want him finding out how I did such things), get him to check the plate – again- and sort it. An extra day or so shouldn't make any difference.

4

The next day came and went in a blur of typing. Phillips sell steel. It comes in various shapes and sizes, but they mainly sell tubing and pipes, and fittings to go with pipes, with some of them made to order in the workshop. I thought I was finally getting the hang of the order system and the sizes of tube and stuff they stocked. Half an hour before the end of the day I checked my bag, but the notes were still there. When Mr Phillips walked through the office at 5.15 as arranged, I shook my head and his smile faded. I got home to find no more paint, just the red gas bill. I hoped Mr Phillips was a prompt payer.

After I'd eaten I thought I'd better text Pete and get him tracing that number-plate. He and I were at school together. He likes to show off his computer skills, so is happy to help me out now and again. He may be as computer-literate as they come and be able to access things that most of us don't even know exist, but he's definitely not a nerd. Even back when we were teenagers, Pete was cool in a grown-up, different sort of way. I met him by chance in the Princes Quay shopping centre a couple of years back and was surprised he remembered me. He'd always had a bunch of girls hanging round him at school, and he had a sort of mad, bad, dangerous-to-know reputation, which was in part due to what we girls would call 'come-to-bed' eyes.

Steve's heard me talk of Pete but I always say his name in connection with some girl or other, and certainly don't mention number-plate tracing. He went out with my best friend Sarah before she settled down, so if his name crops up, Steve doesn't connect it with my work.

Pete never says much about his work, or about the recent past. He occasionally talks about our schooldays, or Oxford University where he studied Computing, but the following five to ten years are shrouded in mystery. Rumour has it he may have sailed too close to the wind, even hacking into financial companies, but there wasn't any proof. I think people may just be jealous of his success. He returned to Hull with enough money for a small mansion with a pool and a gym, and a sleek black sports car, so I'd heard, but no-one was quite sure where he'd been or what he'd been doing.

He's just under six foot with brown eyes that twinkle when he smiles, thick dark brown hair and not an ounce of excess flesh.

So I generally text Pete, rather than ring him, in case his warm masculine voice lures me in and I end up agreeing to meet for a coffee to pick up the car owner's name, rather than just having him send me it. He won't commit to email in case someone catches him out and links him with hacking into the

DVLA. He has his own business solving computer problems with a quiet sideline of gaining information by knowing where and how to look. He's probably not too familiar with the Inland Revenue, though I expect he could manufacture records for himself on their computer if he'd a mind to. Anyway I couldn't text Pete unless I charged up my phone, so I decided to leave the phone on charge, so people could at least get hold of me, and call in at Pete's house while I was picking up a pint of milk. I knew he'd be there but he wouldn't want to ask me in. How did I know that? The same way I knew how easy it was to feel flattered by his attentions and come away thinking there was something going on, something that might ignite with just the slightest encouragement - because only the previous week I'd bumped into him in a café in town.

Before I'd known what was happening, he was pulling out a chair and setting coffee and cake in front of me and it was during that conversation that he'd mentioned Man U had made it to the quarter-finals of the Champions League and I should watch as it was going to be on 'ordinary' TV. Pete's a sucker for football, and he only supports winning teams, so that rules out Hull City, or Leeds United, generally supported in the past by young lads in Hull. I don't know whether Pete's ever been to Manchester but he's still one of their biggest fans. I picked up a six-pack of lager along with my pint of milk and knocked at the door of a small mansion in Sutton, hoping that it wasn't too near kick-off for him to answer the door. If I was in luck, I hoped I'd get the registration number, give him the goods from the off-licence and get home in time to put my feet up with a cup of tea, watching something more to my taste.

Pete's face lit up with that smile that draws a woman in. 'Nice to see you, Rach. You've just brightened a dull day. Come on in. What can I do for you this time?'

'I only need a plate running, Pete, then I'll be out of your hair. I know it's footie tonight.'

'No, it's tomorrow night, Rach, so you can stay a bit and help me unwind. It's been a long day.'

I was confused, and rather flustered. I hadn't bargained on being invited to hang around. Some private detective I was. I must have got the days confused. Why hadn't I checked in the paper? I followed him into the hall, which was roughly the size of my bedroom. Very impressive. Pete held out a hand for my coat and I found myself handing it over, succumbing to his smile.

'You'll have a drink?' he asked.

'I can't stop, really, Pete.'

'I won't take no for an answer. It's no trouble. It's always good to see you.'

I tried to avoid his eyes but failed miserably. Before I knew it, I was in his lounge, sinking into a sofa, holding a cup of tea and telling him about how little I've been seeing of Steve and how we don't seem to go out much any more.

'If you ever get tired of being left out in the cold, you know where I am.'

If he'd asked me out then and there, I'd have

said 'Yes' straightaway, and somehow squared it with my feelings for Steve. Hell, I'd even have done his ironing, if he'd asked. The thought of rummaging through his washing brought a blush to my cheeks.

'Something wrong, Rach?'

'Er, no. Is that the time? Could you run this plate for me please, and text me the details?' I muttered.

He grinned at me, that twinkle in his eye. 'OK, I know you want to get going, so let me get your coat.'

He didn't play games. He didn't need to. His hand just brushed against my neck as he helped me on with my coat. My legs were wobbly and my heart thudding as I said goodbye and stumbled back down the drive. I felt like a daft teenager and was glad no-one was there to see it. Back in my flat, I rang Steve's mobile, thinking I'd connect myself back to real life, but it went through to voicemail. Why did I expect anything else? Still, I knew what I was getting with Steve. Pete, well, he was dangerous. But, as we girls used to say, he was also pure sex on legs.

On Wednesday morning I stared round the office, willing someone to feel it was their lucky day. Gloria was working again. She was singing somewhat tunelessly, but hey, if the government get their way, by the time I'm thinking of retiring, they'll have pushed the state pension age up to 80 and offices up and down the country will be full of Glorias. I can imagine it now, as they forget the name of the firm when they answer the phone, forget what they're supposed to be doing and as for using the computer, well they'll be expecting it to make the tea.

I was wondering if Geoff might be in financial trouble. He did the wages and there'd been talk that he liked a drink or two during the day from a hip flask. It could well be that his figures didn't add up and he had to pinch the odd note to make things right. It goes without saying that Phillips Tools and Pipe Fittings paid their employees in cash. I know you think I'm having you on, but I know of at least half a dozen other firms in Hull that do the same.

I was really busy all day. The pile of orders seemed to grow instead of get smaller, and Mr Phillips kept calling me into his office. When we were getting a drink in the kitchen, Charlene told me to be careful. 'Don't be taken in by his charm. He's only trying to get in your knickers. He's married, you know.' Not only did I know he was married, I knew he had no charm either, but I refrained from telling her so.

At 5.15 I looked in my bag and one of the marked notes was gone. When Mr Phillips walked down the office a couple of minutes later I nodded. His face went from a smile into an 'are-you-sure?' then back to a smile again in the blink of an eye, and he strode purposefully to the main door and locked it quietly. Then he asked me to stand next to him and announced to all and sundry that I had had some money taken from my bag, and he was going to have to ask everyone to let him search their bags and desks while I kept an eye out for anyone trying to hide anything.

There was a lot of tut-tutting and frowning and glancing at watches, but everyone seemed to take it in their stride, amazingly. Ten minutes later and he'd found nothing, so I suggested we call in the workshop staff. They filed in and waited with me while Mr Phillips searched their little lockers, desks and whatever. Then he came and searched them. I was gob-smacked. The note was in young Dave's teenage wallet. He'd been in from the workshop a few times to query the orders I'd typed up and had seemed such a nice lad. He was nearly in tears and so was I, to be honest. Mr Phillips told him straight away that he was sacked and he'd have to consider whether he brought in the police or just let him go without a reference.

Then Dave finally found his tongue. There was only five pounds and some change of his own in the wallet. The rest was his collection of sponsorship money for the charity abseil down the church tower. He'd done it over Easter. He remembered who'd given him the twenty pound note and taken all the change he'd already collected though. As he looked down the office to the three ditsy girls, Sue burst into tears.

'I'm so sorry. It's my hormones.'

I had a feeling it was more a case of wanting some nice things for the baby, but I left it to Mr Phillips to deal with. He took her into his office and left the rest of the staff divided between condemning me for doing a dirty sneaky job, and those who were quite impressed really and wanted to know what it was like being a private detective. I popped my head round the door to tell Mr Phillips I'd send him the bill, then jumped in the car and headed home. It's always good to get a result, even though you wonder what the consequences will be sometimes.

In this case I rather thought Mr Phillips would swallow her story and just let her leave straight away but forget it otherwise. He'd not have any more money disappearing and he could feel noble for not prosecuting a pregnant teenager. The next morning I got a call to say I'd done a good job, but to stick to what I knew in future as I'd typed in an order for his best customer as 5 lengths of steel 1.3 metres long instead of 13 lengths of steel 5 metres long and it was only by chance that the foreman had noticed before it was sent out. I prayed the rest of my inevitable errors didn't surface until I'd got his cheque and banked it.

That night Pete rang. He'd traced the plate and it belonged to a Mrs Elsie Young, aged 74. She seemed an unlikely vandal, but I took her address from Pete and said 'Thanks a lot. You've been a great help'.

'What are you involved in, Rach? Is there anything I can help you with?'

I thought of Pete's eyes and almost weakened but said it was probably something or nothing.

A while later I rang Elsie. She wasn't hiding.

She was in the phone book. She told me she'd had her car stolen the previous week, and I believed her, bless her. I'd mention the paint to Steve when I next saw him, in case Craig had stolen Elsie's car, though I'd leave out of the conversation that I'd had the car number plate traced but it was a dead end. Or maybe I'd just forget about it and put it down to one of those things.

I was just about to eat when the light bulb went in the kitchen. Grovelling around in semi-darkness, I pulled out the kitchen drawer where I keep a torch and spare bulbs, only it stuck. I had to manhandle the drawer above out of its runners and then yank the offending drawer out. It came out unstuck at the corner and the bottom dropped out and everything fell on the floor in a heap. I sat on the floor and swore. Why did nothing ever go right for me? Good job Steve was coming round later.

The phone rang. It was Steve, ringing to say he couldn't come round after all. I filled him in on the drawer and he recommended I get a tube of the stuff which sticks everything together real easy, without the need for nails. Not quite the answer I was looking for, and no sign of sympathy. He'd had a rough day though, and wouldn't be leaving the station till the early hours for certain, so I couldn't take it out on him.

There'd been another body discovered early that morning. This time the body was found in some woods inland from the coast at Dane's Dyke, up past Bridlington. It was in a shallow grave. Steve said though the earth was freshly dug, the first impression was that it'd been there several weeks, though not above a month. That meant the murder pre-dated the first body found. The victim was another young blonde. The Chief Inspector was dragging in all of Hull's sex offenders. At first he'd made a feeble attempt to cling to the idea that Peter Taylor might have committed both murders, but it seemed highly unlikely. Steve felt vindicated in his belief that he'd been chasing the wrong man. Everything matched the first case, including the photos in a plastic folder under the body. The previous time it had stopped them getting wet. This time it had kept them clean and away from the teeth of animals. So, it looked like they were hunting someone who'd killed twice and might kill again. With no other leads to follow, that's why they'd resorted to pulling in the sex offenders and recently released prisoners.

Steve was going to be snowed under for the next few days. He'd have to go to the post-mortem but not until they got the forensics back on the bugs found in the body and they knew how long the body had been buried. Sometimes Steve gives me far too much detail. I now knew that both girls had been strangled. Steve said he was glad he'd been right about it not being Peter Taylor, but hadn't wanted it to mean there was a serial killer on the loose. Until they solved the case, Hull wouldn't be a safe place for young women to be walking around on their own. He warned me to stay in. The next day, I would be wishing I'd taken his advice.

5

Having caught my pilferer, I had a few errands to run in town the next morning, like paying in the cheque from Mr Phillips before my account went into freefall. The wind howled through the town centre, its icy tentacles reaching down necks and whipping up under skirts. To make matters worse, a shower started and though light, the rain hit my face like needles, plastering my fringe to my forehead and drenching me within minutes. The brolly was useless and I hurried to get indoors. You don't get wind like that in the rest of the country, or so Steve tells me.

Once I'd dried off, I thought I'd nip to Tescos to stock up on essentials. I got white spirit and paint in a pretty shade of blue so I could try to clean the paint off the letterbox and the worst off the walls before repainting them. I bought food – well, biscuits, cake, chocolate, quick-cook pies, pizzas and other unhealthy items but also some bananas which are about the only fruit I like. So, I'm not a healthy eater. Accept it - I do. And then of course I strayed from the food aisles and bought a cute white cotton blouse I couldn't resist and a paperback because their top hundred are too cheap to pass up and I had no new assignment to keep me busy.

Although I'd spent more than I planned, I felt I had to clear the flat of all traces of the mysterious paint-pourer, so I went to the big carpet warehouse over the road from Tesco and got a leftover bargain that would just fit my tiny hall. I was wondering about placing an ad in some post offices for more work, whilst waiting to turn right at the big crossroads, when a small red Volvo came out of nowhere and rammed into my rear end, spinning the car round 180 degrees. I was stunned. I'd seen it coming in the rear-view mirror for the last twenty yards or so, like it was in slow motion and in a film, happening to someone else. I couldn't understand it. The driver must have seen me so why didn't he brake? He had plenty of time to steer round me. As fast as it came, it had gone. My glasses came off with the impact and I couldn't see them. They seemed more important than anything. I groped around and found them in the footwell, then opened the car door to go and look at the damage but a lollipop lady was standing there and she wouldn't let me out.

'Are you OK? Don't get out of the car. I've phoned for an ambulance to check you out. What happened? I'm afraid I arrived too late. Did someone hit you and drive off? That's disgusting.'

I searched frantically for my bag.

'Just sit still, dear. You've had a shock. I don't know what the world's coming to. They'll let anyone drive these days.'

I told her I needed my mobile. I had to ring Steve. He'd know what to do. She found my bag and I fished out my phone. I rang Steve.

'It's me. I've been in an accident, but I'm OK. I don't know what to do about the car or anything though.'

'You sure you're alright, sweetheart? Where are you?'

I told him. When I said the car had been spun right round by the Volvo, he swore. Then his anger faded and he was concerned again. 'I can't come, love. I'm real sorry but I can't get away. Give the uniforms my name when they come and they'll help you. I'll try and call round tonight, or ring at least. Are you sure you're alright?'

'Yeah. My bum hurts where the seatbelt dug in, but otherwise I'm fine. It wasn't my fault, Steve.'

'I didn't say it was, love. Just sit tight. How's the other driver?'

'He left in a hurry.'

'You mean a hit and run?'

'Yes. Have to go now. The ambulance is here.' The fussy lollipop lady was talking to the ambulance driver as if I was incapable of speaking for myself. She was probably right. I tried to look at the back of my beautiful, almost-new car but they led me into the ambulance and sat me down. While they were checking my blood pressure and asking if I was hurting anywhere, the police arrived. I told them I was Steve's girlfriend and they said they'd try and get the car moved for me. They asked lots of questions but were very kind.

I only carry my driving licence, so they said I'd have to show my insurance document at a local police station, before they rushed off to put out an alert for a red Volvo, possibly damaged on the front wing. I persuaded the ambulance men that I didn't need to go to the hospital. I just wanted to go home and lie down and shut the world out. Then the policeman popped his head round the door to say the car was out of the way on the verge and I'd have to get the insurers to take it away.

I didn't have the insurers' number. I rang dad but no-one answered. I can usually cope with anything but it had been a bit of a week, and I wanted someone – anyone really, to sort it out for me. I felt too wobbly to do it on my own. Then Pete popped into my head. I thought he could take care of just about anything, or knew someone who could, and so it proved. He rang a mate with one of those breakdown vehicles, and he came up for me himself in his car. When my last car went up in flames I'd had to wait about an hour for the breakdown truck from the insurers, but this time Pete had only just gently strapped my bruised body into his sports car and collected all my belongings from the boot and interior, when his mate arrived. I kept saying I had to get hold of Dad, and Pete kept saying I should wait till I was home and had got the insurers moving.

He took me home, didn't even comment on the paint-strewn hall, made me a cup of tea and then rang the insurers while I drank the tea, saying stupid things like, 'It wasn't my fault' and 'I didn't see the driver' and 'Steve said I shouldn't go out today' -

even though he'd said that for a completely different reason. I used my mobile to call home as Pete was hanging on while the insurers woke up in India or wherever. Mum and Dad had just got back from town. Mum went ballistic and blamed my job again and then insisted Dad should pick me up in an hour or so and take me to theirs for tea, and I agreed. Sometimes it's nice to be mothered. Somewhere I'd missed lunch and it was three o'clock already so I opened a packet of biscuits.

Pete handed me the phone after another half an hour when he'd finally got through to the insurers and I'd eaten half a packet of chocolate chip cookies. I was told to get the car to their designated garage and I could then have a hire car. Again. Pete said he could take me to the garage and we'd meet my poor car there, but it was nearly teatime and I was feeling like I'd been drugged, as well as kicked in the behind, so I thought I wasn't really a suitable candidate to pick up a strange hire car. And I wanted my dad. Pete didn't take offence. He said he'd get his mate to pick me up at ten the next morning and take me and the car to the repair place, and then he left. Then Dad arrived, full of concern for his little girl and that was when I burst into tears. It's amazing how you hold it together till someone hugs you. I'd rather it had been Steve, but Dad was a reasonable substitute at the time.

My family all thought I should have taken the number plate. I would have done, given half a chance but the car had gone before I realised what had happened and I'd been without my specs. It was amazing I'd recognised it as a red Volvo. Other than that, I think they realised I was in shock and in no fit state to be questioned any more. Gran kept telling me I should have gone to hospital as it would help in my compensation claim.

'You'll get thousands, maybe tens of thousands if you play your cards right.'

I ignored her. I felt fine and I detest the increase in compensation claims putting up costs for everyone when people are perfectly healthy after a couple of days. Tripping over paving stones when they should be more careful and then claiming from the council. Don't get me started. It makes my blood boil. I'd got a real sense of satisfaction every time I'd done work for the council, proving that the dire injuries which people claimed kept them bed-bound, didn't stop them playing for the local pub football team or going line-dancing.

After tea, I resisted Mum's attempts to get me to sleep in the spare bed cos I wanted my own bed – and also I did hope Steve might call round, so Dad drove me home. I was almost asleep when Steve rang to say there'd not been any sightings of the hit-and-run driver and was I okay? He seemed a bit miffed that I'd rung Pete to come to my rescue, rather than Dad, but I pointed out that Dad had been out of the house when I'd rung and anyway, he didn't have access to a breakdown truck. He said he was pleased Pete had been such a help, though I could detect the gritted teeth as he spoke. I was glad he'd rung and also a teeny bit glad that he'd been jealous that Pete had helped me out.

The next day Pete's mate called to take me to the garage to get the hire car and inspect mine. I'd dressed gingerly, eyeing the rapidly expanding bruise in resignation. I've always bruised easily anyway, so am used to the various shades of body ornament I wear, but this was in the Champions League of bruises. At the garage a chief technician declared my beautiful brand-new car a write-off, and said because of that, I could only have the hire car for three days. Now where in the TV adverts do they tell you that? They say you get a free car when yours is off the road due to an accident, not that if it's permanently off the road, you can forget it. And to make a double whammy, my car only looked slightly damaged and yet this bloke was telling me it wasn't worth fixing. A new car with a bent wheel and a bit of damage to the wheel arch and it's not worth fixing! I spluttered, 'Surely it can't cost £7000 to fix?'

'Your body cage has gone love, and if the car's less than 2 years old, that means it's a write-off.'

'But the chassis itself is completely intact, and the engine. It's only this wheel and back corner', I protested.

He pointed to a miniscule dent on the bodywork above where the door closed. 'That's where the cage has gone. It's no good. They won't authorise repairs. I'll write a report.'

'I just can't believe it. I thought it might take a few days to repair, but this.'

'You better empty the car. Take the tax disk

and that.'

Those were obviously the only words of comfort I was going to get. I'd used the little nest egg dear old Uncle Keith had left me to pay for a new car because I was sick of repair bills and time spent off the road, and I thought I'd have ten years trouble-free motoring at least. A girl from the office gave me a black bin bag and showed me the controls of the Peugeot I was getting for a measly three days. How was I going to get another car in that time? I couldn't take anything in, so got Pete's mate to sit in with me while I drove to get petrol and then had a cup of tea in Tesco's café. I had three sugars for the shock, then dropped him back at the body shop place and went home. I bet they salvaged everything from my car - engine, upholstery, the lot - and made a fortune while saying it was a write-off. It all seemed a big con to me, a stitch up between the garage and the insurers.

I didn't like driving the Peugeot, so I decided to go to my friendly Ford dealer after I'd had a sandwich. Howard was in. He was the salesman who'd sold me my pretty new Fiesta. Luckily I'd taken his advice when haggling for extras and had taken the option of a guaranteed brand new replacement if anything happened to my new car within three years, rather than alloy wheel trims. With my track record in cars, there was no contest.

Howard greeted me with a surprised smile. 'Having problems with the car?'

'You could say that, Howard. It was lovely,

but I need a new one.'

'Oh?' His smile broadened. Maybe he thought business was good or I was in the fleet business. I soon put him straight, but give him his due, he pulled out all the stops to order me another new Fiesta, same model, same blue. It would be delivered in 10 days and till then I could have a courtesy car from them instead of the hire car, thank Heavens. I think he reckoned I needed a bit of help, though mentioning my boyfriend's a police inspector can't have done any harm.

Howard was so kind. He followed me to the garage to return the Peugeot. I drove carefully as it'd started raining and the windscreen wipers and indicators were the opposite way round to how they were in my car. My poor Fiesta lay condemned outside waiting to being scrapped. I was glad to get in Howard's car and go back to the dealership to take possession of his Ford courtesy car. They could stick their Peugeot and the measly three days. After all the driving around and the shock of having to buy yet another car, I felt a bit sick, and that was before I looked in the mirror. My face was washed out and there were black shadows under my eyes caused by reliving the crash instead of sleeping. I looked like a sick panda. I had another cup of tea then took my documents to the police station. It was another fun packed day. I was starting to think someone had got it in for me.

On the answerphone there was a short message from a Mr Parry who said he'd call back on Monday morning. He said he'd like to discuss some work. I wasn't sure I was up to work. I felt exhausted. I actually fell asleep on the settee, and was woken by the phone just as it was getting dark. It was Pete. He wanted to take me out for a meal to save me cooking. I was so surprised I said 'Yes'. After I put the phone down I started panicking in case I'd let myself in for something I couldn't or didn't want to handle. What did I mean 'in case'? Of course I didn't want to handle anything else with my poor tired brain but it was too late. It was no good thinking about it though. He'd be on his way soon. I had to change the sick panda into an attractive sexy woman and fast. Forget what I said about not wanting to handle a date with Pete – we women have standards to maintain, and that meant looking good, even though I had no intention of cheating on Steve.

I was almost ready when Steve rang. He was still at the station, but could call round later. I felt guilty and nearly lied and said I was having an early night, but I knew it would make things worse cos I can't lie for toffee, so I told him I was going for a meal with Pete to thank him for the help with the car. There was a silence so deep you could hear a butterfly's wings beat, never mind a pin drop. Then he just said, 'Don't drink. I'll be round about five or six o'clock tomorrow, however busy we are here,' and put the phone down.

'Phew! Now that's what I call jealous!' I thought. I didn't want him doubting me, but having him realise someone else might find me attractive wasn't a bad idea. Steve was so busy that I hadn't seen much of him lately and it was nice to have company. I was wondering how I was going to get through an entire evening with Pete in a 'date' type situation though. I would have to take Steve's advice (or was it an order?) and tell Pete I couldn't drink because I was still light-headed after the crash. It was actually true, but that didn't make me feel any less worried that I didn't entirely trust myself to drink in Pete's company.

He arrived right on time, which was a pleasant surprise. My mum says it shows a man respects you when he turns up on time. After all, our time's just as important as theirs and what're you supposed to do for five or ten minutes when you're all ready, except wonder if your bloke's going to turn up. Suffice to say that Steve's not known for his punctuality. I wish he'd think of the time he wants to arrive, add ten minutes and tell me that time. Only he'd have to aim for the original time of course, or it'd defeat the object.

Anyway, Pete looked good. He wore a pale blue open-necked shirt, dark blue trousers and jacket and he looked fit to eat. He's not as tall as Steve but lean and sexy. He has a look of David Tennant, probably known best for being Doctor Who. Mind you, I reminded myself, Steve's good-looking too. He has a lovely strong chest and shoulders, and being taller, he makes me feel protected.

'You look lovely', were Pete's first words. Steve rarely pays me compliments any more, though he says he saves them for when I look special, which makes me feel like I must look a mess most of the time.

I must stop dwelling on Steve. I'm going out with Pete, and if I'm not careful, I'll end up talking about Steve and that's not a good way to repay someone for taking me out, now is it? I gave myself a talking-to whilst smiling and saying, 'Thanks. What was the traffic like?'

Stupid thing to say, I know, but I was out of practice being out with a man other than Steve.

'No problem. Everyone's home from work by now. Shall we go?'

Pete helped me into his sports car, which was very chivalrous and highly necessary as it was practically at pavement level. I was glad I hadn't worn a skirt or Pete would have got an eyeful. We set off at speed and I had to stop myself from asking what the hurry was. With the police connection, I drive within the limit, as does Steve. He'd be teased unmercifully if either he or his girlfriend got a ticket. We got to a small Italian restaurant in Ferriby, a village just to the west of Hull, in record time and were soon looking over the menus. I eat anything. I'm thin. Sorry, girls, but I can't help it.

I don't diet and don't exercise apart from always rushing around like crazy. It's just a mixture of inherited genes and metabolism, plus I stress a lot and that tends to keep the weight down. Even all the choccie and cakes make no impact. Mum says I'll hit the menopause and start looking like I'm pregnant; a stick insect with a fat belly. Thanks, Mum, that's what I say. She's right about the stick insect bit though. I'm not attractively slim. I'm skinny and bony and lack all those nice womanly curves, so before you want to kill me, I deserve some slack after being teased at school for having no breasts.

The food was delicious. I did skip the starter, but only because I know my limitations and I adore puddings when I go out. I hardly ever have them at home, but can't resist them on the few occasions I get to a restaurant. Pete asked me about my recent cases. I told him about the near-death experience in the cellar and he said, 'I wish I'd been there when they rescued you. What colour bra where you wearing under that red top?'

'A decent one for once, black lace', I replied. Pete smiled. I realised what I was saying and that I'd forgotten my earlier promise to Steve, as I stared at the glass of wine that had materialised in my hand. I was losing it, heading off into wide-open flirting country. I'd have to stick to one glass of wine somehow. I tried to steer the conversation onto more neutral territory and asked Pete about his work, but he deflected my questions with the ease of someone who does it on a daily basis. The music was good, consisting mainly of oldies of the romantic kind. 'Endless Love' by Lionel Ritchie followed 'Loving You' by Minnie Riperton. Wine plus those sort of songs makes me go mushy. When I heard Sinead O'Connor start on 'Nothing Compares to You', I asked the hovering waiter for a glass of water.

Pete looked at me, a twinkle in his eye. 'Not want to help me finish this wine then? I'm driving, so you really ought to. We don't want your boyfriend to come across me at the station being breathalysed, do we?'

It was the first time Steve's name had come up. I blurted out, 'We're not engaged or anything', then wished I hadn't. I really didn't know what to say next.

'Have you not thought about settling down, Rach? Me, I think I'm getting to the age when I'd like to think about having a family before too long.'

Was he trying to imply I might be the one he'd like to settle down with?

'I'm not sure whether I want children.' I tried to deflect the subject.

'Well, maybe you don't, but surely you'd like to move into a house and away from the flat-dwelling lifestyle of a twenty-something?'

'I'm not sure whether I'm ready to give up my independence yet.'

'Maybe the right person hasn't come along. Or maybe he has but he hasn't asked you'.

Did he mean him or Steve? He was being ambiguous, flirting with me, and the wine I'd drunk was making it hard not to flirt back. 'Shape yourself, woman' I told myself. He's just feeling sorry for you after that crash and he'd move onto the next conquest if he had his wicked way with you. Maybe for once I believed every word I said, because I muttered, 'Well, it's been a lovely evening but I need some sleep I'm afraid. That crash took it out of me. Do you mind if we leave now?' To tell you the truth, it was hearing Aerosmith's 'I don't want to miss a thing' start up in the background. If Steve and I have a song that's 'our song', then that's the one.

Again, the smile. Maybe he was playing a

long game. It seemed like it when he drove me home and left me at the door, saying, 'We'll have to do this again some time, if you'd like to', and sauntered back to his car, but not before taking me by surprise and kissing me gently but lingeringly on the lips.

I let myself into the flat, legs shaking. That kiss was really really nice, but I hadn't weakened and asked him in for coffee. Actually he hadn't given me the chance to ask. So he probably wasn't interested. But that kiss wasn't a goodnight peck, so he was probably prepared to take his time. That thought made me go hot and cold and panicky. I put Maroon 5 on the CD player, thinking to calm myself but the undertones of the lyrics kept me going back to the end of the evening, so I turned it off and put the news on the TV instead. That's always guaranteed to stop me thinking of romance and such matters.

The phone rang at 11pm as I was in my nightie, about to get into bed. I was tempted not to answer it, but what would Steve make of that?

'Hi Steve', I said.

'How did you know it was me?'

'I'm psychic. Any news?'

'Someone called the incident room to report they'd seen a small silver car on the lane near the top of Mappleton cliffs very early in the morning on the day Susan's body was found. Her body was found on the beach very close by, and it would have been about the right time for it not to have been touched by an incoming tide. But a silver car's hardly a lead. No make even, let alone the number plate. But what about you? Been home long? Had a nice night?'

'Got back about ten. Went to an Italian in Ferriby. Food was good. Had tiramisu. I'm just about to go to bed. I'm really tired. I can't seem to get my energy back after the crash.'

'It'll still be delayed shock. Low blood sugar levels and all that. Glad you're doing your best to lift them.' He laughed a bit self-consciously. I could tell he was dying to ask if Pete was there, or if he'd been up in the flat. It would do no harm to let him wonder. He rang off, still promising to call round the next day, and I went to bed.

6

I got a second call the next morning from Mr Parry. He sounded very formal and asked if he could see me about a private matter that he wanted me to investigate. I was free and needed the money so I suggested we meet that morning, and perhaps a café would be a suitable place. He said he'd meet me in the BHS café at ten thirty. I wasn't sure what to expect so I got there early. I'd told him I had long hair and glasses and would be reading a book. He was prompt to the minute.

'I'm Graham Parry. You must be Miss Hodges?'

We shook hands rather formally.

'How can I help you, Mr Parry?'

'It's rather delicate.'

I waited. In my line of work, it's always delicate.

'This tea's dreadful. You can never get a decent cup outside the home, can you?'

My heart sank even lower than it had done when he'd walked over to the table. I'd taken in his acrylic maroon jumper over a white shirt with tightly knotted tie, his severely parted grey hair brillcreamed to a darker colour in places. I bet his nature's like his hair, I thought, severe and greasy. I'd met his sort before. My uncle John was one.

'I'd like you to follow my wife. I think she's having an affair.'

'I see. What makes you think that, Mr Parry?'

'Her whole personality's changed since I took early retirement.'

'In what way, exactly?'

'Well, she's always worked. She likes a bit of money of her own for clothes and make-up, presents for the children and such, but when I took early retirement I assumed she would as well, so we can spend more time together. She said she didn't want to. She said she likes her job and her friends. Well, that might have been the case. When I was at work she needed friends to talk to. Anyway, I wasn't happy but she only works mornings, so I said I'd do the chores so we could spend time together in the afternoons. To be honest, that was one reason I wanted her to give up work. The house is never as clean as it might be. I can't remember her ever cleaning the windows or the oven, and she only vacuums once a week.'

I managed to avoid spluttering my coffee and smiled sweetly. It's not my job to comment. The client is the one paying the bill.

'And then?' I asked encouragingly.

'Well, she's hardly at home in the afternoons. We often drive to Hornsea at the weekend and sit on the front, watching people go by, listening to sport on the radio, and I thought we'd be able to do that more often. I took her to the Freeport place and she seemed to enjoy shopping. Bought some rubbish but it made her happy. I've suggested we walk in the park, or join one of those clubs for retired people but she said, "I've a lot more years before I'll be ready to mix with a load of old fogies". The last few times we've been to Hornsea she's got out of the car and gone paddling. I can only think she's seeing someone else because she doesn't want to be with me and her whole personality's changed.'

'How old's your wife, Mr Parry?'

'Fifty-three. I'm fifty-eight.'

'I don't want you to take this the wrong way, Mr Parry, but fifty-three is very young these days. Maybe she just wants to enjoy herself a bit before she settles into old age.'

'That's ridiculous. She can do that without behaving like a twenty-year old, surely. No. Someone must be influencing her. She's wearing clothes for a much younger woman. You wouldn't believe she was the same age as Jill and Mary.'

'Are they her friends?'

'Wives of my friends. We all go out together for meals occasionally.'

'It still doesn't mean she's having an affair though. Why would you think that?'

'She's bought clothes that, well, I suppose are attractive to men. Skimpy things with tiny straps and the like.'

'Just one more question. I know this may be

embarrassing, but is everything alright in the bedroom?'

He stared at me as if I'd grown two heads. I thought for a minute he was going to get up and leave. He'd obviously only picked a woman detective because he thought it'd be easier for me to follow his wife. It can't have occurred to him that I'd ask things like that.

'If you mean what I think you mean, things are normal for people of our age. We haven't had relations (I swear he spat the word out) for some time, but Judith is at that age where I wouldn't expect her to be bothered any more. It just tailed off. I would still have a shave on Saturday nights and say she was looking nice. We'd get into bed but she'd turn the other way and say she was tired or she didn't feel like it, so I stopped asking. But that was a long time before I retired. Must be well over ten years ago now. The last time was when our daughter had been for her birthday and Judith had had a few drinks. She doesn't usually drink.'

'And your daughter. Have you spoken to her about the change in your wife?'

'No. I don't want her to think there's anything wrong with our marriage. It'd really upset her.'

'What exactly would you like me to do then, Mr Parry?'

'Follow her on the afternoons she goes out and see where she goes and what she gets up to. I followed her one evening when she said she was going to her book group at Alice's, and she went to her friend's house as she'd said. She doesn't go out much in the evening, occasionally to the cinema with a friend to see a romantic film that I don't want to see. Mostly she watches the television. Other than that she spends half an hour or so every night on the computer. She emails our daughter in Sheffield. It's cheaper than ringing.'

I named my hourly rate and as I expected, he tried to beat me down, saying he was retired, but he agreed to my terms in the end. I don't think he wanted to go through the details of his marriage all over again with someone else, otherwise he might have rung another agency trying for a cheaper quote. He gave me a recent photo of Judith and the address where she worked, and asked if I'd be free to follow her sometime soon. He understood I had other jobs but hoped I'd be able to start work the following week for him. He wanted it sorted and 'things back to normal'. He told me he was taking Judith for a drive to look at a caravan in Filey on the Monday, but he hoped I could start on the Tuesday. He was thinking she'd settle down if she got away from her friends and they could start enjoying long walks on the clifftop.

As he left, fastidiously wiping the table with his napkin, I thought of Judith screaming inside, kicking off her shoes and tucking her skirt in her knickers as she ran to the water's edge to paddle. I suppose I'd always thought of people in their fifties as living the sort of life that Mr Parry wanted, but I realised that I'd want to be like Judith. I only prayed that I ended up with a man, Steve or whoever, who still had fun in him at that age. Who'd paddle and splash, who'd sneak up behind me and whisper suggestive things in my ear, who'd never stop wanting sex in the kitchen in broad daylight as well as on Saturday nights in bed.

When I got back at lunchtime, I kicked off my shoes and stretched out on the settee with cheese on toast and a mug of tea. I had some choccie biscuits for afters. After the morning I'd spent with the frankly obnoxious Mr Parry, I'd be cheating on him myself if he was my husband, but there again, I needed the job. As it was, I thought I deserved to treat myself anyway after less than an hour with him. I was flicking through the clothes section in Cosmopolitan when something made me look up. Maybe a sixth sense, causing the hairs on the back of my neck to stand up. I thought I was hallucinating at first. I just sat there, perfectly still, looking at this small brown furry thing sitting on my carpet, midway between the TV and the coffee table. It was a mouse and it looked just like Jerry Mouse in Tom and Jerry. I've seen them in pet shops and cages, but not in a house, not in a flat, certainly not in a flat three floors from the ground, and above all, not in my flat.

I found I couldn't make a sound. You'd think I'd have screamed, but I was actually scared of making it run in my direction if I startled it, so I sat there, stunned for a whole second or two. Our eyes locked. I must have blinked, because it ran off under the armchair. I took my chance to slide my feet in my shoes, and head for the door, carefully closing it behind me. I hammered on Les's door downstairs. He wasn't in, so I raced upstairs past my flat to Adam's. He works out in the gym and is as big as his girlfriend is small. Luckily he answered his door. I didn't know him too well. The number of his brain cells might be in inverse proportion to the square footage of muscle he had, for all I knew, but he would surely want to brag about catching a mouse.

An hour later, I wasn't so sure, and was almost glad when he said he had to go to the gym, but to call him that night if I saw it again. My lounge looked like the aftermath of a robbery. He'd upended the settee, chair and coffee table and built barriers to corner it, but after it had done the two metre dash like its life depended on it several times it had disappeared when we weren't looking and was nowhere to be seen. I had to go out. I grabbed my mobile and bag and locked the door. Adam passed me on the way out, pushing a note with his mate's phone number on it. 'If it doesn't turn up, you can ring Mike and he'll come round with poison,' he said.

Maybe I'm weird. I wanted to be rid of the mouse, but seeing it dead in a trap wasn't something I fancied. I couldn't face staying in the flat and thought I'd ring Steve for advice. Of course, I couldn't get hold of him, so I left a message. Once again Dad must have been out with Mum as there was no answer there either. Despite thinking it wasn't a good idea – who was I kidding? – I rang Pete next.

'Get yourself some humane traps then, Rach,

if you can't face poisoning it.'

I was rather hoping he'd come and offer to lay the traps or even hunt the mouse himself, but he offered instead to have me stay at his house while the traps did their business. I didn't know how I'd feel about picking up a trap with a mouse in it, but hoped someone would come with me to check on them. I didn't think I wanted it to be Pete. I sure as anything didn't want to stay with him.

'Thanks for the offer, Pete. I might well take you up on it, but I'll see how I feel when I've got the traps. May make me braver, eh?'

'Doesn't sound like you will be. Anyone would think you're more scared of me than the mouse!' He laughed but I didn't join in.

'Well, better go', I said brightly. 'I'll get back to you, OK?'

'I'll wait for your call.' He seemed very confident I'd change my mind about staying with him.

After we'd said our goodbyes I wondered what other options I had. Mum and Dad would be worried as to how a mouse got up three stories of a small modern block of flats. I was wondering that too, but I refused to worry about this being another incident caused by the same person as the paint thrower, whilst a small furry thing was stopping me from watching TV and reading magazines in the comfort of my own flat.

There was no room at Sarah's and to be honest I'm not comfortable with the idea of being woken by a baby crying in the night. Despite Gran's ideas on the topic, I'm not cut out for motherhood, or at least not for a while yet. I put off the decision as to whether I should sleep at Pete's or whether I should sit up all night waiting for the sound of a trap being set off, by going to the pet shop. The traps were surprisingly inexpensive, though it seemed really weird to me that they sold traps for small furry animals at the same place you went to buy small furry animals.

When I got home I'd told myself that the mouse was more scared of me than I was of it, and so managed to open the front door and tiptoe in. I opened the lounge door and saw it nibbling at a newspaper on the floor. I shrieked in surprise, horror or whatever and the equally terrified mouse legged it into my bedroom. He'd put Linford Christie to shame, I'll say that for him. I didn't just get an ordinary mouse. I got one that'd qualify for the animal Olympics. I slammed the door on it, a gut reaction so that I wasn't in the same room.

I was glad I'd cornered the mouse in the bedroom, away from the food in the kitchen and away from my living space in the lounge. I knew I had to put the traps in the room with the mouse because I couldn't live like this. I set them up with chocolate, wishing I could eat it instead. The instructions said they prefer chocolate to cheese. Wouldn't you just know it? I armed myself with a wooden spoon and banged on the door loudly so the mouse would head for cover, then opened the door and sprinted in, closing it behind me. I was trapped with the mouse but I couldn't risk leaving the door open and having it get back in the lounge. I left one trap near the wall to the left and one as near to the bed as I dared. I imagined it inching out from under the bed as I pushed the trap into place with the spoon, then I legged it, opening and slamming the door behind me in one smooth move.

Now at least I'd be able to eat in peace and stretch out on the settee till I could decide what to do. Steve hadn't rung me back so that only left Pete's offer. I could call him and say, 'Yes, please, I'm now so scared I'll risk sleeping under the same roof as your sexy body; that body belonging to the only man in my life who seems to want to spend time with me.' And I could use the phone without thinking the mouse was going to run out from under the chair next to the coffee table that the phone sits on. Then I realised I wouldn't be able to pack anything to take to Pete's apart from bathroom essentials like a toothbrush. My clothes were with the mouse (I refused to think of it as Jerry in case it had to be poisoned if my humane traps didn't do their job).

I was just wondering whether Pete would get the wrong impression if I turned up without a nightie, when there was a knock at the door. Maybe Pete wasn't waiting for a reply to his offer. Maybe he'd come to take me away from danger and he'd have a couple of mates with him who just happened to be rodent removers. He seemed to have mates who did everything else.

It was Steve. I'd honestly forgotten he'd said he'd come round when I'd spoken to him after my date with Pete. After all, he didn't respond to the message I left him about having a bit of a crisis.

'Hi sweetheart. Sorry I didn't ring you back. I've only just got the message. I haven't got long but I said I'd be round, so I'm here. What's the crisis?'

'Oh Steve, there's a mouse in my bedroom. It was in the lounge while I was reading at lunchtime. I looked up and it sat there next to the TV like Jerry out of Tom and Jerry and I squealed and it ran under the chair and I got my shoes and ran downstairs for Les and he wasn't in so I asked Adam and he tried to catch it and couldn't so I went to get some traps and when I got home it scared me and I shrieked and it ran in the bedroom and I shut it in there. Then I thought I had to be brave and use the traps or I'd never get rid of it so I put chocolate in the traps and crept in and closed the door behind me to keep it there and put them down and ran out again but that took all the bravery I had and now I daren't open the door and I've got to pack cos I can't sleep here and Pete said I could sleep at his.'

'Whoa there, Rach. Slow down. Take a breath. You mean a real furry mouse?'

'Yes'.

'And you're planning to sleep at this Pete's?'

'Yes. Well, I haven't seen you for over a week and we hardly ever have time to speak. Sleeping at Pete's was the last resort if I couldn't raise you.'

'Sorry, sweetheart. I've hardly been home. How long since you put down the traps?'

75

'About half an hour maybe.'

'Have you looked in them?'

'No. I told you. I've not got an ounce of bravery left.'

'Shall we look together?'

'Can you just look please?'

'Come on Rach, it'll be alright. You better point out where you put the traps and you can keep an eye on the door so it doesn't get out. You don't need to come right in the room with me.'

There was nothing in either of the traps. I didn't know whether to be pleased or disappointed. I was scared at the thought of seeing a wriggling trapped mouse but I just wanted it to be over with and have my flat back.

'How on earth could a mouse get up three flights of stairs and through a closed door?'

'That's just what I thought. I wondered if it might have been put through the letter-box like the paint.'

'What paint?'

I told him and could feel a lump in my throat as the two incidents and the car crash all seemed to gel together. He had the same idea.

'You must have upset someone good and proper, Rach. I'll get the number plate traced. See what that tells us.'

I hadn't the nerve to save him the trouble. Let him find out himself it was stolen. It wasn't like he'd be able to do anything else about it. Thoughts skittered in and out of my head almost between breaths. 'That's why I couldn't face going home and getting Mum and Dad worried.'

'Look, I really have only popped in for literally half an hour to see you, but things can't carry on like this. I think it's time you stayed out of harm's way till we can track down who's behind all these incidents. For now though, let's see where that mouse has got to.'

I shut my mind for the time being to the probability that someone was out to get me, and concentrated on the present. 'Do you think you might be able to catch it? It'd be great if you could.' I didn't hold out any hope, but I was so grateful for his company that anything seemed possible, and while he was looking, at least I wouldn't be on my own. I could rescue some clothes if I had him in the same room. He made me feel safe and even a bit silly for panicking instead of walking straight in and getting what I wanted.

Steve moved around the room, pushing things to one side and banging on things to frighten it out of its hiding place.

'It's eaten some tissue out of the box on the dressing table. Oh that's awful. It must have been running around my stuff. How did it get up there?'

'Ever heard of Hickory, Dickory Dock, the mouse ran up the clock? They can climb, Rach.'

Steve picked up a perfume bottle and said quietly, 'It's behind these bottles here. Have you got something to catch it in?'

I got an opaque plastic beaker I use for water in the night. I'm so clumsy, I daren't use glass on the bedside table. I handed it to Steve. He moved the bottles of cleanser and stuff and the mouse leapt to the floor. Steve pounced and that was it. I was waiting for the blur of movement as Linford mouse legged it across to me and over my slippers or up my legs, but there was nothing, except a scratching noise.

'Did I kill it?' Steve asked calmly.

'No, it's in there, wriggling. Oh, Steve, that's brilliant. You're my hero. How the hell did you have quick enough reactions?'

'I think it stunned itself when it jumped. It just seemed to stand still for a few seconds and that was enough. Get me a piece of card or something to slide underneath and I'll take it outside.'

I found him something and he calmly slid it under the beaker, lifted it, and went out of the door.

I was shaking. He seemed to be gone ages and I wanted to shut the door behind him but thought it would be dreadful to shut out my rescuer, so I just kept watch in case he'd lost it and it ran back inside. Then he was back.

'Quick, shut the door, it's coming!'

I looked at his face and realised he was joking.

'Don't, Steve. Has it really gone?'

'Yeah. I took it to that grassy area at the corner and let it out under a streetlamp. Poor thing. It sat there shaking.'

'Poor thing! I'll give it poor thing. It terrified me and denied me my flat. Don't expect me to feel sorry for it.'

'It'll probably get eaten by a cat before the

night's out. You've sent it to its death.'

'Well I'm sorry and all, but the cats round here only go after birds and anyway, it'll have a taste for going in houses now. Now come here, my hero. I just can't believe you did that. You're so brave.'

'I'm just glad I turned up when I did, Rach. I really do have to be off now though. Back to work. I've been tied up re-interviewing all the sex offenders and newly-released prisoners with silver cars, checking for those with dodgy or no alibis. Anyway, you don't need to go to Pete's now. I'd rather take care of you myself. Get round to my flat as soon as you've tidied up and packed a bag. I don't think you're safe here at the moment.'

I agreed with my hero. Now Steve had caught the mouse, there was no way I was going anywhere near Pete's. Steve was a superhero in my eyes, so much so that I almost offered to have his babies. He may not be around much, but he makes every minute count. I remembered that Pete hadn't offered to come over and catch the mouse. He'd just recommended I get the traps. His was more a managerial style of helping, rather than hands on. At that moment I much preferred the hands-on approach, and Steve and I indulged in an all too short hands-on session of kissing before he broke away and left, but not before handing me the key to his flat.

He'd only been in my flat for about half an hour, but things felt good again. I set about righting all the furniture that Adam had moved earlier and finished packing the bag. I still felt nervy and expected another mouse around every corner. Yes, I was definitely better leaving my flat till I could face it without imagining animals wherever I looked. And of course I wasn't unhappy at the thought of staying with Steve for a while. I decided not to ring Pete. He'd helped me a lot over the previous few days but not ringing would send him the message that I wasn't about to become another of his conquests.

7

I'd like to say that Steve and I had the best sex ever that Saturday night. I'd like to, but I can't. The fact is, in real life, female private detectives, like all women of child-bearing age who aren't pregnant, have periods and the previous night before Steve got home I'd just started. So instead of waking with a sexual afterglow, I felt like shit. I'd hardly slept because I'd had those awful cramps I get right at the beginning of my period, and I hadn't liked to disturb Steve and go rummaging in his bathroom cabinet or ask him where he kept his paracetemol, so I lay there rubbing my stomach and occasionally dozing off.

In the morning I told Steve and got a fair amount of sympathy, some paracetemol, a cup of tea and a gentle cuddle, which immediately set me on the road to recovery. Only another day or so of real awfulness and then I'd be on the upward slope back out of the period pit. I went back to bed for a while till the tablets kicked in, then I decided to get some fresh air and exercise and wander around the old town near Steve's flat. Steve's flat's really modern even though it's in a courtyard off Dagger Lane, which sounds ancient as well as highly appropriate for a policeman.

I let myself out, putting the spare key on my key ring as if it belonged there and walked the short distance to the Market Square. One of the best things about living at Steve's is being near to this nice café in the square. It does a selection of coffees and other drinks and lots of yummy home-made food, including the most enormous scones you've ever seen. I'm not kidding. They come in two flavours and are as big as a tea-plate. There's a gift shop on the ground floor, selling craft items, unusual cards and jewellery as well. On the odd occasion I've actually been in there with Steve, I've tried to linger by the jewellery, in the hope he might treat me to something pretty in silver, but I should know to just ask straight out or buy what I want myself. You know what men are like, they don't pick up on hints; you have to be direct.

Upstairs I took a seat by the window and looked across the square to the old Fish Street School. There are lots of interestingly named streets and alleyways around the square, like the narrow street called The Land of Green Ginger. It's the oldest surviving area of Hull. I've always loved the gold statue of 'King Billy' as he is affectionately called - William of Orange to those seeking accuracy. It's a massive statue of him riding a horse, and although I'm no history expert, you don't see gold-coloured statues littering town centres so we in Hull are justly proud of it. I mean, even kids know it's not solid gold, but there again, maybe it is and they pretend it's not, to deter thieves with large articulated lorries.

It was a sunny day and as I walked past the end of Holy Trinity Church, Hull's equivalent of a cathedral, I glanced across the street and the church looked fantastic, reflected as it was in the golden gleam of the modern glass office block opposite. Glancing down I could see tiny fishes engraved in the concrete.

I carried on away from the market, past the marina and back past Steve's flat and came to the pier on the banks of the Humber. Away up river in the far distance was the Humber Bridge. In front was the massive river itself. Strangers always seem amazed at its breadth.

I walked to the end of the short pier, watching the muddy brown water lap at the ironwork of the old jetty where you could once board the ferry across to New Barton on the south shore. Then I turned and popped in the public conveniences for old times' sake. They've won prizes and were just as I'd remembered – complete with hanging baskets and garden gnomes. The old fashioned taps on the sinks shone and there were still old-fashioned overhead cisterns on the wooden-seated toilets, with handles dangling on chains. It's kind of nice that some things don't change. After a few lungfuls of bracing river air with the tang of seaweed mixed in, I headed back to Steve's flat and watched an old film on the telly. I'm a sucker for romantic comedies. 'Sleepless in Seattle', 'Pretty Woman', 'Dirty Dancing', you name it, though my all-time favourite is 'While You Were

Sleeping'.

I didn't see much of Steve all day but he made the effort to get back in the evening. He reported back that the car parked outside the flat during the paint incident, had belonged to an old lady who'd reported it stolen. I'd forgotten to ask Pete anything about the car, other than the owner's name. Steve told me it was a red Volvo, which strongly suggested the paint incident and my crash were linked. He said he'd had the car listed as "stolen, believed used in a crime". The police would be looking out for it now. Other than that, it left us up a blind alley.

I asked him what was going on at work. He said the results of the first post-mortem and the forensics were back. Susan had been strangled, but there was no sign of any recent sexual activity nor of any other wounds apart from the marks on her wrists and ankles where she had been chained up. I was glad I didn't get to go to post mortems and see photos of bodies. I'd never make a policewoman. I don't expect they flip when there's a mouse in their flat. But I try to show an interest in Steve's work. Sometimes he clams up and wants to leave work at the police station, but then there are days when it actually seems to help him to talk things over with someone not involved. This was obviously one of those days.

'I keep wondering if there's another girl out there at the moment, Rach, chained up and lonely, with tape over her mouth. If there is, I'm not sure we're doing enough to help her.'

'I'm sure you're doing all you can, Steve. Do you know who the second victim was? Was she an au-pair as well?'

'She was called Nicola Kennedy, and no, she wasn't an au-pair. She worked in a museum in the town centre. And you're wrong about her being the second victim. She was found second, but killed earlier, so she is technically the first victim – that we know about, anyway. Nicola was a quiet girl like Susan, and she was blonde too, but that's about all they seemed to have in common. She lived at home with her parents.'

'They must be in a right state.'

'You're right, and it's even worse because she's been missing a couple of weeks, and so they were called in to look at Susan's body, because Susan hadn't been reported missing when her body was found. So they've had to go through it twice. Their daughter didn't go out much in the evening, just to night class, no night clubs or anything. We're interviewing everyone who knew her and it's not a long list, I'm afraid.'

'Maybe Nicola and Susan shared some friend, or maybe they went to the same class or something. Did Susan go to classes?'

'No she didn't. Mind you, apart from nightclass, Nicola rarely went out until the last few weeks of her life, when she went out frequently. She must have been seeing the murderer then I reckon, and there was some reason she kept it quiet from her parents.'

'Well it looks like the bloke doesn't live

with his own parents then, or he'd have had nowhere to take his victims back for coffee and a cuddle.'

'If you're right, then the boss has us barking up the wrong tree. He thinks the murderer must be one of those socially inept types, still living at home.'

'Well, it was just a guess on my part. Your boss could be right, but surely the bloke has to have had somewhere private to take the girls where he could keep them prisoner, and it could be the same place he took them after a date.' I was trying to be helpful, but I could have been muddying the waters.

'I was wondering about the noise, thinking it had to be somewhere in the country, but if he kept them silenced with tape...'

'He'd have to take it off for them to eat though, surely?' I felt sick at the thought that he might not even do that.

Obviously that had occurred to Steve. 'Who says he fed them? But yes, I think he would, and although he must've threatened them, he couldn't guarantee one of them wouldn't scream when the tape was removed, even if just for a moment till he hit her. Which brings us back to it being somewhere deserted.'

'Any clue in the photos?' Did I really want to know what was in the photos, I wondered?

'No. In both cases, the girl is sitting on the floor, chained up. The wall just looks like white plaster. Could be anywhere. Anyway, love let's forget about work for a while.'

'Sorry I wasn't much help.'

'Maybe not this time, but sometimes you say something that triggers an idea.'

We cuddled up on the settee listening to Heart FM and before I knew it, like the other nights while I'd been staying there, he was asleep, and I was heading that way too, so I shook him awake gently and we went to bed and slept like babies.

On Monday morning I got up and nosed around Steve's flat. I'd been there before of course, but never on my own. I was browsing through Steve's CD collection to see how his tastes had progressed since university and discovering he didn't seem to have found time to buy much at all that was new, when my mobile rang. I wondered if Mr Parry's wife had changed her plans from spending the afternoon with him. I know I would have done if I could. But no, the voice belonged to Mr Phillips, of Phillips Tools and Pipe Fittings Ltd.

'Er, Rachel, I'd like you to come in this morning. I know it's your morning off, but it's absolutely urgent and I'll make it worth your while. There's a wages matter that can't wait till you get in work tomorrow.'

He sounded nervous and was using my first name. Something was going on and he wanted me to pretend to be his wages clerk. I knew it might be trouble, but the words 'make it worth your while' sound very attractive when you've got bills piling up.

'It's not very convenient, Mr Phillips, but I'll manage somehow. I can only stay till lunchtime though. Will that be long enough?' I said in my sweetest voice, unsure whether this was going out on speaker phone or not. I could have stayed longer, but I wanted to sound in character.

'I'm sure that'll be fine, Rachel. I'd be most grateful. See you soon.'

I dressed in the most work-like clothes I had with me, black cord jeans and a sexy little pink jumper. Let's face it, they weren't work clothes at all, but this wages clerk was supposed to be on her day off, right? I didn't waste time and was at their office not much above half an hour after he called. I walked through the main room and everything looked pretty normal. Gloria gave me a wave. She probably thought I was her granddaughter.

'Ah, here's Rachel, the new wages clerk we have now. Rachel, this is Alan. He left before you started with us, about three weeks ago. He has a little problem with his severance pay and his reference, and he wasn't happy with the answers he was getting on the phone so he's come in person. Cath's typing him a new reference but Alan needs his last six months' salary re-calculating to take account of the higher salary he would have had if he'd got the promotion to foreman instead of Frank.'

'Why don't you just tell the woman I've got a gun and let's get on with it', growled Alan.

Right. I knew now why Mr Phillips had called me. He wanted the police but didn't have any opportunity to call them. Why does it always happen to me? Because it goes with the job, Rach. Now sort this out and let's try to get out alive. Thus ran the thoughts in my head as I took off my coat and eyed Alan to see if he was bluffing or enough of a maniac to use the gun.

'Alright, sir. Have you got the new rate of pay and the date it should have started?'

Mr Phillips handed me a sheet of hastily scribbled figures. 'I've done a rough calculation, but you'll have to check it and then work out the tax etcetera.'

He obviously thought I might be crap at maths and pay Alan even more than the increase he never got. I suppose I shouldn't be surprised after my error with the lengths of tube, and my mess with the order file. He was barking up the wrong tree though. I was hopeless with metric measurements and bad handwriting, and I got easily confused with strange computer programmes, but I'm a whiz at maths, and I always got great references from the places I temped in wages departments.

I used Mr Phillips's calculator to check the gross salary figure, then the tables to work out his tax and national insurance. Theirs isn't the only company to pay in cash, nor the only company to use actual tax tables rather than a computer to do it for them, so I knew the ropes. Mr Phillips may have been a bit surprised when I changed his figure from £422.54 to £422.45, and turned the pages looking like a true professional, but give him his due, it didn't show in his face. It came to £293.18. Alan was obviously expecting more. I explained patiently that tax and national insurance between them always came to just over a third, but he wasn't really convinced.

'That's not enough. I need to get my car repaired if I'm going to get another job. You can't live out at Hedon and get work in Hull without a car.' He was shouting now. I'd seen no sign of the gun but maybe that was coming next.

'How much is the bill?'

'I don't want handouts. I just want what should have been mine.'

'Well, maybe Mr Phillips might consider paying you a bonus for the inconvenience he's caused you. You must have had travelling expenses this morning, for instance.' I sounded calm, talking quietly in the hope that his voice would lower as well, but he had grabbed his bag and was poking around inside it. 'How much is the car repair bill?' I asked again.

'Three hundred and seventy-five quid, give or take a few pence.'

I did a speedy calculation in my head, as Mr Phillips offered him an extra hundred pounds. He wasn't going to accept, I knew that now. He wanted what he felt was his due, not a wad of notes to shut him up. I was right. He flipped and pulled out a gun.

'Just get down on the floor. You're going to have to give me my job back if there's not enough wages.'

'Alan, that gun means things are going to get worse for us all. Put it away now, man.' Mr Phillips was trying to calm things but making them worse. Alan was now in the position of crazed hostage taker, though I didn't think he wanted that and he wouldn't know where to go from there, so anything might happen.

'Alan. I've got an idea. I think a suitable inconvenience payment would be a hundred and twenty pounds, that'll come out at, let me see…' I scrabbled in the books, adding the money to his final month's adjusted salary. 'That'll come out at an extra eighty-six pounds 38 pence. That's a total of £379.56.' I looked pleadingly at Mr Phillips.

'Yes, Alan. I think that would be a satisfactory payment in lieu of bank interest you've missed out on, your phone calls, postage and travel costs today and your time spent in getting your wages corrected.'

Alan was silent for a couple of minutes, the gun shaking in his hand. He was still pointing it in our general direction. Then he spoke in quite a shaky voice, 'Yes, that seems fine, but what about the gun and everything. I can't just go now, can I? You'll call the police.'

'We just want this over, Alan', I said gently, 'as much as you do. There's no need to involve the police is there, Mr Phillips?' If Alan was surprised at a lowly wages clerk taking control, he didn't show it.

'I don't know how to get out of this.'

'Mr Phillips will get you the money and you can leave.'

I prayed there was enough cash in the safe and that Mr Phillips would keep quiet till this was over. I thought he was scared enough. The gun was still waving erratically in our direction and Alan was sweating. Just one slip of his finger near that trigger. I didn't want to think about it.

'But how do I know you won't call the police the minute I walk out the door?'

'You don't, but if we are regarding this as the correction of an injustice, and the payment of wages due, then that'll be the end of it, won't it? If Mr Phillips disagrees with your fair and just settlement, he can always go to an employment tribunal, but that'll cost him a lot more than settling with you. I don't think he wants to waste his time with the police and he knows you've suffered enough.' I hoped Mr Phillips was agreeing with all this I was spouting. He'd get costs if he went to a tribunal, but Alan wasn't to know that, and anyway, short of hauling in the bailiffs, I doubted if Alan could pay the tribunal costs even if they were awarded against him. As for the police, well, I'd let Mr Phillips decide on that, but afterwards. After what seemed like an eternity while I held my breath, Alan dropped the gun back into his bag, and said wearily, 'Okay. Give me the money. I can't go yet though.'

'Why?'

'My Eileen's coming in her car at one o'clock. We agreed she'd wait round the corner.'

It was only twelve thirty.

'Can't you ring her and tell her to come early?'

'No, she'll be under the dryer still. She's at the hairdresser's, having a set.'

'Has she got a mobile?'

'Oh no, she'll have no truck with one of them. Neither will I.'

'Well, it's my day off and I've come in specially, so I really want to get off home now. Why don't I give you a lift to the hairdressers?'

And that's what happened. Mr Phillips counted out the money for Alan and slipped me three twenty pound notes, mouthing, 'I'll ring you', and I drove Alan and his gun to the hairdressers to meet Eileen. The siege was over and none of the other employees was any the wiser. As for the gun, Alan told me when I dropped him off that he'd never have hurt me. It was one of those cigarette lighters, not a real gun at all.

I still felt like I'd been held hostage by a crazed gunman, because it'd felt like it at the time, so I went into Marks & Spencers and bought some new sexy undies to change my mood entirely. I planned on staying at Steve's for at least a week, and my period would be no problem in a day or two. I also bought some of their gourmet ready meals and delicious desserts fit for my mouse-conquering hero. I stopped off briefly at home to tell Les I'd not be around for a while, and to pick up more clothes and my favourite bath foam but I didn't hang around long. I kept one eye out for unwelcome intruders the whole time.

I'd not been long back at Steve's when Mr Phillips rang me on my mobile to say 'thank you'. When I told him of my conversation with Alan in the car, he was relieved. 'I suspected it wasn't a real gun, or if it was, then it was some relic that a relative had used in the war that wouldn't be loaded, but I couldn't be too careful. Alan was a good worker, just not suited to being in charge of the workshop. I'd already just about decided I didn't want to take it further and what you've told me confirms my decision. I'll see if I can't put in a good word for him with another firm. I don't want to see him and Eileen struggling.' I told him I couldn't help but agree that in this case, nothing would be served by bringing the police into it, and he thanked me again and said he'd have no hesitation in recommending me to any of his friends and business acquaintances who might need a private detective. Then he rang off.

I ran a hot bath and washed my hair. I felt marvellously pleased with my day's work and felt I had to tell someone, so I made a cup of tea and rang Sarah for a chat. I brought her up to date with the latest in my seemingly endless string of calamities and she told me that it looked like Josh was teething again. Bless him; he'd been trying to chew his way through the bars of his cot. She was looking forward to a night out with John just as soon as her mum got round, so I didn't keep her on the phone long.

Steve didn't get home till after I was in bed, but then I drifted back off to sleep in his arms, without a care in the world.

8

The next morning I woke early. My mind had been replaying the scene where I came home to find the paint poured through my letterbox and the one when I saw the mouse in my lounge. It made me wonder if my car crash was an accident after all. I lay there, thoughts of my tormentor whirling round my head. When Steve woke, I shared my thoughts.

'Who the hell could it be, Steve? Who'd want to make my life a misery?'

'It has to be someone connected with your job, Rach. These kind of things don't happen to ordinary people who work in offices, schools, shops. People with safe jobs. It has to be revenge for something you've done to someone. The only other reason for a series of nasty incidents like these would be jealousy - like if I was having an affair with you, and my wife found out. Then she might want to wreak similar havoc, but as far as I know, I'm not married.'

'Neither am I, so it can't be my jealous husband either. I suppose you're right, Steve, but the only sleaze-bag I can think of is Craig Dobson. He'll be far away by now, though I suppose he could have come back into the area, or he could have got someone he knew in Hull to carry out the attacks.'

'It's a bit petty for someone like him, and anyway, I can't see the point of Craig or any of his mates coming after you, Rach. After all, he hasn't ended up in jail yet and he'll want to stay well away.'

'Well I can't see any of my ex-clients doing it. Despite what you and Mum say, my job's not dangerous. I just can't think of anyone. Maybe the events are all unrelated and just bad luck. Like I first thought, the car crash was probably an accident, the driver going too fast in a stolen car, maybe even joy-riders. The paint could have been kids, vandals, and as for the mouse, well maybe it climbed up the drainpipe or hid inside someone's straw packaging for a new lamp or something. It could have wandered in when my door was open, or even just walked up the stairs.'

Steve shot me a look which translated as 'in your dreams'. 'You'd better face it love, you've upset someone, and the sooner you work out who it is, the better, because the police haven't the time to spend hunting down unidentified people who pour paint through doors and deliver mice. Your only hope is that they find the stolen car, with the driver still in it.'

'Well my money's still on Craig. I don't usually get involved in anything dangerous. Can't we track down any friends he might still have in Hull? What about Dean Hornby, the landlord of The

Steam Packet?'

'He did a runner when Craig disappeared. We found out he'd been involved in supplying the drugs that Craig dealt in. Anyway, what do you mean, "Can't we track down his friends?" Surely you mean the police, not me and you, and I don't think it's a high priority with these murders, love. You of all people should know how stretched we are at the moment, and my money's on another of your clients, identity as yet unknown.'

'OK. I'll look through my files again', I said, though secretly I was planning to see if Pete knew any way to help me. I refused to believe there was a queue of people out to endanger my life. I knew it must all lead back to that dodgy case and Craig.

After Steve had gone off to work again, I slipped my jacket on over a stripy jumper and yesterday's black cord jeans. I'd had a call from Mr Parry to say his wife was going out straight from work and she'd told him she was going shopping. He wanted to know if it was still convenient for me to follow her. I agreed but had time to kill till lunchtime so I thought I'd go round to Mum's beforehand.

I rang Pete first and asked him if he could track Lucy Turner down. I wanted to know if Craig had left any calling cards like paint and mice for her. The police hadn't been able to force her into leaving a forwarding address and all I knew was, she'd told me she was going home to her mum's in Lincolnshire for a bit either till Craig was caught, or he'd had time to forget all about her. He said he'd see what he could do. I think he wanted to talk longer, but I cut him short, saying I had an appointment with a client, because I didn't know where the conversation might lead. I still felt guilty about letting him kiss me, even if I was under the influence and not paying attention properly. Anyway, he wasn't to know the appointment wasn't till the afternoon.

As it was Tuesday, Mum was ironing, and glad of someone to talk to while she worked. Martians could land in Hull, but my mum would still wash on Mondays, iron on Tuesdays, vacuum on Wednesdays, visit my aunt on Thursdays, have her hair done on Fridays and go in town on Saturdays. She did do other things but it was hard to budge her from her routines unless she was going on holiday and then some really major planning was involved.

'Hello, Mum. I'm only working afternoons this week, so I thought I'd pop round. Shall I put the kettle on?'

'That'd be nice, love. What are you doing at work? Are you back to temping? I do wish you'd get a permanent job, and so does your dad. He's always saying we paid for you to go to university and you've not done anything with it.'

'Mm. Well I'm following this woman to see if she's having an affair.'

'Anyone I know? What's her name?' Mum had got Dad's moan off her chest so could now indulge her curiosity, even if it meant showing interest in my potentially dangerous detective work.

'You know I can't tell you her name.'

'Oh, go on. I might know something.'

I went ahead and told her the whole thing. After all, I don't work for MI5 and when all's said and done, she was right. She often did know someone involved in one of my cases and her network of gossipy friends and neighbours had saved me time on a number of occasions. This time though, she drew a blank.

'Don't think I can help you there, love. Tell me what else you've been up to. How's Steve?'

I thought of Pete and decided that it was best not to tell her about my meal out or she'd be inviting him and me round for one of her Sunday salad teas and asking if his intentions were honourable.

'I had a mouse in the flat, but Steve caught it for me. A real hero he was.'

'A mouse? A real one? How did that get in your flat?'

'Don't know, but it was a real one. It ran so fast it was horrible, but Steve caught it and it's gone now.'

Mum wanted all the details so I told her while we ate chocolate digestives and drank tea. When I got to the part about staying at Steve's, I decided to be economical with the truth and not mention the paint incident, or Steve's suspicions that I was being targeted in some way, but instead of allaying her worries, I achieved another undesirable effect.

'Well, I'm not sure I agree with you moving in there, Rachel. I mean, is it going to be permanent? I like Steve, but surely he should at least pop the question first. It'd be alright if you were engaged, but there doesn't seem to be any sort of long-term plan for the future.'

'Mum. It was just the mouse, OK! I felt all spooked out, like it was still there and its eyes were staring at the back of my head. I'll probably be going home after the weekend.'

'Right. I see.' It was obvious she didn't and her indignation had turned to disappointment. She was hoping to finally be able to get a special wedding day organised for me. There's no satisfying my mum. I took my leave after promising to go and see Gran the next day, and I was outside the office where Judith Parry worked, ten minutes before she was due to finish. I hoped she'd not sneaked off early. The office was on a quiet industrial estate but I didn't think she'd notice my car outside on the road.

I recognised Judith easily from the photo Mr Parry had given me. She had shoulder-length auburn hair, dyed presumably, and looked a good ten years younger than her husband. She said goodbye to a couple of other women who were leaving at the same time, either for lunch or for the afternoon. She got in her pale green Vauxall Corsa and set off in the direction of town. I hate this bit of my job. I consider myself a good driver, but it's never easy to follow someone when you haven't any idea where they're heading. I drove as near behind the Corsa as possible. Normal people don't expect to be followed and in town traffic it isn't unusual to have the same car behind you all the way to the shopping centre at lunchtime. Traffic lights almost intervened, but for once I was lucky and we arrived at the Princes Quay shopping centre car park within half a minute of each other. I was able to park on the same level, a short distance away, and congratulated myself on the good start to the afternoon.

It seemed Judith really was shopping, as she went into one clothes shop after another, sometimes stopping to try on a selection. She seemed to have decent taste. I managed to find a blouse I fancied in New Look. Might as well have a bit of fun on Mr Parry's time, I thought, and it makes me look less like a shoplifter than if I was just browsing the hangers but never buying. Bit of a mistake that turned out to be though.

We went in Boots and I bought shampoo while Judith bought some other things. When I came to pay, to my horror I discovered my debit card was missing from its usual spot in my purse. My Tescos and Sainsburys cards were both present and correct, but no debit card. I couldn't believe I'd done it again. I blame these PIN machines that swivel round and face the customer. The assistants expect you to remove the card and very rarely remind you. I wouldn't mind but I felt so stupid because it had happened to me before, a mere six days ago, and I'd sworn then to be really really careful in future. Yes, I know. There was nothing for it, I'd have to see where Judith went next, then pray she hung around a while or risk losing her, while I legged it back to New Look for my card. She went in Debenhams and I ran like the clappers back the way we'd come.

The previous week I'd had to show ID and had been made to wait, but this time the girl just handed the card to me, ignoring the long queue waiting to pay. I raced back to Debenhams and arrived out of breath and stressed in case I'd screwed up and lost her. I'd have to cut down on the cream cakes, though I couldn't promise on the chocolate. I wandered around, forcing myself to calm down and breathe slowly, but I couldn't see her.

I walked back to the entrance and scanned the crowds. I was just beginning to think I'd have to admit defeat when I spotted her coming out of a bakery across the road. Thank God. She was still on her own. If she'd been flirting with the baker, good luck to her, was what I thought, as I followed her down the road. Now I just hoped she was going to stop for a drink soon, as I was getting desperate for the loo. She wouldn't have had time to drink coffee in Debenhams, I didn't think. Luckily I was right. She went in a coffee shop and I was able to nip in the loo before ordering. After a pleasant half hour sipping coffee, eating a Danish pastry and sending a number of texts on her mobile, she got up to leave. I wondered who she was texting. I also wondered if she really emailed her daughter every night, or a man friend.

Bit of a dilemma for me that really. I rather hoped she had a man friend, but I didn't want to see her with him, because it was my job to report back to the dreaded Mr Parry. I couldn't think of him as Graham; he didn't seem human enough to me. 'Oh well', I thought, as we headed back to the car park, 'that's the trouble with relationship cases, they rarely produce satisfactory outcomes.'

That night it was after nine when Steve got in. I told him what I'd been doing, and then asked him about his day.

'We've had the pathology report back on Nicola Kennedy, whose body was found at Dane's Dyke. The cause of death was as expected, strangulation, and time of death was confirmed at around two weeks before the body was found. Again there was no sign of any sexual activity nor of any other pre-death wounds apart from the marks on her wrists and ankles where she'd been chained up. She did however have post-mortem wounds from being attacked by animals.'

'Too much detail, Steve. That's horrible.'

'The poor girl wouldn't have felt a thing, love. She was already dead.'

'I know, but I just don't like to think of it.'

'Well, both bodies were dumped after being killed elsewhere. We need to find out where they were held and killed if we're going to stand a chance of solving the murders. The other leads we have aren't that strong. Susan Hardy's stomach contents showed her last meal was probably pizza. We're contacting all the pizza delivery firms in the Hull and East Riding areas.

'Anything else?'

'Our enquiries into photographic suppliers haven't borne any fruit so far, but it's really hard without a name or description for the suspect, so attention's shifting to calls from the public, interviews with friends of the girls, and possible sightings of people and cars in the areas where the bodies were found. Extra officers have been drafted in from the West Riding to help.

It makes the forensic scientists' job much harder when they don't have a murder scene to search. They've been scouring the woods and the cliffs and beach area, but as the girls weren't killed there, there's unlikely to be much in the way of solid forensic evidence to give us any leads.'

'Not a lot to go on, then.'

'Some of the officers drafted in are also going round hardware shops to see if anyone's recently bought metal chain at the same time as duct tape. The duct tape just looked the usual silver-grey that's sold everywhere including market stalls, DIY stores and even some supermarkets, but chain is less common. Of course, the chain could have been bought many years ago and been lying in a shed or garage somewhere. The boss doesn't think we can gain anything by appealing to the public about the chains. He rather wants to hold back the information that the girls were kept restrained and were photographed, so we can eliminate cranks who confess even though they had nothing to do with the murders.'

'It all sounds a bit like you're clutching at straws. You just need a break though, Steve. Don't worry, it'll come.'

'I hope so. There's one other thing. The underwear. Unfortunately it looks like both girls were wearing the same set in the photos, so it wasn't as if the murderer had bought more than one or gone back to a shop for more. He could have gone back for a different size, but we don't think that's likely. And you wouldn't believe the number of saucy underwear suppliers on the internet these days.'

'I would, you know. There's loads of ads in Cosmo for a start and they all have websites. And I bet for every one legitimate enough to advertise there, there'll be dozens of other smaller places, not to mention shops who buy wholesale. Whoever's got that job must be having a whale of a time trawling through the internet looking for saucy underwear that matches.'

'It's a WPC actually. Men don't notice the details, I'm afraid.'

We laughed and it lightened the mood.

Even so, I knew the police had to investigate every avenue and they'd be trying to establish the manufacturer involved, so they could try and track suppliers and shops. It was the kind of lead they turned to when nothing more substantial came up. It looked like they were in that position already. Both girls seemed to have disappeared into thin air until their bodies had turned up.

And that was another equally tenuous line of enquiry – trying to find out where the girls had been kept. Steve told me that local bobbies were investigating abandoned buildings throughout Hull and the East Riding. The Post Office were often particularly helpful with such matters it seemed as their regular postmen and van drivers tended to know which buildings didn't get post. Of course the building might not be abandoned, but it was a start, and that's all they could do sometimes, just keep chipping away and hope for a breakthrough.

We watched TV. The murders had made the top item on the national 10 o'clock news. There were reporters camped out as near as they could get to Dane's Dyke, as well as at the cliffs near Mappleton and outside the police headquarters in Hull, and Steve's boss made yet another appeal for anyone with useful information to come forward. Steve said that although widespread publicity could help produce a vital clue, there was a danger that they could be swamped with too much information and people made things up because they wanted to get involved. I found that hard to believe but apparently they do get a lot of crank calls and all calls have to be logged and investigated so time was easily wasted.

Also the press kept saying things like, 'The public want results, and they want them now', as if the police didn't want results and were just dragging their feet and not taking the murders seriously. Too much pressure meant that the police could overlook something vital or not take adequate pains to substantiate information because they were rushing. At that point we shut the nasty world out and lay snuggled on the settee watching a film till late.

When I got to Gran's on Wednesday morning, she opened the door wearing a Barbie pink velour jogging suit, with her hair freshly permed. 'You're late'.

'I didn't realise we'd agreed a time. I told mum I'd call in this morning, that's all, Gran.'

'Well I expected you earlier. What do you think?' She did a sort of twirl.

'Mmm. Lovely', I said, unsure what I was commenting on.

'I thought I'd wear it to the bingo this afternoon. Got to move with the times, you know.'

I refrained from saying that Barbie pink might be undergoing a revival somewhere in the country, and doubtless some people were wearing velour jogging suits, but I didn't know you could still get the combined effect in the twenty-first century. All that with tight steel-grey curls as well.

'I'm not sure about the slippers, Gran. You might want to go for trainers instead.'

'I couldn't wear trainers, our Rachel. You don't want me to look stupid, do you?'

I wiped the grin off my face before it even started and led the way as usual through to the kitchen.

'Oh good, a cup of tea.' As if Gran would dream of serving coffee. She'd already laid out a slice of swiss roll each on a plate. Her idea of luxury. 'This looks nice, Gran.'

'Never mind the cake, tell me what you've been up to. Have you set the date with that bobby of yours yet?'

'Steve? No, not yet, Gran.' Mum must have not dared tell Gran that I'd moved in, even temporarily, or Gran'd have bought a hat already. I was grateful for small mercies. 'He's been really busy on those murders. You know, the two blonde girls. It looks like they might have been killed by the same person.' I might as well give her a titbit to tell her cronies at bingo, I thought, and Steve said there was a press conference following the second postmortem so I wasn't breaking police confidences; well only by about an hour, and the bingo'd not be over till a couple of hours after. She'd be able to impress her friends with a granddaughter important enough to find out snippets of new information for them to mull over.

'Well, I better start keeping a more careful look out when I'm walking around alone, then.'

'I don't think you need worry if he's targeting young blondes, Gran, but I suppose you can't be too sure.'

'Well I hope you're locking your car doors after you get in.'

'I'm careful Gran, honest. Have you any news?'

She launched into a long tale of how Marjory Leach had got ripped off by an unscrupulous builder who'd knocked at her door with some left over tarmac. 'Plain stupid that Marjory. I mean, doesn't she read the papers or does she think she's too nice to be ripped off? They'll not catch him neither, not with these murders to cope with. There aren't enough bobbies to go round. That's why you never see your Steve.'

She took me upstairs to show me a coat she'd bought in the sale. 'It's a serviceable colour, grey, so it should last. It'll see me out anyway. In fact, maybe I should have just managed with the one I've got.'

I protested that she'd live for years yet, probably outlive the lot of us. It was true, but also a game she like to play every time she bought anything, and I knew better than to deviate from the rules, so I played along, until I caught sight of my watch.

'Got to go now, Gran. I've got a case this afternoon.'

'Oh yes, your mam said. The cheating wife.'

Before I got drawn into a discussion of the rights and wrongs of infidelity with Gran, I grabbed my bag and sidled to the door, where I said my goodbyes, and promised to come again soon.

I stopped for a sandwich and drink at Steve's then got myself to Judith Parry's office on time. That afternoon she drove to a house in leafy Ganstead. I called Mr Parry from the car and he confirmed the address and car on the drive as belonging to Judith's best friend. I saw them through the window and unless they were indulging in a threesome, the afternoon seemed to be an innocent female get-together. She stayed there all afternoon, and I was glad when she left. I'd parked up the road a bit and got out to stretch my legs once or twice, but I was stiff and in need of the loo when she came out and drove off.

When I'd seen her back to her house, I rang Steve from my car and suggested it might be to his advantage to get home a bit earlier that night. Alright then I admit it, I told him in graphic detail what I'd do to him when he got home and what I'd be wearing. I put on my new underwear and black stockings. I'm not really into women's lib and their ideas about not letting yourself be a sex object for a man. The fact is, stockings make me feel sexy too, so why not? I covered myself up with a silky peach dressing-gown and put some music on. At eleven I gave up and went to bed.

I lay in bed thinking I was none too sure about this 'living with Steve' thing. I mean, I know I wasn't happy about stepping out of the shower and drying my feet, only to discover the bathroom floor was covered with wet footprints so my feet got wet again – and they trailed in over the bedroom carpet, making that slightly damp too - and the wet towels dumped in a heap on the bed didn't exactly enthral me either, but I bit my tongue after I'd mentioned it the once, and things didn't improve. Hey, it's his flat after all, but you'd think someone with a swanky place by the marina would be able to afford a dishcloth. Only like I said, I wasn't moaning about it, whereas Steve was snapping at me all the time.

'Can't you manage to put your empty chocolate wrapper in the bin, Rach, please?' and 'This kitchen looks like a bomb's hit it. Can't you keep it tidy?' Presumably it was usually tidy because he never cooks. When it wasn't the kitchen and the rubbish, he complained about my things taking over his bathroom shelves. I mean, what difference did a couple of bottles of shampoo, conditioner and the like make in the general clutter of a bathroom? Granted, his flat was devoid of clutter when I arrived, but I was his girlfriend, and although there wasn't much room for both our clothes in the wardrobe, did he have to shout at me and say I was squeezing him out of his own flat? He just needed an extra wardrobe, that's all. You have to make allowances when you share. Maybe we'd both lived alone for too long.

I hadn't heard him come in. At breakfast I left him in no doubt about how I felt that he'd been late even though I'd dressed up and told him what I'd be wearing and added to that, he hadn't even phoned. Then I felt really bad because he told me there'd been a third body found. He was so tired I don't think he'd heard much of my rant. The apology passed him by too. He said they'd got a list of convicted sex offenders with silver cars and had interviewed them all. They were checking further into the ones with little or no alibi. He said he couldn't imagine getting away early at all at the moment, but to make up for it, he'd insist he had a break on Sunday as he was long overdue a day off .

I gave up expecting him the rest of the week, ate chocolate and watched videos.

9

On the Thursday, Judith Parry set off out of Hull. She parked up in Beverley and went round the market and the small shops near the Minster. It's a nice little market town, about eight miles north of Hull with narrow pavements and winding streets, and I don't think of going there often enough. I only went there as a child to go to Beverley Westwood, which is just outside the town itself and where we'd run up and roll down grassy banks and hide in the bushes and behind the trees and generally have a right good time, until Mum noticed how many grass stains were on my clothes and that I'd ripped something as usual. Amazingly my sister Laura always stayed neat and tidy. It's no wonder I'm the one who always has the calamities while her life sails on serenely.

The streets were bustling and I lost sight of Judith once, but then I almost literally ran into her on a corner outside a shoe shop. A bit flustered, I hung around outside, looking in the window, as she went in and looked over the racks. I told myself that if she looked up, she would have probably seen me watching her, but the truth is my eye was caught by a gorgeous pair of red shoes. They were shiny patent with the cutest heels and a tiny strap round the ankle, and I just had to try them on. Luckily for me, Judith selected a couple of pairs of shoes and sat down while the assistant went to get them in her size to try on. I slipped in and asked for the red stilettos in my size.

I had a momentary flashback as I said, 'red stilettos' to the young girl, but if you're serious about shopping, and about your job, I reminded myself sternly, you have to learn to separate your own life from a life where people are found with shoes protruding from their eyes. Judith, a woman after my own heart obviously, tried on the same shoes in black, as well as another open-toed pair with thicker heels. I wondered about them, but knew I couldn't afford two pairs. To tell the truth, I wasn't sure I could afford the stilettos, but you know how it is with shoes, you can never find what you want when you're looking, so if you see a perfect pair sometime you're not looking, you'd be mad not to buy them. And they fit perfectly, so they may as well have had a flashing sign saying, 'Rach, these are your shoes'.

Judith and I arrived at the counter together. 'These are gorgeous aren't they? I haven't seen any patent shoes for ages. I wish I could have got the red too, but I'd have nothing to wear them with.' Judith had a lovely laugh and I warmed to her instantly. It was going to be awkward following her if she recognised me though, so I muttered, 'Yes. I love them. Got to dash. Got to buy a red dress now', and left the shop pretty quickly. I could just see us having a chat over a cup of tea and cake, and that would be treacherous when I was working for her husband. People seem to talk to me though, and I guessed Judith was a similar sort of person, and if I'd not been working, we could well have ended up in a café together, exchanging first, shoe stories, then life stories.

As it was, I hovered in the doorway of a book shop down the street, let down my hair and put my glasses on. I wear contacts usually when I'm working, and wear my hair tied tight back in a pony tail or in a French knot. That way, if I ever see my clients or people I've staked out and followed, when living my 'normal' life, they don't connect the two. Obviously two pairs of shoes had stretched Judith's budget. She had a cup of tea in a little café but she didn't go for cake. I hovered around, looking in various windows. It kept spitting with rain and I was glad when she eventually finished sending texts to all and sundry and left the café. She returned to her car and drove home. Another wasted day, but at least I'd earned some more money, even if it went on the shoes.

On Friday morning I went to see Sarah and talked her into leaving the baby with her mum so we could go shopping. I wore my new red shoes to break them in a bit. You'd have thought I'd have seen enough of the shops following Judith, but it was the usual dual purpose trip. I poured out all my feelings about Steve – and Pete.

'I'm getting so fed up with hardly seeing Steve and I felt a right fool getting all dressed up for him in my stockings and then he didn't get in until I'd gone up to bed. It made me feel a bit tarty instead of sexy in the end. Strange how that happens, isn't it?'

'I wouldn't know. We don't get five minutes to ourselves unless Mum comes round to babysit and then we're straight off out, and when we get back we're either too tired, or the mood's gone by the time John takes Mum home, or Josh wakes up crying. I haven't had sex for four or five months now. I just don't think I have the energy for dressing up.'

'Oh Sarah, you could wear sexy underwear to go out in and be waiting for him downstairs when he gets back from your mum's instead of getting ready for bed.'

'I suppose so, but I've got an ear out for Josh all the time.'

'You know you'd hear his healthy lungs even over the loudest noises you and John could make, so you should really stop worrying and go for it. But tell me what you really think of Pete. Do you think he's looking for someone to settle down with or just out for a good time?'

'Tell me about all about this date you had then.'

'It wasn't really a date. I was shattered after the crash and he offered to buy me a meal to save cooking, but I had a really nice evening with him. We went to an Italian in Ferriby and he made me feel really special, pulled my chair out, helped me into the car and stuff like that - things that Steve doesn't bother with. It might have been the wine or the romantic music, but when he talked about settling down, I thought maybe he'd be more suitable material than a policeman.'

'Really! He asked you to settle down with him?'

'No. It was in general terms, but Steve never mentions settling down. I wish I could say he missed me when he moved back out of my flat a while ago, but he's always so busy with work. I don't think he ever had a minute to think "I wish I wasn't sitting here on my own; I'd rather be with Rach." And now I'm in his flat temporarily and there doesn't seem a lot of difference. Sometimes I just think I'm just a convenient friend to have sex with.'

'Oh Rach, I'm sure you mean much more to him than that.'

'You could say the same of me as well I suppose, but I missed him a lot when he moved back out. I tell myself I don't and that my life isn't conducive to being in a full-time relationship, but I don't think I mean it. I know he comes round and rescues me and I think he loves me in his way. I know he hasn't the time to look for, let alone spend time with another woman, so I don't think he'll go off with someone else, but it's not like we have a permanent arrangement. I mean why can't we live together and still retain some independence?'

'Have you asked him, Rach?'

'Well, I suppose not. I keep up this façade of

it not mattering, because I'm scared if I ask I'll get the answer I don't want to hear.'

'It's time you asked him.'

'I know, but how, without making it seem like I'm needy? And what if Pete's really the one for me? He is gorgeous and he makes such an effort. I've not given him much encouragement either.'

'Yeah, but Rach, maybe that's why he does make such an effort. Don't forget in school, Pete could get any girl he wanted, me included, and I don't expect that's changed much really. He might just see you as a challenge.'

'You think he's just having a bit of fun and playing with me?'

'I didn't mean it to sound like that, you know I didn't. You're really attractive Rach. You don't think you are, because you think you're flat-chested and a bit skinny, but it doesn't put Steve off, does it?'

'No, but men seem to go for one distinct type and Pete, well think of all the curvy girls he went out with at school, like Pamela Shirtcliffe – and you of course, but you couldn't compete with her on that front. She was enormous.'

'He might want a change, but Rach, I don't think he's the settling type either, whatever he said. I think that's a ploy because he knows it's what women want to hear. I don't think he's slimy or underhand. I just think that honeyed words slip off his tongue because that's how he is, a flirt. He genuinely feels a lot for the girl he's going out with, but he's attracted to so many girls, and he's the sort who'll always have a roving eye and not be able to tie himself to just one person. I tell myself that's why he dumped me. Not that I wasn't good enough. I could be wrong Rach, but are you sure you want to find out and risk having your heart broken? Because I know you, you pretend you don't care but you do. And what about Steve? You might lose him if you get serious about this thing with Pete.'

'But have I really got him? I don't play games, otherwise I expect I'd be actively trying to make Steve jealous with Pete. I played it down when Pete helped me with the car, and when he took me out for a meal, I made out it was a last minute thing because he'd rung and I was feeling faint so he thought he'd make sure I ate.'

'There's no hope for you, Rach really. You're a full-blown romantic and you're one of those people who can't love two people at once. I hate to say this, but you have to decide. If you're not sure of Steve, then you could go out with Pete if he asks, but at least you should ask Steve if he thinks he'll ever want to get married.'

'Bit blunt that. I suppose I could ask him if he thinks he'll ever get on the property ladder and suggest two salaries is the only way these days. Anyway, I forgot to say. I got a text from Pete while I was on my way here, asking if I want to go and see a film.'

'Go then. You'll only work out how you feel by spending time with him. Steve's too busy to take you and you never know, it might make him think about what he's got and what he might lose.'

'Even if I'm just his easy route to sexual gratification?'

'You're putting yourself down again Rach. If Steve only wanted you for sex he wouldn't worry half as much as he does about you. He got really cross when you nearly got yourself killed, didn't he? And he's always discussing his cases with you. He values your opinion.'

'Maybe. Though he thinks I'm a bit dizzy. Thanks for listening anyway, Sarah, I wish I knew what to do for the best. I think I will go to the pictures with Pete. I'll be sober and won't do anything silly. And Steve - well, when this murder case of his is wrapped up, he won't be so tired and maybe then I'll find the right opportunity to ask him about the future.'

We picked up our bags and left the café, heading back to Sarah's.

In the afternoon it was dry for once. Judith Parry drove home from work via the garden centre. Not having a garden, I wasn't tempted to buy anything, but she bought some bulbs. Mr Parry was out but I could see her in the garden cutting down overgrown shrubs. Presumably she planted the bulbs as well. I couldn't hang around too near or she might have noticed, so I parked on the next street and just walked by a few times, but no cars arrived and it would have been risky to entertain a male friend in her own house in broad daylight so I wasn't too bothered that I didn't sit right outside the whole time. I was beginning to think Mr Parry was paranoid about there being someone else. It looked like she didn't want to be with him, but that was all.

While I was cooking tea, talk of the devil, Mr Parry rang for a progress report and to tell me she was going to the dentists at nine on Saturday morning and then she was going to look for new curtains. He was reluctant to spend any more money, but said I should follow her again as she said she'd be out all day, and then send him my typed report and invoice.

Just afterwards, Pete rang. He gave me Lucy's mum's number and then asked if I wanted to see the new James Bond film. It was the first night but he'd managed to get tickets and wondered if I was free. Bearing in mind my conversation with Sarah, I said I'd love to, and he said he'd be round in an hour. I rang Lucy's mum straight after putting the phone down. I explained who I was and her mum told me she didn't know where Lucy was. I was sure she was lying but couldn't blame her. I might not be who I said I was. I played along and told her about the paint, the car and the mouse and asked her to tell Lucy to be careful, should she hear from her. She must have felt a bit sorry for me, because she said she was sure nothing like that could have happened to Lucy (for that I read that nothing had), but she'd be sure to pass the message on if she were to hear from her daughter.

Pete hadn't given me too long to dither about what to wear because I had to eat first and shower and wash my hair. I settled for my favourite purple jumper and a pair of jeans. I was going to put my hair up, but it's not comfy leaning back in cinema seats. He was on time, again, and I enjoyed the film and the company. Steve liked James Bond as well, but I couldn't see him getting to see it before it ended up on TV. Pete asked me to go for a meal afterwards, but I said I'd already eaten and I had an early start in the morning. He dropped me at the door, leant across and kissed me briefly on the lips, and asked when he might see me again. I said I'd ring him. If he was disappointed, he didn't show it.

On Saturday Judith went to the dentists all right, but she was in and out in half an hour. I felt sorry for her, living with Mr Parry, but at least she wasn't tied to the house, and she had her job. I dreaded to imagine what her life would be like when she had to retire, but it wasn't my business, and I told myself I couldn't get personally involved in my cases.

She set off, heading east out of town, which was strange if she was going to pick new curtains. I followed her right through Hedon, way out towards the coast, past the wind turbines at Skeffling. I love these good old Viking names and although it's not considered historically accurate any more, I can't help picturing them marauding their way across the Holderness plain. Then we passed the North Sea Gas terminal at Easington and drove right down to Spurn Point. She set off down the narrow track right to the very tip where the coastguard station and the jetty for the lifeboat are. There was no other way off the point, so I took the time to go to the loo and put a bit of distance between us before paying my three pounds and following her down the track.

I could only drive slowly and it was a weird feeling with the grey North Sea on one side and the brown river Humber on the other. There were paved ridges and blocks all along the track to prevent it becoming slippery when the wind blows wet sand across it. There were also narrow rail lines. Dad had once told me that a military railway had been built along Spurn Point to the tip to take troops and guns to the end to defend the mouth of the Humber. The reason I remembered was that the trains had been powered by sails so the wind blew them down the rails, and that caught my imagination. Very eco-friendly, but I wondered what they'd done when the wind was in the wrong direction. There'd be no worry about a lack of wind. It always seemed windy at the east coast.

I hadn't been out to Spurn since I was a kid. The point had doubtless changed its position since then, as erosion takes sand from one side and deposits it on the other, changing the shape and lie of the curving spit of land. There was no real reason why I'd not been in all those years, but maybe it was because it's remote and there's not a lot there unless you're into bird-watching. Another thing I'm not into, is walking far, and when Judith got out and set off down the path over the sand dunes to the beach, I realised I was hardly dressed for the conditions. I'd got a nice warm jacket, and a sweet little fleece hat I found in the car to keep the wind off, but I seemed to have misplaced the handy flat shoes I keep in there for creeping around after people. And what was I wearing? My shiny red stilettos. Oops on a big scale.

Judith's figure was rapidly disappearing into the distance. Either she had some definite purpose in mind, or she was walking quickly because it was cold. I walked so far down the path, hoping to see she'd stopped on a bench, and then when I saw she was still striding on ahead down to the beach, I whipped off my shoes before they got ruined and stuck them in a carrier bag I'd snatched up from the car. It was freezing, but I couldn't think what else to do. Suffering in the name of work, I walked along the beach in my bare feet. It was so cold and the strips of shingle hurt my feet, but at least my shoes were OK.

I was a long way behind her, but I soon caught up as she kept picking up pebbles by the shore, pocketing some and throwing others back. I daren't risk her recognising me, so I turned and walked a bit in the opposite direction, just casting the odd glance over my shoulder. As I walked up towards the Point itself, a large tanker was coming into Hull. I got the most incredible view of it seemingly sailing straight into the side of the sand dunes, as it passed by the end of the Point.

Frostbite was setting in, when a tall grey-haired bloke strode down onto the beach. He walked past me as if I wasn't there, a boyish grin on his face. I guessed where this was heading, and walked up off the beach to the dunes. It was steep climbing back up and a case of two steps forward, one step back, as the sand slipped away beneath my feet. I turned at the top and as I expected, they flung their arms round each other's necks and kissed like they hadn't seen each other for ages, or were in the first throes of romance, or maybe they just always felt that way about each other. Either way, it looked like Mr Parry was right. I had my camera with me, but hesitated. It didn't really matter that I was exposed, instead of snapping furtively from my car. I could pretend to be snapping sea birds or anything remotely nature-related. What mattered was that I genuinely liked this woman and I didn't like her husband.

Somehow I've always avoided this dilemma so far in my unusual career. That's pretty amazing. Even more amazing I suppose, when you realise what sort of person I am. I agonise over how to avoid upsetting people in my private life, yet I ended up in a job which by its very nature, means I frequently have to tell people what they don't want to hear. I have to tell employers that it's their favourite clerk who's stealing from them, parents that their child doesn't want any more contact with home, and men or women that their spouse is cheating on them. None of it's easy, but I generally manage to keep my distance because of the short timescale involved. Sometimes I feel that, although unpleasant, it's better they know the truth instead of guessing at it. After all, if they hadn't had doubts, they wouldn't have come to me. I'm not spilling the beans to a best friend who was in complete ignorance that her husband's cheating on her.

But Judith Parry touched a nerve. I felt some sort of sisterly affection for her, and she was the one who was doing the cheating, instead of being cheated on. Would I have felt differently about all my other cases of marital infidelity if I'd known or liked the person I'd caught out? Or was it just that Graham Parry was the first really obnoxious client I'd had, someone to despise, rather than pity.

While I pondered all this, I took no photos, but watched from the dunes as they walked along the beach, his arm around her shoulders. They left the beach too, and walked up to a bench, both laughing. I moved behind a bush to watch as they looked into each others' eyes. The man stroked her hair and she laid her head on his shoulder. I knew with certainty I couldn't do this. I walked back to the car before I saw any more and had to make my lies even bigger ones.

I got back into the car and tried to rub life back into my feet. I drove back down the track and bought myself a cup of tea in the café. Should I wait or should I go? I wondered what Mr Parry would think if or when Judith left him. Would he think I'd been useless at my job if I kept quiet, or would he think she'd been scheming and careful? Did I care? And would she leave him? Meeting at Spurn Point suggested her male friend couldn't take her back to his house. He was probably cheating on someone too. Maybe his wife deserved to know. Relationships are a minefield enough when they're your own, but meddling into someone else's, well, it's best that I don't usually think of it. Maybe he didn't want to hurt his wife, but was unhappy for some reason, or maybe he was just so happy with Judith, he gave in to temptation. Maybe they were planning a future together, or maybe they were just getting what happiness they could. Perhaps it would be better if Mr Parry found out and it forced the issue, but on the other hand if her boyfriend was not able to be with Judith, then I'd be taking from her the only happiness she had in her life.

There were too many maybes and I had to report back to Mr Parry that night. I pictured them walking back to their cars, arm-in-arm, and Judith driving up to the cafe and asking, 'What are you going to do Rach?'

I turned the key and drove away. I wrote up my report that night and reported Mrs Parry had been to the dentists then had a ride to Spurn Point and took a walk. It was true, as far as it went. I wasn't the police. I hadn't sworn to tell the truth, the whole truth and nothing but the truth. I even charged Mr Parry the full rate, though I thought about reducing it a bit. In the end, I thought of myself in my fifties and knew that I would want a life, and that Judith deserved a chance of happiness. She might not get it. She might still get discovered, but I couldn't influence that. I could at least buy her a little more time.

10

On Saturday night Steve filled me in on the details of the third body. This one had also been found near Dane's Dyke, this time in the wooded area surrounding the steep path that led from the car park right down to the beach. The police were waiting to hear how long the girl had been dead. By now they had a comprehensive list of missing blondes, so it was only likely to be a matter of hours before she was identified. There'd also been a bit of a breakthrough. They'd found a link between Nicola Kennedy, the girl whose body had been found second, and a convicted rapist, Gavin Parker. He'd worked for a while as a driver for a stationery company who supplied the museum where Nicola had worked, and he'd made several visits there in the months leading up to her disappearance. He was down on the list as having a small silver car, and couldn't come up with much of an alibi.

He was being interviewed while officers searched his digs, looking for something that might enable them to arrest him on suspicion of murder. There hadn't been much evidence on either of the first two bodies, so it was the unwanted and unspoken thought of Steve and his team that the third murder might give them vital clues or forensic evidence. However, knowing that a possible suspect was in custody didn't lighten the mood at knowing a third girl had been killed, and we went to bed subdued.

I was ready on Sunday morning a full ten minutes before Steve. He'd taken the day off, just like he'd promised. I told myself to take my time but I didn't want to give him any excuse to change his mind. He looked tired still but sexy, dressed in jeans and one of my favourite pale blue shirts. He flung a thick jacket onto the back seat of his car. 'Have you got a thick coat, Rach? It might be chilly by the coast.'

'I'll see what I can dig out. I wonder if we'll get a summer this year for a change.'

I was so looking forward to the drive and to being in Whitby again. I still remembered when we'd driven there for a day, back when we'd been at university together. Steve had borrowed his mum's car to ferry some more stuff over from his home in Leeds and had taken me up to Whitby while he had the use of it. I used to go with the family of course when I was younger, but that was our first real trip out together and we got on so well. We didn't run out of things to talk about, though we were comfortable being quiet together too. When we'd got to the top of the hundred and ninety-nine steps by the abbey and sat on a bench, Steve with his arm round my shoulders, I knew then that we fit together and had something special. It seems incredible when I look back, that we went our separate ways after completing our degrees.

I did go down to London at weekends when Steve was posted there after his police graduate training course, but he often had to work and I was working during the week. Soon the gaps became longer and I didn't seem to fit in with the London crowd. I saw him talking to a girl once, smiling down at her like he did with me, and I suppose I started to pull back then. I was so sure he'd find someone more sophisticated, prettier, certainly more available, that I didn't go so often, trying to save myself the inevitable pain before it came. He didn't ring so often or we missed each other and left messages. Until one day I realised we'd not spoken for months.

When he moved back up to Hull and we got together again, we only spoke briefly about it once, and he said he let me go because he always seemed to be too busy and he couldn't visit enough to be what I wanted. He knew I hated London and wouldn't move down there, so he'd thought it was for the best. He's never said why he came back to Hull. I suppose it was the only place where he could get up the ladder to Inspector, but sometimes I wonder why he didn't go home to Leeds instead. Maybe less opportunities there, I tell myself, but I've never asked him, and he's never said.

Inevitably we had to stop to fill up with petrol. I was in a hurry to get going and when Steve's mobile rang, I jumped out to fill up the car for him. I was just reaching into the car for money to go and pay, when he ended his call and looked past me, out of the window. 'You haven't, Rach. Tell me you haven't filled up with petrol.'

'Thought I'd save us some time, love. Why, what's wrong?'

'We won't be going to Whitby today, I'm afraid. I can't believe you didn't remember.' I stood there, handbag in hand, totally confused.

'What are you on about, Steve?'

'My car's an Alfa Romeo TD, Rach. You know that.'

'Are you bragging or something, just because mine has no initials after its name? I don't get it.'

'TD as in Turbo Diesel, love. It's a good job I hadn't turned the key and started it up.'

Then the penny dropped. I wasn't usually with him when he filled up but I've heard tales of people filling diesel cars with petrol and vice versa. 'I didn't realise it was a diesel, Steve. Really. I know it's stupid. Oh hell, will you be able to get it sorted? We could leave it here and take my car to Whitby.'

'Rach, we're not going to Whitby. I need my car. I need to get it sorted today and I'll have to call out the breakdown service and sit here till they come. How could you be so stupid? I need the car first thing tomorrow to go out to the coast with work.'

If I'd thought, I'd have known he was just tired and couldn't take any more hassle, but I was upset he called me stupid because I'd never known his car was diesel and didn't notice the letters TD on the back. Though even if I had, I wouldn't have known what they meant. 'Look, I was only trying to help. Ring the RAC and I'll go get my car, follow you to the garage, and we'll go from there. I could drive you tomorrow if you want.'

'Just forget it Rach. I'll have to go in work to sort out a car. I'll get a passing patrol to pick me up from the garage and take me to the station to get a car. It'll probably be an hour or so before a breakdown truck comes anyway and then I'll have to hang around the garage while I book it in. You go home. It's pointless us both wasting our day off.'

'But surely we can still go to Whitby in my car.'

'It's going to be lunchtime love. I don't fancy tearing up there and back. Let's just forget it.'

There seemed to be no point in asking if he wanted me to wait with him or saying anything else. He was determined not to find a way round it and I felt ready to cry. I got my coat, and walked off down the road. When I got back to his place, I collected my things together and drove back to my flat. I'd said I'd stop a week and a week had passed. As I walked out I wondered when or if I'd be back. Alright, maybe I was being a bit melodramatic, but it seemed there could be no serious future for us if we couldn't manage one day out together without it going wrong. I'd hoped we'd be back early evening in plenty of time to make love, after a lovely day out. He couldn't even bear to have me sit and wait with him, to try to laugh about it. What was the point any more? I felt frustrated, but far more than that, I felt very sad and lost.

When I got back to my flat, I walked in carefully, hoping nothing else untoward had happened whilst I'd been away. No mice, snakes or alligators, no paint. It all seemed fine, if a little cold and unwelcoming. I put the kettle on and rang Sarah to tell her the latest. I could hear Josh screaming and could tell it was a bad time, so I just said I'd gone back home, Steve was cross with me cos I'd messed up his car and we didn't get to Whitby, and if she had a spare five minutes later, I could do with her shoulder to cry on. I decided I couldn't face the flat on my own. It was either go to Mum's or hit the shops.

I'd spent quite a lot that week, so thought I'd go to Mum's again. She'd be wondering what'd hit her as I was only round there on Tuesday, but at least I'd not mentioned going out for the day with Steve, so I could act as if I'd expected to be on my own. I couldn't do with Mum's sympathy and home-spun wisdom. I'd rather thrash out my problems with Sarah.

I listened to my answerphone messages in case someone hadn't followed the request to ring my mobile if it was urgent. There was a message from the day before, asking me if I could do a check on a street where they were putting in an offer on a house. I gave them a quick ring back, took their details and the address of the new house and agreed standard terms. I told them they were lucky as I'd just wound up on a long job and hadn't taken on any new cases because I didn't know when I'd be free. A small white lie. Mr Perry's case was a full week, so quite long for me, and I hadn't taken on any new cases. I hadn't been offered any either, but they weren't to know that. I always like to give the impression of being in demand.

I knocked at Mum's back door.

'Hello. Are you busy? I thought I'd pop in and see what your new curtains look like.' On the way over I'd remembered that Auntie Lesley was making Mum's new living-room curtains and I'd only had a description of the material so far. I knew Mum'd be pleased to show them off and she'd have picked them up from my auntie's by then.

'Come in, Rachel. What do you think? She's done a good job, our Lesley has.'

'Oh yes, they're lovely. They match the carpet and the suite just right. You made a good choice with this blue, and the material's good quality too. You'd not have got them that good ready-made, and there's just not the same choice of colours in the pre-packed ones either.' Personally I had nothing against ready-made, shop-bought, but I knew what Mum wanted to hear.

'You're right. I'm so glad you like them. You can never get an opinion out of your dad, apart from "They're OK", and that's only if you point them out to him. Could be a totally different colour and he'd not notice they'd changed.'

'Where is Dad then?'

'Out the back. He's been at that garden

every bit of fine weather we've had, and we've not had much so far this Spring, have we?'

'I'll just nip out and say 'hello'. I don't suppose you'll have enough dinner for me as well, will you? Only I was planning to eat out, but I'd rather eat your cooking any day. It doesn't matter if you can't manage though. I don't want Dad to go short.'

'I'll just peel some extra veg while you're talking to your dad. I've got a chicken so it'll do you easy. Gran's not coming today. She's entertaining one of her gentleman friends. I don't know which one. I can't keep up with her and she always has more than one on the go at the same time.'

I wandered out and exchanged a few words with Dad about plants, seeds, bulbs and the like and Hull City's chance of staying up. When I got back in, mum had dinner on the go and she'd got out a letter from Dad's sister Kath. There were photos of my cousin Suzy's wedding. I didn't feel like looking at wedding photos so I said a few appropriate things then changed the subject.

'Do you know anyone who lives on Garden Village, Mum? You know, off James Reckitt Avenue?' I'd gone to school not far away but that was years ago.

'Can't say as I do, Rachel. Why?'

'Oh, it's a new job I've got. A woman's hired me because she and her husband are buying a house on Maple Avenue and they want a neighbourhood check done. They want me to see what it's like at different times but particularly late at

134

night, and at weekends. They want to know if there's a problem with kids hanging around, noisy neighbours, that sort of thing.'

'Do people pay for that instead of doing it themselves? Well I don't know myself, but your Gran might know someone. I'll ask her for you, shall I? Or will you be popping around to see her soon?'

'I went last Wednesday, so if you wouldn't mind asking for me, that'd be good.' Relieved that I'd steered the conversation away from weddings, we went on to discuss the latest eviction from the programme where soap stars sing, or make fools of themselves, depending on who they are. I can never remember the name of the programme. Soon dinner was ready. After I'd eaten I felt a bit better and decided I'd make a start on my surveillance.

I'd just got back in the car when my mobile rang. It was Steve.

'I'm sorry, love. I didn't mean to lose my temper. I know you don't know anything about cars and I should have told you before I took my phone call. I didn't mean for you to pack your bags.'

'Well I did say I was only stopping a week or so 'til we were sure nothing else had happened, but thanks for apologising. I'm sorry too that I was so upset, but it was quite a big deal to me, going to Whitby, as well as the fact that I've not seen you all week. And you've been so tired when you've got in, I've felt a bit surplus to requirements.'

'Oh no, sweetheart, far from it. It's been lovely to walk in and see you on the settee or in my bed. This case is just taking it all out of me, but it's

135

not often you get a serial killer. It is exceptional. Anyway, have you eaten?'

'Had dinner at Mum's, sorry, but I could come and watch you eat.' I was hoping he wouldn't just go off on his own.

'I've managed to borrow a car from work while mine's sorted. The breakdown people towed it to a garage and dropped me off at the police station, which was very good of them. I've got to eat but I'll get a pizza out of the freezer. It won't take long. Are you still at your mum's? If you've not made plans for the rest of the day, we could salvage what's left and go out. It'll have to be somewhere a bit nearer though.'

'That'd be lovely. I've just left Mum's and I've no plans.'

'What about Sewerby, then? We haven't been there in ages.'

'Mmm, yes. Good idea. I'll be round soon then.'

'I'll be waiting. I'll try to make it up to you a bit while my pizza's cooking – as a sort of starter. I'll save the main course till I get you back tonight. After a nice afternoon out we can chill out with a couple of glasses of wine and catch up on what we've been missing.'

I could have told him I had other plans and made him sweat, but life's too short. I love Steve and like I said to Sarah, I don't play games. I must have been missing when that female gene was handed out. The only thing I decided was I wouldn't move back in with him – at least not while he was on the serial murder case. I wasn't going to be waiting in all night most nights for him to come home.

Until he had the time to take me out like Pete, I still wanted him to make an effort if he wanted to sleep with me, to ask and not assume I'd be there waiting. And if Pete wanted to take me out again, I'd go. I'd tell Steve and let him draw his own conclusions. If he asked though, I wouldn't pretend that there was something between me and Pete or that I wanted there to be. I'd be honest and say I was fed up of staying in every night.

Steve and I hugged and kissed while his pizza finished cooking, but it was ready soon after I'd driven over. He was starving after messing around with the cars, so that made it a bit easier to pull apart when his kitchen timer went. We were a bit like boxers, just getting into our stride when the bell broke us up but after Steve had eaten, I found us some ice cream to share for seconds. I knew Steve needed to get right away from work and I wanted to go out with him, so although part of me wanted to stay and cuddle, we got in the car and headed off up the coast to Sewerby Hall on the outskirts of Bridlington. Besides the hall itself, there's a small children's zoo, a few craft shops, a small golf course with a putting green, and lovely gardens, and it's set right on the cliff top.

It didn't take us that long before we were pulling into the car park and walking through the gates. There was no charge for the hall and gardens at that time of year, so we decided to look inside the hall. There was a room dedicated to Amy Johnson, and I particularly wanted to see it, as she'd been a heroine for me when I was growing up in Hull, even though she'd died years before I was born. In the photos I'd seen of her, she'd looked so pretty and feminine, and yet she'd learned how to fix planes and was the first woman to fly single-handed to Australia in 1930, as well as making other world-record flights. No wonder she was held up as an example to girls in Hull of what we could achieve if we put our minds to it.

She was the celebrity of her time, feted by crowds in Australia as well as at home. And then she disappeared, presumed dead, while flying a transport plane in 1941 during the early years of the Second World War. She was only thirty-eight. She wasn't allowed to fly in combat even though she'd much more experience than many of the men, but she undertook flying duties behind the lines. Strangely, I felt that somehow it would have been better if she'd died actually defending her country.

There were several photos of her, and they reminded me that, more than just pretty, she was hauntingly beautiful with large soulful eyes. I discovered that she'd studied law at Sheffield University in 1922. It was so rare for women to go to university at that time, I thought it was no wonder she had the guts to fly all that way on her own.

We looked at the paintings, then went downstairs. Most of the downstairs rooms were empty except for a large hall filled with rows of chairs. When I saw a pile of leaflets on a table by the doorway about arranging your wedding at Sewerby

Hall, I tried to picture Steve standing in a suit, waiting for me to walk down the centre aisle in an elegant white gown, but it didn't seem me somehow. I don't think that's because it looked more like a ballroom than a church, because I'm not at all religious and expect I'll go for a registry office if I ever get that far. It could just be that I find it hard to picture the whole wedding thing, even after looking at my cousin's wedding photos with Mum. Steve didn't comment so neither did I.

When we got outside, the sun was shining, so we strolled around the gardens for a while.

'Do you want to take the miniature train into Brid? I'm not bothered either way.'

'No, let's stay here, Rach. It's quiet and relaxing. Do you fancy a coffee? We can sit outside.'

'Yeah, it's mild enough and I could just about manage a cake.'

'You can always manage a cake, sweetheart.'

'Are you saying I'm fat?'

'Far from it. You can eat all the cakes you want and not put on an ounce.'

The cake was yummy and I washed it down with dandelion and burdock lemonade instead of coffee. I'd not had that for years.

Afterwards we walked away from the cliff and found the putting green. Steve's your typical competitive male, but I've got a competitive streak too, so it was no wonder we decided to have a game. I knew Steve had flirted with playing golf with his boss when he joined the force, so I wasn't surprised he beat me, but I surprised him by not losing by much. I was 9 strokes behind over 18 holes, and that wasn't bad. Steve was in a brilliant mood as we walked back to the car, having got a hole-in-one.

'That hole-in-one was like sinking a twenty-five foot put. Even Tiger Woods would be proud of that', I told him. 'I've been thinking, Steve, why don't we stay in a hotel tonight and drive back early in the morning for work.'

I was hoping he'd go for it while he was in such a good mood and I'd get a night of passion away, so I was thrilled to bits when he said, 'Go on then, why not.' I gave him a taste of what was to come, with a passionate kiss in the middle of the car park. We climbed in the car giggling like love-struck teenagers and drove off to look for a hotel. I was surprised when Steve swung north onto the road to Scarborough, as it's further away from Hull, but Steve said he knew of a decent hotel if he could find it. His sergeant had just spent a week there and it was cosy, friendly, clean and well-decorated, overlooking Peasholm Park.

The park is a favourite place of mine from when we'd spent family holidays in Scarborough. There's a large boating lake with an island in the middle. Every summer on Thursdays and Saturdays there's a mock naval battle on the lake with loud bangs and fireworks. My sister and I had loved it, and I was glad to see it was still advertised. We'd fed nuts to squirrels in the park and we'd sailed our little yachts on the stream that flowed into the lake. Dad had rolled up his trousers to rescue mine when I'd let go of the string and it'd floated out of reach. The café and other buildings are bright coloured and built like Japanese pagodas. It had seemed very exotic to us as children.

After we checked in we had time for a walk down through the park to the North Bay. The sun was setting and though it was getting cold, it was glorious. We played our game of inventing lives for people. We'd done it when we were students, but that day we picked out potential criminals or couples having affairs depending on whether it was Steve's turn or mine.

Back at the hotel we made ourselves as respectable as possible, and went down to eat in the dining-room. Steve insisted on a bottle of wine, knowing I'd have at least two glasses, so when we got up to our room I was all for stripping off and leaping into bed, but Steve slowed me down. We'd rushed our coffees and brought the after dinner mints up to the room. He undressed me slowly, kissing me all over, placing pieces of chocolate on strategic parts of my body and eating them off, licking the bits that got left behind. I did the same to him. By the time we were completely naked, we were both desperate for each other. I knew I was being far too noisy, but that's the good thing about a hotel. They're not your own neighbours you're disturbing. We'd already paid and we had to leave early the next morning so we wouldn't have to look any other guests in the face.

11

We drove back home on Monday morning, me still filled with that warm glow I get when I've been kissed and stroked to within an inch of my life. When Steve and I eventually find the time, we can't get enough of each other. And, because we went to bed early, we got most of a decent night's sleep too.

Steve dropped me at my flat and seemed to accept my explanation for still moving back out, namely that he was working such long hours and it would be easier for me to be back where my clothes and the computer for my job were.

After a cup of coffee, I went out. I had to call at the Ford dealership to drop off the hire car and pick up my own new car. I was running out of names. The number plate had the letters DVE. Looks like you're going to be my Dave then, I said as I got in and eased my way into the traffic. I like to give my cars girls' names really, but Davina just seemed to be stretching the point for the sake of it and Dave sounded solid and dependable, which is what I needed in a new car right then. I was hoping for better luck with this one.

When I got back, I checked everything in my flat was alright and decided it was time I did some housewifely things. I went round the bedroom collecting up part-worn clothes, stripped the bed and bunged it all in the washer with the dirty stuff and turned it on. I have no room for a laundry basket, so the washer doubles quite effectively. I particularly wanted to get rid of the shredded newspaper and any droppings left over from the mouse so I vacuumed like a crazy thing, emptied bins and tidied up, then made the bed. While waiting for the washing I even cleaned the bathroom. The freezer needed defrosting and the kitchen was in need of a good wipe down. Nothing was likely to be happening on a Monday morning in Maple Avenue, so I thought I'd tackle both before the cleaning mood wore off.

I was working off calories by the bucket-load, and when you added in the previous night's activities, I'd be able to wolf down a couple of family size bars of chocolate and still weigh what I'd been the previous afternoon. Better still, I didn't need any chocolate because of the warm glow effect. I suppose that's the way it goes, you comfort eat when you're down and not in the mood for exercise, but when you feel good and you're getting plenty of exercise, you don't need to comfort eat.

Talking of food, I knew I had nothing in for meals because I'd been at Steve's all week, so I put the washing in the dryer and was just about to nip out to the supermarket when the phone rang. It was Steve. He sounded really upbeat, though his words said the opposite.

'Hi Rach. You won't be seeing me for a while I'm afraid. We've had a major breakthrough with this Gavin Parker. You know, the one who delivered to Nicola Kennedy's workplace? When we searched his digs we found a pile of photography magazines. There was no camera but he must have one. We're holding an ID parade right now to see if any of Nicola's friends, relatives or neighbours recognise him.'

'That's great news, Steve. Thanks for taking five minutes to let me know.'

'Well I know it won't go any further than you, and I wanted to give you some other news as well. I'm afraid your theory about Craig Dobson being behind all the attacks on you is definitely a non-starter.'

'Why? What's happened?'

'He's in custody.'

'Told you he could have come back to Hull. Why can't it have been him then?'

'If you'll just let me finish, I was going to say he was arrested a couple of days ago after getting in a fight outside a pub one night. He was in Douglas on the Isle of Man. He's been there since he left Hull after trying to burn you and Lucy to a crisp in that warehouse. He was working as a bouncer in a nightclub, and he has an alibi for the times you were attacked, because I rang through and it checks out. I didn't want to say anything till I'd got all the answers.'

'It still could have been one of his mates.'

'I don't think so, sweetheart. When they

mentioned your name, Craig couldn't even remember who you were. Then he said, and I quote, 'why the fuck would I bother with her? If I went after anyone it'd be that slag Lucy'. So I think that's a dead end Rach. Have you had any more ideas?'

'No, I haven't. I really thought it was tied up with Craig. I'll have to wrack my brains again. Anyway, thanks for letting me know. I'm just going out to get something to eat.'

'You can come back here tonight if you want, love.'

'Do you really think you'll get home?'

'I hope so. One of the lads is going to pick up my car for me once the petrol's been drained.'

'Well, I'll see. I need lunch anyway and there's a few things I need to do here either way.'

'OK. Send me a text.'

When I got back from the supermarket I had a spot of lunch and then I remembered I hadn't checked my answerphone. There were two messages.

Pete's voice slid into my ear. I could picture his smile as he said, 'Hi Rach. I've been trying to get hold of you. I was hoping you might like to go out for another meal, unless you fancy going to a club. I hope there's nothing wrong. I'm here if you need me. Give me a call sometime, eh?'

I felt guilty for not ringing him back after the trip to the cinema. I couldn't remember when I'd last spoken to him. I knew I'd told Sarah I'd go out with him anyway, but after the previous night with Steve, it seemed like it'd be unfair to Pete to agree to go out. On the other hand, I'd not be seeing Steve for a while, and it was hardly stringing Pete along, if I was honest with him. But I had told Pete that Steve and I weren't engaged, and although it was the truth, it might have given him the wrong impression, one which didn't exactly compute with the serious love-making. While half of my brain carried on this conversation with itself, the other half pressed the button to listen to the second message.

'You'll have to come home sometime, and when you do, I'm going to make you pay.' A distorted voice spat out the words and they echoed round my little office before settling into every corner of the flat, filling it with fear. Steve had logged the paint, the car ramming and the mouse incidents as possibly being harassment, but he said it was unlikely anything would be done other than a record kept on file in case of other incidents. I couldn't prove they were linked or that anyone was out to get me. This was different though. However busy he was, Steve wouldn't mind me ringing him at work about this.

I rang his mobile and he answered, brightly, 'Ringing me back already, sweetheart?'

I filled him in on the call, played it over for him and he said someone would be round, and as soon as they'd been, I was to pack a big case and go back to his place. I felt guilty that I'd been thinking of going out with Pete, so I turned Steve's offer down, and said I was thinking of staying at Mum's to help with my nephews as I wasn't likely to see much of him at his place anyway. He seemed satisfied with that. To be honest it was tempting to go back to Steve's, but I had promised myself I wouldn't until his serial killer was caught. The reason why he sounded so chirpy was that they'd got enough now to charge Gavin Parker with murder. The old biddy who lived next door to Nicola had identified him as the chap she'd seen with Nicola in the park a few days before she disappeared.

'I know you won't breathe a word, and the press'll get hold of it soon anyway, but it's looking good. We were going to have to release him if we couldn't charge him, so this has come just in time. Now we have more time to interview him and we'll have to hope he confesses. In the meantime we can look for his camera and the place where he took the girls.'

'That's great, Steve.'

'The only problem is, the neighbour is elderly and wears glasses. The prosecution could do a demolition job on her, saying her eyesight's dodgy. Also Parker's still saying he doesn't own a camera. We need to find something that clinches it before we have a case that'll stand up in court, unless he confesses.'

I did think about going to Mum's but by the time I'd got off the phone, the call didn't seem as frightening as when I was telling Steve about it. I told myself, 'Sticks and stones' etc, and hey, the caller couldn't know I'd moved back home anyway. It certainly wasn't as scary being in my own flat as staying in the same house as Mikey and Johnnie, who were a bit of a handful. I'm sure my sister ruled them with a rod of iron, and that's why they tried to take liberties when they stayed with Mum, but I'd already rashly volunteered to take them out for a day and I couldn't face spending even more time with them.

With Steve so busy, by the time he tried to contact me again, the nephews would've gone and I could always move in with Mum in reality if things were still scary. I ironed to keep my mind off things till a policeman arrived. He collected the tape, took a brief statement as to the length of time I'd been away from the flat, made a note of the crime number I'd been given before and left. In case my mystery attacker was watching, I packed a few things in a suitcase, slung it in the boot and drove to Steve's anyway. If my attacker hadn't touched me there before, he wouldn't bother if he thought I was there again. I'd go home later. I let myself in with the spare key I'd managed not to give him back. I made a cup of tea and then it was almost three pm, so I left again. I decided I had to do something rather than brood so I drove over to Maple Avenue to see what the area was like when kids were leaving school and passing through.

Garden Village is as nice as it sounds. It may be only a short distance from the busy main road to the coast, but it was planned when planners made an effort to create an environment where you'd like to live. The houses are not all the same, though of the same materials. They've bay windows, are large and well-proportioned with garages and big gardens. The streets are leafy with garden-like verges, and the interlaced avenues wind round in curves, large trees sheltering the houses from being overlooked. The area suits its name.

It was amazing to realise that the lucky first owners were factory workers for Sir James Reckitt. You may have heard of Reckitt's Blue bleach bags, when they made toiletries and medical supplies, or maybe you've heard the name when it joined forces with the mustard manufacturer's to become Reckitt and Colman's. Well, Sir James was a true philanthropist and he took his workers from their squalid back-to-back terraces with no facilities, let alone luxuries like gardens, and installed them all in this little estate of about six hundred houses that he had built specially. There was even a community hall. They must have thought they'd moved to paradise.

I found Maple Avenue on the A-Z. There was a 'For Sale' sign outside number three. Its garden and those of the adjoining houses all looked neat and tidy, there was no evidence of peeling paint and it was quiet. I parked and got out. The house was for sale, so it was legitimate to walk round the back and take a look. The back garden was enormous by today's standards. I could imagine myself sitting on the lawn, soaking up the sun, maybe pottering in the flower-beds. I like my flat, or I did until it became the target of my mystery attacker from hell, but it did lack a garden. There wasn't even a communal one where you could hang out washing.

I peered through the windows. There was nothing to see. The rooms had been stripped but the

149

house didn't look neglected. The décor was recent and I caught myself drifting off into an imaginary world where I pictured my furniture in these rooms. Of course, with prices these days, I couldn't afford it myself. A vision of Steve in the kitchen, calling to the kids...fast rewind there, I thought. I hadn't committed myself to kids. I rubbed them out and then I could picture Pete walking down the hall – towards Steve. I shook the daydreams from my head and examined the boundary hedges and fences.

They all seemed in good condition and when I glanced over them, it was to find more neat and tidy gardens. Come to think of it, someone must have been cutting the lawn at number three. I was walking back to the car when the side door of number five opened. 'Can I help you? Are you meeting the estate agent here?' a woman in a plum-coloured jumper asked. I explained that I wasn't interested in buying number three myself, but was just investigating for prospective buyers, and could she tell me anything about the owners of number one? I was fairly sure from her manner and her clothes that she was a considerate type herself, but she might be persuaded to spill the beans on any troublemakers.

'Oh, there's no trouble with any of the residents of this street. Most have been here for years. Mr and Mrs Fox only left to go and live near their daughter in Cornwall. I've been keeping an eye on the place and Ted, my husband, he's kept the garden neat. It's no trouble for him and it's better than looking at an overgrown garden, as well as being nicer for the people who move in. Who did you say they were?'

I waffled a bit about client confidentiality, but secretly thought this job was a bit of a doddle, and I wondered why my clients hadn't thought to do it themselves, but maybe they were too busy, or they didn't know where to start, asking questions. I was lucky to have found such a helpful neighbour I suppose. 'Are there any drawbacks to living here then, would you say?'

'Well we hardly go out in the evenings, but Mr Brooks down the road is our Neighbourhood Watch representative and he says he's glad he has his car because he wouldn't like to be walking past the youths that hang around on the grassed area at the far end of the avenue. He thinks they deal drugs. Not that anyone from round here would be involved in anything like that, but we're not far from the main road as you can see, even though we're far enough away from prying eyes. But they're no real bother. There's no noise and no fights and Mr Brooks, he goes round every morning and clears up any mess. He's rung the police and the council but not got anywhere. My Ted thinks all the resources get diverted to the big council estates. I expect they'll move on in a few months anyway.'

'And pigs might fly', I thought to myself. 'Thanks for talking to me. You've been really helpful. Anyone would be really pleased to get such nice neighbours.' At that, I got back in my car and drove off. I intended to go back late that night and see for myself. I suppose it all depended on whether my clients had teenage daughters, or younger ones who would eventually be teenagers. If they lived on their own and liked the quiet life, maybe the drug-pushers wouldn't be a problem. You'd have to go a long way to find such perfect neighbours and lovely houses, and the residents of the estate obviously thought so because I didn't see another 'For Sale' sign, even though I drove down all the little avenues. No-one wanted to leave.

I drove back home, made myself a healthy mushroom and chicken stir-fry with rice from the contents of my newly re-stocked fridge, had a shower and curled up on the settee in front of the TV. At about ten I was nodding off when I remembered the Garden Village estate again. I wrapped up warm and set off.

I drove onto the estate, took a slow drive right round and then returned to the entrance near the main road. There's also an exit from the estate onto the road where my old school is, but I reckoned if there was any action, it'd come from the main road. For a long time, it looked like I'd drawn a blank, and I was just thinking of driving round again when I saw a group of lads in my rear-view mirror, coming down off the main road. They were quiet, none of your laughing, joking and messing around that you'd associate with a group of lads at around that time of night.

I started up the car and moved further onto the estate. I didn't want them to wonder why I was sitting there, but rather assume, if they thought anything, that I had just left someone's house and was going home the other way. I parked outside number three because then if anyone saw me and asked questions, the lady at number five could vouch for me. I couldn't see the grassed area she'd mentioned from the car, so after about ten or fifteen minutes, I got out and crept round the corner, keeping low. There wasn't much to see. The group were hanging around under the trees, but talking so quietly, they wouldn't disturb anyone. Occasionally another lad would walk up, an exchange of cash for goods would be carried out, and he'd go on his way. Some of the lads came and went. There were about six at most there at any one time. I waited till I felt I'd seen enough. No big changes in numbers or noise, so I went.

I figured I'd go down one more week night and a couple of times over the weekend, during the day and in the evening, then I'd submit my report and let them choose. When I got home I was shattered and went straight to bed. In the morning I remembered Mum. She'd had my sister's two lads a couple of days already and was quite exhausted by them when I turned up to make good on my promise to take them out. Sis and her drip of a husband were having an exciting trip by North Sea ferry to Holland. She had a nerve dumping the kids on Mum when they were off school for Spring Bank Holiday. I almost envied her a few days in Amsterdam till I thought of her husband, Rob.

He was like a third child. He relied on her to organise his entire life and seemed incapable of making a decision, though he would talk about the options for hours. If shelves wanted putting up, or even a light bulb changing, then my sister had to do it herself. I had to admit that he was really good-natured and wouldn't harm anyone; he was honest as the day is long and would never cheat on her but he was so time-consuming, no help at all and worst of all, incredibly boring. I dreaded to think what their sex life was like.

Anyway, when I picked up the boys it was one of those rare warm and sunny late Spring mornings so I thought I'd take them to East Park to check out the new café and playground. The council have spent a lot of money on renovations and I'd not been in years, even though I didn't live far away. We drove down and parked where there used to be tennis courts when I was at school. The splash-boat was running and the lads were clamouring to go on it. I knew they couldn't go on alone and I wasn't sure I had the nerve these days, so I tried to fudge my answer, but kids are direct and won't settle for any old 'maybe' or 'if you're good', and in the end I agreed, hoping for a quiet life. I told them they could go on before we left the park but they'd have to go and play first. Somehow I thought I'd be out of money if we went on first and then had to have repeat performances. I needn't have worried about repeats.

They went into the new play area and for a while I actually enjoyed myself, reading a book on the grass nearby, glancing up every now and again. After about ten minutes they were at my side demanding ice lollies. I didn't like giving in to everything they asked for but, I reasoned, I hardly ever saw my nephews so I should make the effort. I couldn't let them go across the road to the shop on their own, so abandoned my book and stood in the queue with them. I treated myself to a Magnum, explaining to the boys that these were only allowed for adults. Luckily they wanted lurid green lollies in the shape of a monster or something, so I was spared the pleas that they have Magnums too. Back at the play area, I enjoyed my icecream and liberal dose of chunky chocolate and picked up the book again.

I was disturbed by shrieks and crying. Mikey had kicked someone and pulled their hair for 'pushing in'. I had to soothe the feathers of an irate mum and lead them away to the old fort to play there for a while until things calmed down. They played hide and seek, and I was forced to join in to keep an eye on them. We lost Johnnie after a while. After half an hour of frantic searching, we found him playing football with some other lads on the field the other side of the aviaries. I wasn't best pleased and came over the heavy Auntie, dragging them round the aviaries and the emus and peacocks. Those male peacocks sure can yell, but not as loud as I can.

The lads had calmed down quite a bit so we went back to the playground and I promised them that if they behaved for half an hour while I read, they could go on the splash-boat before we went back to Mum's. Amazingly, it had the required effect, even though it was over far too quickly.

We queued up at the splash-boat for a while. Maybe they could have gone on their own, but I was taking my responsibility seriously. When we climbed in, Johnnie was all for leaning over the side, so it was probably just as well I was there.

The lake looked a long way down and the track steep, and I was beginning to regret I'd agreed to go on at all, when suddenly we set off with a lurch, gathering pace as we swooped down to the water. How could I have forgotten that the only place to sit is in the middle. We were drenched. The kids squealed. They loved it. We were hauled back up to the top and the gates opened.

We squelched back down the steps. I couldn't see how we could have got so wet from a little spray. My hair was hanging in wet rats' tails and because I felt cold after the soaking, my nipples were standing to attention through my wet t-shirt. It was at that moment, it had to be really, that I looked across to the car park, wondering if there was anything I could use as a towel in the car, when my eyes caught Pete's – and his slid up and down my body.

'You look…. interesting. Kind of sexy really.'

'What are you doing here? Shouldn't you be working on a Tuesday morning?'

'It's a warm day. I fancied an icecream and thought I'd come over here to see what they've done to the park. It used to be our backyard and I still don't live far away.'

Our old school overlooked the lake. It looked just the same, ivy-covered and mellow in the sun. I remembered lunchtimes spent in the park playing bowls, rowing boats and buying icecreams with school dinner money. I expect inside it had changed as much as everything else had, but from where we were standing it looked the same as ever. I looked back at Pete. I'd been trying to avoid the smile in his eyes.

'I'm here with my nephews. They dragged me on the splash-boat, and this is the result.' What a stupid thing to say. I watched as his eyes slid down to my t-shirt. I couldn't think of anything remotely interesting to say that would distract him, but he spoke first, interrupting the lack of thoughts in my brain.

'So, are we going out again, then? You did say you and Inspector Rose aren't an item, didn't you? Or maybe you've changed your mind?'

'Auntie Rachel, can we have another go on the splash-boat?'

'Can we? Please?'

The insistent voices penetrated the fog of indecision and sheer embarrassment and I pulled myself together.

'No, I'm afraid not. Come along, Johnnie, Mikey, got to get you home to your grandma and get you dried off.' I turned to Pete, 'Can I ring you?'

'Sure'. He sauntered off and I gathered the boys together, wishing I could manage to act my age when Pete was around, instead of about fifteen.

'Who was that then, Auntie Rachel? Is he your boyfriend?'

'Yeah, do you snog him?'

Kids, I hated them.

Sis and her husband came back from Amsterdam on the Thursday and I thought I'd better put in an appearance before they went back to Doncaster. I didn't really hate the boys, after all. They were just hard going when you weren't used to it. They were keen to show me the presents Laura and Rob had brought them back. Not clogs or a windmill thankfully, but some Lego kits that Laura hadn't seen in England yet. Apart from marrying Rob, Laura's always had reasonable taste. After Laura had told me all about their trip, I braced myself.

'Hi Rob. How's things? Did you have a good time?'

'Yes, thanks. It'll be good to get back home though. Work's really busy at the moment. A few of our smaller competitors have gone to the wall in the recession, and we had to cut staff too. Now the work's starting to come in, well obviously more is coming our way. I've been out and about nearly every evening measuring and pricing up. And I've got the VAT and tax returns to get done this month. You wouldn't believe the amount of work involved. The accountants charge a fortune. I try to do as much as I can first. And we need to cut down on expenses. I need to go back over the last two, possibly three years...' I tuned out at that point. With Rob it was always more of the same. He was so boring. What did Laura see in him? And a double-glazing salesman too; I ask you! I smiled and made appropriate noises until he drew breath and then I made my excuses and went to find Mum in the kitchen.

'I should never have let your dad have a mobile phone. He can't look after anything decent.'

'What's he done now?'

'He had it in his pocket in the garden. God knows why. He leaves it on the mantelpiece nearly all the time. He never takes it when we go out, when it might be useful in case we break down, and then he takes it in the garden. It's only ten yards away. Anyone would think he was expecting a call from another woman.'

That would be laughable, as we both knew.

'So why did he take it out there?'

'He said he might keel over with a heart attack one day, doing all that digging I make him do. I only suggested he break up some of the geraniums and put them in a bag for Laura to take home.'

'And?'

'Well, he was filthy when he got in and he got changed and put his gardening trousers straight in the washer. I'd got it turned on already when he came in the kitchen, asking if I'd seen his phone. And that's when he remembered it was in the pocket of his trousers.'

'Oops. So it's had it then?'

'There was only a bit of water in the washer and the phone didn't look wet. When we opened it up though, the battery was all wet and so was the little metal thing, the SIN card or whatever it's called.'

SIN card sounded quite appropriate for some of the uses mobiles are put to, so I didn't set her

159

straight. 'Are you going to get him another phone or not bother?'

'Oh, it's working. We dried it off and turned it on and it worked. I couldn't believe it.'

'That's good then.' I was still waiting for the bottom line.

'Yes. It must've been worth paying a bit more for a good make. But anyway, I think I should look after the phone, don't you? He obviously can't be trusted with it. You do agree, don't you?'

'Mm. Maybe you should just get one yourself anyway, and you can take yours when you go out. His'll probably not work much longer.'

At that, I left. I didn't want to get drawn into an argument over who should take possession of the phone. I knew they'd not consider it worth having two phones. Are other people's families like this, or is it only mine? I just know I needed another cup of tea and some chocolate to get over popping round to Mum's for tea and biscuits.

12

I went out to Garden Village again on Friday after school had finished to see how rowdy it got. I parked the car and wandered round the whole of the small estate. On the greens there were children playing games, someone walking a dog, and cleaning up after it too, I noted favourably. I didn't see anyone at number one or number five. In fact the only people I passed in Maple Avenue were a middle-aged couple who were holding hands. They looked blissfully happy and I wondered if Steve and I (or should that be Pete and I?) would look like that in twenty-odd years' time.

I didn't hang around long. I had a date and wanted to get ready. I'd make one more visit and then type up my report and send it with my bill. I'd given in and rung Pete a few days after seeing him in the park. Maybe I just wanted to show him I didn't always walk round looking like a drowned rat, or maybe I just fancied a night out.

I was ready by the time Pete knocked at the door – just. I'd allowed plenty of time to have a shower, wash my hair, dress and make-up. I'd even decided what to wear. Amazing or what? Out of the shower, hair dry, I'd pulled on my best jeans and had to reject them – I was having a fat day. Even us skinnies have fat days – a fat day's any day you can't fasten your clothes properly and have room to sit down comfortable – no matter what the size. I decided to go for a strappy blue top and black skirt with my black suspenders and stockings. Well, a girl's got to go out feeling sexy if she's with a sexy-looking bloke, I reasoned.

When I opened the door I was almost convinced Pete could see I was wearing stockings but if he could, he didn't comment. 'You look nice, Rach. Don't know if I've ever seen you out of jeans. Are you ready?'

'Yes.' I was tongue-tied again.

'I thought we could go to The Old Oak in Sutton. Have a bite to eat then stay there if you want or move on. Does that sound OK?' I'd suggested a quiet drink when I rang him, partly because there wasn't a film that I fancied, and it seemed less like I was expecting too much from the evening than suggesting a meal.

'Yes. That sounds good.' My conversation skills were really improving. A whole four words.

Pete was wearing navy cords and a white shirt under a dark jacket. He looked expensively dressed but still casual, and very, very sexy.

The pub wasn't overflowing, but there were enough people there.

'What would you like to drink, Rach?

Wine?'

I asked for a glass of medium white. I like dry wine really but in pubs you often get vinegary stuff masquerading as dry. While I replied, I'd been thinking about the fact that dry would have sounded more sophisticated, and I suddenly realised I should have asked for a spritzer or I'd be needing another drink soon and you know what I'm like with wine. Oh well, in for a penny, in for a pound, as they say. Steve didn't even know I'd come out with Pete so he wouldn't know if I drank a dangerous two glasses, would he?

I brought Pete up to date on my recent calamities and as expected he said someone was obviously out to get me. I agreed that there was a chance they were all linked. I didn't realise how quickly I'd drunk that glass of wine till Pete said, 'Another glass, Rach?' and he was off to the bar before I could say "No". I swear, I couldn't have stopped him if I'd tried.

We talked about people we'd known from school. Then I tried asking Pete about his job and how he'd earned so much money, but I just got the answer 'computers' for my pains. I knew other guys with degrees in computing, and though doing nicely, they certainly weren't living in almost-mansions in leafy Hull suburb-cum-villages. He did open up slightly about holidays. Made me green with envy with talk of the places he'd been – toured the States, east coast and west, been to Egypt, South Africa, you name it, it seemed. Though he never said who he'd been with. I even wondered if there might be a Mrs

Pete lurking somewhere, or at the least an ex-Mrs Pete. I told him about the trips I'd made to various European countries while I was at university and then my recent spate of non-holidays, and about having no-one to go with. If I'd been sober I'd not have laid myself open to the words, 'I may ring you when I'm next off somewhere then, Rach. I'm sure we could have a good time together.'

I muttered something about it getting late, but he shrugged it off and stood up to go to the bar again. I knew I'd had enough alcohol. I wasn't drunk but I was sitting much closer to Pete than I had when we'd got to the pub, and he looked dangerously attractive, so I said I'd quite like a coffee.

Brilliant stroke, Rach, particularly as pubs don't sell coffee.

'That sounds like a good idea. Let's go back to mine and have a coffee, put our feet up.' There was no hint of seduction in his voice. It was all very pleasant, but I didn't need seduction, I was doing quite nicely, all on my own. His house was as spotless and palatial as I remembered. He must have a cleaner, I mused, as he hung my coat in a neat little cupboard off the hall and led me into the lounge. I sank into his sofa then thought better of it, and went to talk to him in the kitchen instead. That was an even worse idea. I could feel myself longing to lean against his slim body and try his mouth for size. He turned from the worktop and nearly spilt the coffee.

'I think I'd better put this down a moment and hold you instead', he said softly. He stepped towards me, raised my face to his and kissed me. It was a slow, gentle kiss and my lips parted at the same time as his. He put one arm around my back and pulled me closer. I was struggling to stay upright as my legs turned to jelly.

Then I heard music. 'Wow', I thought. 'That's new'. Abruptly it sunk in - my mobile was ringing. I tried to ignore it, but I knew it was a signal to me to stop Pete – that it was only the drink that had got me into this position. Steve was right about the 'two glasses of wine and you're anyone's' bit, after all. As I rather suspected at that time of night, it could only be the man himself on the phone.

'Rach, I've got some bad news.' His voice cut through the alcohol like brakes on a speeding car.

'Nothing's happened to Mum or Dad, has it?' They were my first thought, when someone mentioned bad news.

'No Rach, they're fine. It's your flat. Someone put newspaper and rags soaked in petrol or white spirit or something through your letterbox, and tossed a couple of lit matches in afterwards. Mainly smoke damage but the hallway and some of the lounge caught fire before the firemen arrived.

'Oh my God. Was anyone hurt? Was it just my flat?'

'No-one hurt, Rach, and just your flat. Mr Jenkins raised the alarm after a woman came tearing down the stairs and knocked him flying. He managed to get to his feet and look out of the window and he got her number plate. Then he went to investigate, saw flames and called the fire brigade.'

'A woman?' I'd think about that later.

'Yes. About your age he thought. Look, I'm sorry about the flat.'

'So am I. I hope nothing I really like's been burnt, but I'd put up with that if you can catch this woman and put an end to everything.'

'The fire brigade referred it to us as a possible arson. The girl on the switchboard recognised your name and told me, but it's not my case, Rach. Don't worry, though, they'll be doing everything they can to find her and I'm sure it won't be long now. She may have left something at the scene. The number plate's the same as that of the car Mr Jenkins saw before – probably the same red Volvo that hit you. It must have been kept in a garage or something, because it's still down as stolen but there've not been any reports of sightings. Mr Jenkins got a better look at the driver though, so that gives us more to go on. Long dark hair, quite small but pretty, he said. He's wondering if the small thin bloke he saw before was really this girl, hiding her hair under the baseball hat. Does the description match anyone you know? Anyone who might have a grudge against you?'

'Not really Steve, but I'll think about it. I'll go to my place and survey the damage, see what I can rescue.'

'It's a crime scene, love. You won't be able to get in at all.'

'I'll have to go though, Steve, just to see.'

'I know how you must feel, but it won't be pretty. You'd be better off staying at your mum's, and getting a strong cup of tea and some chocolate down you. To be honest, I'd really like you to move back in with me.'

'They'll be able to tell me how much damage, even they won't let me in, Steve.' I felt really awful. I daren't tell him I'd been still living in my flat and wasn't staying at Mum's, at least not till I saw him in person. And as for the fact that I was at Pete's, and the position I'd got myself into, after those glasses of wine....

'Alright, sweetheart, but don't hang around. Get yourself back to your mum's, soon as you know how things stand, and keep me up-to-date. I'll try and call round when I leave, or at least ring you again later. We're interviewing Parker's neighbours, workmates and known associates and trying to link him in with Susan Hardy and the third victim, Emma Chamberlain.'

'It's OK, Steve, I know you're busy. Don't worry. Tell you what,' I made a snap decision, 'I think I will move back in your flat though, if you don't mind, just in case anyone's following me around. I'd rather they don't take trouble to Mum's.'

'Good. I'm glad. Pack a big case this time. I'll see you whatever time I get home then. Take care. Bye.'

'Bye, love.' I'd avoided the awkward problem of letting him know I'd never been at Mum's and that I was at Pete's, but now there was Pete to deal with. When I'd taken the call, he'd wandered out of the room, but he was back now.

'I've got to go. My flat's been fire-bombed.'

'Oh, Rach, that's dreadful. Did they catch

who did it?' I described the woman fleeing my flat and that the red Volvo had been seen again. 'She sounds familiar.'

'Sounds like lots of young women to me.'

'No, I think it's in connection with a red Volvo, but I can't place where or when I'm thinking of. Never mind, it'll come to me. Is there anything I can do to help?'

'Nothing, Pete, and to be honest, I've drunk too much and I think I may have given you the wrong impression just before the phone rang.'

'It seemed like you knew what you were doing, Rach, but I wouldn't want to take advantage of you. What can I do to help?'

He was being so sweet and reasonable that I felt really awful.

'Pete, you won't like this, but I'm going to be honest. I've decided to take up Steve's offer to move in there. I just need to pick up some stuff from my flat. Would you mind terribly calling me a taxi?'

He laughed. 'You could stay here, you know.'

'That's really sweet of you, but I don't want to draw my attacker to someone else's house, or I'd be going home to Mum's.'

'And Steve, doesn't he count?'

'He's hardly ever there, and he's a cop. He's paid to cope with sticky situations. You're not. That's the difference.'

'Is that the only difference?'

'I don't know, Pete. I really don't, but I don't feel now's the time to think about it too much.'

'OK, but I've not drunk much at all. I can drive you.'

'No thanks.' I didn't want him to know where Steve's flat was. If he came round one day, what would I do? 'Just a taxi'll be fine, thanks. I'll get what I can tonight and go back to the flat in the morning for my car.' It looked like I'd have to risk driving to Steve's, or else he'd wonder why my car wasn't outside his flat, why I hadn't driven from my flat to his with my stuff, why I'd not been at Mum's or able to drive or… No, I stopped myself. It was all too complicated but I couldn't drive anyway. Maybe I could have managed if I drove very, very slowly and drank some coffee at my flat first, but the bottom line was I simply wouldn't allow myself to drink and drive.

The taxi took me to my flat. On the way I justified moving back in because of the dangerous situation I seemed to be in. Somehow right now Pete seemed more dangerous than the arsonist. Either way, I knew I'd be safe at Steve's and that was all that mattered.

I needed some clothes and toiletries at the very minimum. I hadn't packed a suitcase as I hadn't moved to Mum's. There was only the one fire-engine and a panda car, but there were a couple of other cars that looked unfamiliar. They might have belonged to forensics or plain clothes. I climbed the stairs and smiled at the young constable manning the door. I didn't even try forcing my way in, just asked if I could speak to the policeman in charge. When he opened the door to go in, I peeked over his shoulder.

The hall was black and reeked of smoke. The fire must have been long since out as there was no actual smoke. There was water everywhere.

He was back a few moments later with a man I didn't recognise. 'Sorry about this, love. You're Steve's girl, aren't you?'

I nodded, though I wasn't sure myself. 'Could I just get some clothes and toiletries for now please, or did the fire get into the bedroom?'

'No love, you were lucky your neighbour rang 999 so quickly. Most of the flat's OK, but ten minutes longer and the whole lot would've gone up. We'll be on our way in a few minutes ourselves after we've boarded up. I'll have to go in with you though, and then you'll have to leave the flat till the fire investigator's been.'

'That's OK, thanks.' I grabbed what I wanted and left. If he thought it was odd that a grown woman picked up a somewhat bedraggled teddy bear, dressed in a natty scarf her mum had knitted for it, and said, 'Don't worry, Sundi, it'll be OK', then he didn't let on.

By the time I got down to the road I felt the whole experience had sobered me up without any need for coffee but drinking and driving is unsafe and illegal, so I'd asked the taxi to wait. I'd realised Steve would never notice my car wasn't parked on a side street near his flat. I could pick it up in the morning after he went out. When the taxi dropped me at Steve's, I let myself in, stood under the shower for five minutes, drank two glasses of water and

Sundi and I went to bed in each other's arms. Sometimes a girl's best friend is her bear.

13

On Saturday I woke and could still smell smoke in my hair. I washed it in the shower, but stretching for the shampoo that I'd put on Steve's windowsill, I slipped and landed heavily on my hip. Another bruise for the collection and a good way to start the day. I smelt smoke again while I was drying my hair. Luckily I glanced at the hairdryer and noticed the smoke was coming from that – followed by a small flame. Eek! I turned it off, unplugged it and put it in the bin. Why do hairdryers burst into flames on me? I can't remember it happening to anyone else I know, but that was the third one to self-combust when I was using it. It wasn't even mine either. I'd have to get Steve a new one. At least he hardly used it. I think his mum must have got him it and he used it on clothes instead of hair when something he wanted to wear wasn't quite dry.

Outside the rain was coming down in sheets so my damp hair wouldn't matter, as long as Gran wasn't watching, or she'd be there saying, 'You'll catch your death, going out with wet hair, our Rachel.' I had to go out to pick up the car from outside my flat. I hunted round in vain for a brolly, so decided to squander some money on another taxi instead of walking across town to a bus stop.

I had to remember to pick up my brolly and hairdryer, as well as more clothes. Steve had said, 'Pack a big case', after all.

Mr Jenkins was out of his flat faster than you could say 'Neighbourhood Watch'. 'Someone's made a right mess of your flat, haven't they? Now who'd want to do something like that? Lucky I noticed or we'd all have been burnt alive in our beds.'

'Oh yes, it was brilliant of you to phone the fire brigade so quickly. There must be something I can do to thank you?'

'Nonsense. It's what neighbours are there for, you know that. Wouldn't mind some of those chocolates you got me that time I helped you take the table to the tip, though, but only if you're passing the shop.'

I made a mental note to get him a box of Thornton's champagne truffles and gingerly opened my front door. The smell hit me straightaway. How was I ever going to get rid of it? It was bad enough when I burnt toast or even when hairdryers spontaneously burst into flames, but this was a hundred times worse. I'd have to strip the wallpaper, re-paint, get rid of the carpet... Oh dear. Well maybe just shampoo the carpet and wash everything down in the lounge, and do a more thorough job in the hallway. I quickly revised my plans in view of my limited bank balance.

It was really the hallway that was the worst. I'd only just put down the new carpet and cleaned everything after the red paint incident, as well. On the bright side, I had some paint left over. I grabbed a brush and painted the hall before collecting the things I needed. The smell of paint fought for precedence over the smell of scorching, but after I'd ripped up the carpet, the paint seemed to be winning the battle.

I moved the things I was taking out of the hall and onto the stairwell, along with the carpet for the binmen and then I sprayed Febreze liberally everywhere. It'd do till I came back with new carpet and air freshener. Damn, I'd got paint on my favourite jeans. I'd been really careful, but I should have changed into old clothes first. I'm always thinking I can manage without changing when there's only a small area wants painting. You think I'd learn but I'm always in too much of a rush.

My mobile rang as I was getting back in the car. I felt like an adolescent schoolgirl but ignored it anyway when I saw it was Pete. I'd debated whether to mention our date to Steve. It'd seemed like no big deal when Sarah said he couldn't possibly find anything objectionable in my going for a drink with Pete whilst he was so busy at work. That was before the event though. Now it looked like waving a red rag in front of a bull if I told Steve, even if I gave him a highly edited and sanitised version of events. I'd have to speak to Pete soon though, or he might just ring me when I was with Steve and I couldn't very well ignore the call then.

Not content with no answer, my phone announced the arrival of a text. 'Pls ring when u get this. Have news on car. Px. PS Sorry u had2go.'

My heart sank. News on the car could wait. I had to play it cool. Who was I kidding? I should just come straight out with it and tell him Steve and I were getting serious. Well, we were when Steve was in, I thought. Serious enough for me to wander round Boots looking for wherever they'd discreetly hidden the condoms. I'd already got milk, the new issue of Cosmo and the Thorntons for Mr Jenkins and had only called in Boots for shampoo and a new hairdryer, but if I was moving back in, then I had to play it safe. Condoms were on offer, so I grabbed 2 boxes. That was my excuse anyway.

I'm not embarrassed buying condoms. I wouldn't like you to think that. I'm a modern woman, but I still try not to broadcast it, so when I plonked my basket down by the till and this sixteen year-old girl picked up one of the boxes and waved it in the air so the whole queue could see, I was a tad uncomfortable. 'These are 3 for 2 you know.'

I muttered something like 'It's OK', but she wasn't going to be deflected from her role as most helpful assistant of the day.

'I'll wait while you nip back.' Realising I would only draw more attention to myself if I resisted, I did as I was told. I could feel six pairs of eyes boring into the back of my head as I almost ran down the shop, returning sheepishly with a third packet quite a few minutes later, because I couldn't find the shelf again. I paid, put the points on my

Boots card as requested which made the queue even longer, then crammed them into my bag with the shampoo and hairdryer and walked out of the shop as if my shoes were on fire. Wouldn't you just know it? I bumped right into Auntie Lesley and Mum.

'You look a bit red, our Rachel. What's up?'

I muttered something about being in a rush then remembered I'd not rung to tell Mum I was back at Steve's and my flat had been hit by the mad arsonist. I decided to leave that to one side for the moment and instantly launched into a detailed description of Steve's nice flat and its furnishings. I knew that was guaranteed to put her off the scent and it worked like a treat.

'You know, Rachel, I'm sure he might be working up to proposing soon. We could get a copy of Bride magazine and you could nip round tomorrow for a cup of tea. What do you think?'

I hadn't the heart to blow her dreams sky high, so agreed with everything she said, whilst gently steering her away from Boots and back towards WH Smith's for the magazine. I couldn't believe the price of something that was one big advert filled with lists, but forked out the money and handed it to her. 'Here you are, Mum. You have first look. I'll be round in the morning and you can have the most important bits sorted out for me.'

It was worth it to see the broad smile on her face. I almost felt like ringing Steve and asking him to marry me so she wouldn't come back down to earth with a bump when it turned out she was wrong about his intentions. I watched as Mum and Auntie

Lesley walked off towards the bus station, chattering excitedly. Well, after that Oscar-winning performance, I just had to nip back into Smiths to buy myself some chocolate so I didn't feel tempted to eat the Thorntons myself. Then after lunch I was off to Garden Village to check again before I handed the prospective buyers my final report.

When I drove off the main road and onto the estate, I was still in the realms of wedding talk and was again picturing myself being carried over the threshold into one of these pretty old houses. The sun was dappling through the trees that lined the curving avenues and I envied my clients.

I parked in my 'usual' place and set off at a brisk pace, determined to get a feel for the whole estate. I went up and down every little road, following my progress on the A-Z. There were some young mums with babies in those German-engineered pushchairs that probably cost more than my mum had spent on me in the entire first five years of my life. Good job I wasn't the maternal type, or I'd be taking Mother and Baby magazine round to Mum's as well, the daft mood I was in.

When I'd come full circle several times, I was back at number 3, Maple Avenue. I'd still not seen any other houses for sale, which reinforced my view that properties here didn't come on the market very often, and when they did, they didn't stay on it long. I walked round the back of the house, just to check that no-one had been rash enough to use the garden to dump a load of rubbish, and peeked in the window to remind myself of the size of the rooms. I was surprised to see what looked like some bedding in the alcove of the back room. I couldn't remember seeing anything there before, and wondered if someone had broken in and had been sleeping rough.

I was going to knock at the neighbours for a key, after checking there were no broken windows, but first it occurred to me to try the back door. It opened easily and I shouted out loudly, 'Is anyone there?' before stepping almost directly into the kitchen. My shoes echoed on the bare floor. I stopped and listened. It was totally quiet. I shouted again to be sure, and took the precaution of leaving the back door open in case I had to run for it. Maybe it was teenagers getting in to use the place for their drug sessions but it could have been anyone.

I found the door to the back room, leading off from the hall, and pushed it open tentatively. I held my mobile like a gun at the ready, though I doubt if I could have rung anyone if someone had jumped out at me. I waited for what seemed an age to see if I could hear anyone breathing but I couldn't hear a thing above the sound of my own deep nervous gulps. I peered round the back of the door and thankfully could see nothing but the abandoned bedclothes. I breathed a sigh of relief before looking through the rest of the house, equally slowly and carefully. There was no-one there. No sound at all. Not even a dripping tap.

I went back to the room where I'd seen the crumpled duvet, hoping to find some clues. It was only then that my nose smelt something else besides musty bedding. Gently I lifted a corner of the duvet with my foot, screamed and ran out of the house. The next door neighbour was at the fence before I could say another word. She took one look at my face and said, 'You look like you need a cup of tea, dear. What's happened? Have you seen a mouse?'

'A cup of tea would be lovely, thank you.' I didn't want her screaming as well, so dialled 999 on my mobile while she was busy in the kitchen. I decided to tell her when she was sitting down at the kitchen table that someone had been found dead next door.

The police came quickly and sealed off the house but not before I'd broken the news to the neighbour without giving any details. 'I'm afraid I've some bad news. I've found a body next door. In the empty house. I'm not sure who it is, but I've seen him before, walking down the road with his wife. I was checking on the house and found the door open.'

'Oh my goodness. That's dreadful. Someone local? I wonder who it is?'

A police sergeant knocked at the door. Excuse me, Mrs …'

'Mrs Sanderson. Can I help you, officer?'

'Well, this is a bit difficult, but Miss Hodges here' he indicated me, 'she seems to think the man was local. I realise this is an awful thing, and you can say "No" if you want, but would you be willing to take a quick look and see if you recognise the man. We can then get his next of kin to identify him properly.'

'Of course, officer. It'd be my civic duty. Just wait a moment while I change into my shoes.'

Mrs Sanderson followed him next door and was back within five minutes.

'It's Mr Brooks, our Neighbourhood Watch representative. I told you about him, I think? That he used to keep an eye on the lads who came on the estate. He had a key, you know. He went in regularly to check on things. They only showed me his face. I wonder how he died? Could you see? Did he have a heart attack, do you think?'

'I can't say, but make yourself a cup of tea. The police will have their own ideas, but I'm sure they'll want you to tell them about the key and him coming and going.'

'Oh, of course. It'd be no trouble at all.' I could see in her eyes that she was relishing being someone important, though I'm not sure she'd be so pleased when she found out there was a murderer on the loose on her cosy little estate. Mr Brooks had hardly plunged the knife into his own chest, I was sure. As for my clients, well, who'd want to buy a house where a murder had been committed? My mind must have been in self-defence mode as it wandered off at a tangent, wondering how much the asking price would be lowered by its association with a murder.

The memory of his open staring eyes, and his blood-drenched clothes brought me back to my senses just in time. There was a knock at the back door. It seemed the police had come back in the form of Inspector Jordan. I'd last seen him at the Humber Bridge Country Park. Give him his due, he recovered quickly after finding it was me who'd discovered the corpse next door. 'You're making quite a hobby of finding bodies, aren't you, Rachel?' he said kindly. He must have noticed that I was shaking despite the tea I'd just drunk.

He took me through the details, whilst a constable took notes. I'd been to the house the previous day so the time of death was definitely in the last 24 hours. I could tell he was glad to have some time frame immediately, as well as the victim's name, although no doubt Mrs Brooks would be able to pinpoint the time much more closely. He was very interested in the youths selling drugs, but I didn't know any of them, and doubted I'd be able to identify any either. It seemed like Mr Brooks must have been observed watching them, and someone was worried the police would be tipped off. After I'd told him everything I knew, he asked Mrs Sanderson for Mr Brooks' address and told her he'd be back to talk to her in a little while. He said it was important that they see Mrs Brooks next to break the news and get her to officially identify the body.

I was still a bit stunned and accepted a second cup of tea, so I was there when the Inspector returned, and I had chance to ask him why Mrs Brooks had not reported her husband missing.

'She did and her call was logged, but there was no reason for it to be followed up. He often went out late in the evening for a walk around the estate as part of his Neighbourhood Watch duties, apparently. Then he would go back and watch TV till the early hours. Mrs Brooks likes to go to bed early, so she didn't notice he was missing till this morning. She'd rung the hospitals and police station when she'd realised he'd not slept in his bed last night. Obviously when a grown man goes missing, we can't do anything till a certain amount of time has elapsed, unless there's a strong possibility of foul play.'

'Mr Brooks had a key to next door's', piped up my hostess.

'Yes, so I understand from Rachel here. Can you tell me anything else? Did you see or hear anything in the empty house last night?'

'Sorry, we were out all evening, officer. We went to the cinema. We hardly ever go but my husband's a big fan of James Bond films and this new one's just come out. I was tired when we got in so I went straight to bed. You can ask my husband, but we're both heavy sleepers and he never mentioned hearing anything this morning. Of course, our house doesn't adjoin that one. Maybe you'll have more luck with the Maynards.'

'Thank you. Could you ask your husband to give me a ring if he did hear anything, when he gets home from work, please? Potter, you'd better go round to the Maynards' and see if there's anyone in.'

'Oh, Inspector, you'll be out of luck I'm afraid. I've just remembered. The Maynards are away this week.'

'Right. Potter, you get started on house-to-house inquiries. I'll see who I can spare when I get back to the station and send someone out to give you a hand. Now forensics are here, I can leave and get the incident room set up.'

I said my goodbyes and left through the throng of curious bystanders. I called Steve from my mobile when I got back to the car and filled him in on the murder I'd uncovered. Predictably his first reaction was concern for me, followed by annoyance that I was once again mixing with serious crime. I protested my innocence. Checking up on a neighbourhood for prospective house-buyers was hardly courting danger. It had just been my bad luck.

'Funny how it always happens to you, though.'

'Maybe CID will have some idea who might have done it, or the Drugs Squad or whatever they call themselves.'

'Those young lads you saw dealing wouldn't be at all bothered whether they were seen by someone who didn't even know their names. They would have just scarpered and come back another time. Why would they bother bringing the law down on their heads by killing him? It doesn't make sense. They're only small fry, just out for money. Anyway, you get yourself out of there and go do something quiet like visit your mum. I'll see you later. I might be able to get away early tonight.'

'OK. I said I'd call round in the morning, but I could pop in today if she's in.'

'Yeah, do that. It'll make you feel better and I'd rather you weren't alone.'

If he knew about Bride magazine he wouldn't be saying that, I thought, as I turned the key and drove off the estate and the short distance to Mum's.

As it was, Mum wasn't in. She'd probably gone round to Auntie Lesley's. I couldn't face driving over there, so I drove back to Steve's.

I made myself something to eat, a little early but I needed something to do. I watched the early evening news, then turned off the TV. Nothing to grab my attention. The flat was quiet, too quiet and I felt lonely. I didn't want to go out in case Steve came home as promised, but I just couldn't settle to anything. I started cleaning to take my mind off being alone but when I'd finished an hour or so later and there was no sign of Steve, I sat on the settee and sobbed. I wanted to think it was finding the body but inside those four walls I could admit to myself it was Bride magazine. I wanted Steve to propose to me. I was fed up of coming home to an empty flat with no-one to cuddle up to and share my calamities. It was all being well, managing to cope on my own, but that didn't mean I wanted to.

After I'd had a good cry and checked Steve's phone was working and my mobile was turned on and had sufficient battery, I found some rubbish to watch on TV. Worryingly, I was actually beginning to care if a minor celebrity playing the drums was better than one fire-eating, when the phone rang.

I snatched it up.

'It's me.' I knew the 'me' in question, and the quiet, tired tone of his voice told me all I needed to know before he continued, 'I can't make it love. It's going to be a late finish again after all. We've pulled in a bloke whose girlfriend reported him for tying her up and taping her mouth with duct tape. She said he was giving her the creeps.'

'I thought this Parker was the murderer. What are you doing questioning other people now?'

He rightly ignored my criticism of police procedure. 'We can't ignore any leads, Rach. What if Parker turns out to be innocent and we let someone else get away? We'd be crucified. Anyway, did you see your mum? How are you?'

'She was out. I'm OK but I really wish you were coming home early, Steve. I'm feeling pretty low right now.'

'Haven't you got a friend you can ask round? What about Sarah?'

'She doesn't go out in the evenings cos the baby has bad colic.' I didn't know that, but I felt too sorry for myself to ring her and have her turn me down. I felt rejected enough.

'Sorry, love. I wish there was something I could do. I'll give you a hug when I get in if you're not asleep.'

I put the phone down and tried to pull myself together. If we were married, Steve'd still be out all the time. My mind turned to Pete. It was dangerous to ring him now. It was after nine pm. He'd wonder what I had in mind. But maybe I should give some serious thought to letting him into my life and making it less empty. I questioned my motives. Most of the time I felt I really loved Steve. Would I be just trying to make him jealous? Or was it that I thought I'd never cope with being a policeman's wife? Was it right to go out with someone else just because I felt lonely? But maybe Pete was the right person after all, and I wasn't giving him a fair chance?

My head swirled. In the end I went and got some biscuits and picked up a book. I read the same paragraph several times before giving up and taking a shower. As I lay in bed my head started thinking again, though this time it was about my mysterious fire-bomber. Whilst thinking about Pete, I'd remembered his text about the car. I'd ring him in the morning. Take the bull by the horns and see how I felt when I saw him for the first time since he'd kissed me in his kitchen. At the same time I could see what he could tell me that might find my mystery female attacker and get me back in my own flat.

I didn't hear Steve come in. My head wouldn't turn itself off till it was really late and then I was out for the count.

The next morning I was looking for some breakfast when he strolled into the kitchen, dressed for work. 'Waste of time last night. He was scared stiff, that bloke. He was only after a bit of spice in their sex life. He thought theirs must be boring, because she kept making excuses. Truth was, she just didn't fancy him any more. Not like us, eh, love?'

Steve brushed his fingers against the front of my t-shirt.

'Come on then Steve, you've got time.' I felt for his zip. He grinned at me. I was stepping out of the skirt round my ankles and we were heading for the settee when the phone rang. 'Let it ring, Steve. Please!' But the moment had gone and his

186

hand was reaching for the phone, even though he still held me tight.

'Right. OK. I'll be there in ten minutes.' I was so frustrated I could have screamed. 'It's the boss.'

'Does he know what time you got in last night? And it's Sunday.' I hated myself for sounding like a shrill fish-wife, but it all boiled up inside me.

'Oh, Rach. I know how you feel, but he's my boss and he's giving me the chance to tackle Parker this morning. A change of approach.' He reached out to stroke my hair, but I was twisting away from him by then, getting dressed.

'Just go, Steve. But don't bank on me being here when you get back.'

'You know you don't mean that. Look, I really haven't time for arguments. I'm sorry, but I have to go. I'll see you later.' And with that he went. I knew he hadn't a choice, I knew I shouldn't have been angry with him, and I knew I hadn't meant it when I'd said I'd not be there when he got back. I went from angry to very sad in the blink of an eye, and I sobbed my heart out.

14

It's supposed to make you feel better, crying, but I felt like shit, to be honest. Still, Mum was expecting me. Also I'd promised myself I'd ring Pete, as I needed to get my attacker caught and feel safe enough to move back home. On my own, I might just be able to work out if I wanted either or none of the blokes in my life. I found Pete's number in my bag and dialled. No reply. Damn. I put the phone down. Then I picked it up and dialled again. I had to at least leave a message, but I can never think when I'm not expecting a machine.

'Hi Pete. It's Rach. Sorry I've not been in touch. You can get me on my mobile today. It'd be good to meet up and you can fill me in on the car. Do you mean the red Volvo?'

It was the only car I could think of, but I wasn't sure what he could tell me more about Mrs Elsie Young and her stolen car. Surely the police would have contacted me if they'd located it or the person who'd stolen it?

I drove to Mum's, dreading the wedding conversation as any impending nuptials seemed as unlikely as me winning the lottery – and I don't even buy a ticket.

'Hello, Rachel. I've got a nice apple pie from Brenda next door. She's trying to use up last year's apples from her trees before this year's crop comes along.'

'That sounds nice, Mum. Dad settled in back at work OK?'

'Oh yes. He couldn't wait to get back. I don't know how we'll manage when he retires, Rachel. He'll have to work in B&Q or Asda or become a lollipop man. I'll not be able to cope with him under my feet all the time, and he's always asking what I'm doing, or worse, why I'm doing it the way I am.'

'Oh dear. Still, it's years till he retires. Try to forget about it. He could always go on surveillance for me.' I didn't mean it. Dad would drive me insane too, but I could see it'd got her down and she needed some hope.

'That'd be great. Yes, I can see him now. I can send him out with a thermos of coffee and he'll be gone all day. Well, you have cheered me up. I couldn't stop dwelling on it. I just couldn't think how I'd carry on. Good, the kettle's boiled. Can you cut the pie while I pour?'

I couldn't bring myself to worry her over the arson attack, so decided to continue to draw a veil over the fact that I was back at Steve's. Come to think of it, I wasn't sure I'd told her I'd moved back home anyway. However, I could see the copy of Bride magazine open on the table and didn't like leading Mum on twice in one morning. I'd have to come clean.

'Mum, about me and Steve...'

'Don't you worry, love. Your dad's got a bit of money put by, so you can have the wedding you've always dreamed of.'

I'm just too soft. What could I say? I couldn't tell her I'd exaggerated and I didn't think Steve'd be proposing after all. Mum'd made a list of the page numbers we needed to look at and I spent the next hour discussing dress colours, which church, what hymns, who would need to be invited on our side – we'd have to ask Steve later for his list of relatives and friends – and even the presents I should ask for. I got really carried away and by the time we closed the magazine I almost believed everything would shortly be turning into reality. I managed to rein Mum in when it came down to any discussion of booking anything though, and kept saying it was good to have everything sorted out, but we'd have to wait for Steve to pop the question before we could launch into action.

We were back on the thorny subject of who should be bridesmaids, when the phone rang. I haven't many female relatives and those I have are a little plump, to be kind. Mum said they'd spoil the photos and didn't Steve have anyone who'd do, but secretly I thought they'd make me look like a fashion model in comparison. The call was from Gran, and when Mum came back, all further talk of weddings was suspended.

'Are you free next Saturday, Rachel?'

'I think I could be. Why?'

'Your gran needs a lift to Leeds and she's asked me to go too, and I'll not get through it without you, as well as needing you to drive.'

Confused, I waited for the explanation which I knew would eventually come. I didn't have to wait long.

'Gran's decided to make a bid for fame and she wrote into 'The X Factor'. She's got an audition slot at eleven on Saturday.'

'What! Gran…. singing?'

'Yes love, I know, but you know what she's like when she gets an idea into her head. I've been trying to persuade her that they're not looking for people her age but she says they always put some older people through and it'll be fun to go on the telly. I thought I'd heard the last of it, but she'd obviously only stopped talking about it till she'd found out the date. You will come, won't you?'

'Well…'

'I can't bear the thought of going as it is, but your Dad'll have nothing to do with it, I know that for sure, and I don't fancy going by train. Apart from that, I'll need someone to help me keep her in line so she doesn't do anything silly.'

'Isn't going on 'The X Factor' silly enough when you're Gran's age, and worse, when you're tone deaf?'

'I know Rachel, but she is my mother.'

'Well don't you get any ideas. I can do without you being an embarrassment to me when you get old.'

'That's one of the few things you have going for you when you get old, you know. Doing what you want and not caring who sees you doing it.'

'Right. Well, I'll have to stand up to you better than you do to Gran, won't I? You'd better tell me what time I have to turn up, or is she planning to queue overnight?'

'No. She said she needs to sleep in her own bed so she's in fine fettle to impress that Simon Cowell. I expect he's used to people like her. It'll be a day wasted but maybe we could go round the shops if she gets out early.'

We both knew that wasn't going to happen, but I promised to set my alarm for 7am and play chauffeur to Hull's latest pop diva. 'Has she decided what she's singing yet? Or rehearsed at all?'

'She didn't say and I didn't ask.'

I knew how she felt and I left soon afterwards, with half an apple pie in foil, 'for Steve's tea'.

The phone rang while I was in traffic but by the time I'd found a safe place to pull in, it'd stopped. I looked in 'missed calls' and found it was Pete. I decided to wait till I got back to Steve's flat to return the call as I wasn't sure how much credit I had. Who am I kidding? I wanted a cup of tea in my hand, and I didn't want to be diverted round to Pete's house 'while I was still in the car'.

Pete picked up straight away, as if waiting for me to ring.

'Hi Pete. It's me, Rach.'

'Thanks for ringing back. I was beginning to

think you were avoiding me. Surely not?'

I could hear the twinkle in his eye as he spoke and his flirting relaxed me.

'What's this about the car, Pete?' I wanted to know, but also I wanted to distract him from flirting. I just didn't know how I felt any more. Steve and I had had that gorgeous night in Scarborough, and then we were back to his work taking over, and now we'd just had that awful row. I found it so hard to go from feeling really loved-up to being a low priority again.

'There's this crazy girl I went out with. She was always jealous, even though I wasn't seeing anyone else.' (I filed that away for future reference. If he could be faithful to a crazy girl, then maybe he wasn't a serial flirt or a two-timer). 'She often turned up in a red Volvo. She didn't have a car of her own, but she borrowed one from some relative or other. It might have been her gran's. Anyway, it occurred to me. Maybe the red Volvo that hit you wasn't stolen. Maybe it was just borrowed, only for once the borrower forgot to mention it - and maybe it was borrowed from that Elsie.'

'So maybe Elsie is this girl's gran and she was out to get me because of you?'

'Could be.'

'But how would she have known about me? We've only been out a couple of times and only recently.'

'It's not nice to think about, but she must have been watching me, and followed you after you'd been to my house.'

I wasn't sure whether having a crazed female stalker was better than a murderous ex-client or not, but at least it was something to go on. 'You'd better give me her name and address Pete, and I'll have a word with the policeman who's dealing with my case.'

'Her name's Stella. Stella Cooper. She lives at 45 Horton Avenue. It's off Sutton Road.'

'I hope it's her and we can get it all tied up and sorted, but the first incident, the paint through the letter-box, wasn't that before I came to your house? After all, I came round to ask you to run the number plate.'

'Mmm. Well, it may not even be the same red Volvo, but I thought you should know.'

'The police'll be able to check if she's related to Elsie what-not anyway. Thanks, Pete, that's a great help.'

'So how are you otherwise Rach? No more incidents? Are you still staying at your friend the inspector's flat? Is he looking after you?'

'He's hardly ever there. It's just a safety measure. I can't wait to move back home. Maybe this woman of yours'll turn out to be my attacker, she'll get caught and I can get back to normal.'

'Right. Well, I was wondering if you'd like to go out again?'

'Oh... Well... Yes, that'd be nice.'

I couldn't believe how quickly I agreed. I just can't say 'No', can I? I know I'd never know whether Pete was a possibility unless I gave him a chance, but only that morning I'd been trying to seduce Steve. And failing, I reminded myself.

'Rach?'

'Yes?'

'Did you hear me? I asked if you're free tonight, and if you fancy going for a drink somewhere.'

'Umm, sorry Pete, my mind wandered off there.' As in, it started having an argument with itself over whether I should really be getting more involved with Pete. I remembered how I'd almost given in to him. Why couldn't I just settle for Steve? Why couldn't I be honest with Pete and tell him I was seriously involved with Steve? I'd given Pete the impression we were just good friends. Mind you, I'm not sure he believed me.

'So, tonight's OK then?'

'Er, er, yes, that'd be good. Could we meet up somewhere, if that's alright, rather than you picking me up?'

After I'd put the phone down I couldn't believe how the conversation had run away from me. At least he hadn't asked why I didn't want him picking me up from Steve's. It meant I'd be in my own car so I could drive home after we left the pub, rather than having to go back to Pete's and put myself in a potential situation. And I don't drink and drive, so I'd be able to think straight and not get tipsy and dangerous. I thought I'd got it covered, so I put it out of my mind and picked up the phone to call my policeman. After I'd given him the details, he said he'd get back to me as soon as he'd checked out Stella whatsit.

I decided it'd be safer all round if I went out, so I grabbed my handbag and went shopping. I could always use something new to wear. Thank God shops open on Sundays these days. I was walking past Marks and Spencers when I felt a tug at my elbow, 'Rachel. I'm glad I bumped into you. I need something for Saturday to impress that Simon Cowell. You can help me.'

Bloody marvellous, I thought. I come out to wander around and treat myself and I have to run into the shopper from Hell. 'I'm in a bit of a rush actually, Gran.'

'Are you tailing someone? I could help.'

Pretending I was on a case obviously wouldn't work. 'No, but I'm meeting a friend in half an hour.' I waited for a bolt of lightning to hit me for lying to an old lady, but nothing happened, probably because she was still going to get her way whatever I said.

'Well, we'll just have to get a move on then, won't we? I thought I'd get one of those short sparkly dresses like Tina Turner wears but I can't find anything.'

'Probably because you only see dresses full of sequins at Christmas and in the January sales, Gran. There's a lot of satin things around at the moment though', I said, resigned to losing the next half hour of my life.

'Ok, lead on then', said Gran. It wasn't easy dragging her away from the most outrageous skimpy things that she could find, but eventually we compromised on a tight strappy satin top with lace and sequins around the neck, which she could wear with a black skirt she already had. The top was bright red and suited to a seventeen-year old but it could have been a lot worse. I left her at the bus station, and drank a hot chocolate in a café before plunging back into the shops. I'd seen a couple of things while I'd been with Gran, but I'd not wanted to slow her down by trying them on or I'd have never got her off my hands.

I bought a pair of black cord trousers and a lemon long-sleeved t-shirt, both practical but nice, and then splurged on a silky v-necked short-sleeved blouse in turquoise with tiny black flowers. It was pretty, a flattering style and lovely to the touch, as well as not being strappy, so I could wear it to a pub as well as for a more dressy occasion. Who was I kidding? It'd be perfect to wear to go out with Pete.

15

I called round at my flat before I went to Steve's to get ready for my date with Pete. There was a red electric bill on the mat and a pile of junk mail but nothing else. No cheques, no personal letters, no paint. I was in the shower when my mobile went and thought I'd better answer it. After all, it could have been a new case. I'd got no work just then and even though I was living at Steve's for a while at least, I still had bills to pay, so it seemed. I couldn't ask Steve for money.

It was PC Graham, the policeman looking into the attacks on me. 'We've traced Stella Cooper. There was no sign of a red Volvo outside her house, though she did admit her grandmother was Elsie Young. She said she had driven it occasionally to do favours for her gran, but because it'd been stolen a few weeks back, she's not been able to drive it lately. She denies all knowledge of you, let alone attacking you. She seemed jumpy but all we have is a coincidence at the moment – that she went out with your boyfriend.'

'He's not my boyfriend. She might have just

thought he was.'

'Like I said, we've not enough to question her or put her in a line-up. I'm not sure your neighbour got that good a look at her anyway, and if he didn't pick her out it would just weaken any case we might eventually have against her. Though she might cave in if we can get something that ties her to being in your building, even if it doesn't prove she fire-bombed your flat. She didn't have a cast-iron alibi for any of the attacks.'

'Where did she say she was, then?'

'Shopping. Going for a walk on her own. That sort of thing.'

'Did you ask her about Peter Shannon?'

'She admitted she'd been out with him, but said it was over weeks ago. She said he was a loser.'

'Well she's definitely lying then. He's good-looking and has a posh house in Sutton.'

'She could just be bitter, but we're going to talk to her neighbours and see if anyone remembers her driving a red Volvo recently. I'll get back to you, but please continue to take care. If it's not her, someone's still out to get you, and if it is, we haven't the manpower to follow her, I'm afraid. I'd hope our visit would stop her in her tracks, but if she's unhinged, who knows?'

On that cheery note, he hung up. I'd just got back in the shower to wash my hair when the phone rang again. This time I let it go to voicemail. When I got out it was the police again. I am popular with the boys in blue, apart from the one who matters. I couldn't think why Inspector Jordan would want to speak to me again. I'd told him all I knew about the Garden Village murder, and if I didn't get a move on, I'd be late meeting Pete. I decided it could wait till the morning. After all, I needed to call Steve as well. I was still upset with him for walking out that morning but I had to let him know I'd be out, on the off-chance that he came in early to make it up to me. I hadn't a clue what to say though. I couldn't lie but I wasn't sure he needed to know I was going out with Pete again.

Good job he was at work, so he wouldn't be able to talk for long.

'Steve, it's me. Pete gave me a lead on a possible name for my female attacker. I spoke to PC Graham about it. He checked her out, and she might be a possibility although there's no proof. I'm just going to tell Pete what the police discovered and see if he can come up with any more information.'

'How's Pete involved? And can't you ring him? I don't like you going out on your own while your attacker's on the loose.'

I wasn't sure how much to tell Steve about my involvement with Pete, but luckily I was saved by someone in the background calling his name. After he answered, he came back on and said, 'Now where were we, Rach? Oh, yes. We've had a bit of a setback here. Parker's come up with what could be an alibi for the third victim we found, Emma Chamberlain. She was last seen getting into a silver car one afternoon when Parker was taking part in a fishing competition. We think he could have left unnoticed after it started, but it's made things a lot tougher for us. Anyway, until that's been checked out, things are a bit quieter. I should be able to get home early at least, and make up for this morning. I am sorry about what happened. Do you have to go out?'

That made me feel a million times worse so I fudged it. 'I've already said I'll meet Pete now. I won't be long, but he's busy till about eight so I might be late back for once. If you get home before me, just fix yourself something to eat.'

I could tell he wasn't happy, but he didn't feel he could push it after the morning's argument. 'Ok, but are you alright?'

'Yeah, sure. Had an exciting time with Gran today. I'll tell you all about it when I see you.'

As I dressed in my new blouse I felt a bit guilty but I hadn't lied to Steve, just distracted him a bit.

The phone rang again. God, that policeman was persistent, I thought.

'Hello, Rachel Hodges here.'

'Rachel, what did you think of, letting Gran buy that skimpy top? She'll embarrass us to death.'

'That was the best I could do, Mum. Honest, you know what she's like. Look I'm sorry, but I've got to go. I'll see you one day next week if I can. Otherwise I'll be round on Saturday morning to pick you both up - unless Dad's changed his mind and he's taking you?'

'Not unless hell's frozen over in the last couple of hours. Have you had a chance to talk to Steve about setting a date?'

'Not exactly, Mum. He's really busy, and he's so tired when he gets in, it's never a good time at the moment. In fact most nights I'm asleep by the time he's home. Look, I've got to go now. Sorry, but there's someone at the door.'

I hated lying to her, but I was running late. There were no more distractions though, so I met Pete in the pub we'd agreed on, not long after eight.

'Mmm, you look good, Rach. Are we going anywhere special?'

I was flattered but also embarrassed as he obviously thought I was over-dressed for the pub. 'You mean the top? It's nothing special. I got it in a sale.' I hated lying but I didn't want him to think I'd gone to too much trouble or who knows what he'd expect of the evening. We decided to move to a popular wine bar in the town centre anyway, as the pub was having a karaoke evening.

The wine bar was heaving and it was hard to find anywhere to sit, but we managed to find a couple of stools against a wall-mounted table. I was just filling him in on my conversation with the police constable who'd been to see Stella, when a drop-dead gorgeous girl tapped him on the shoulder and said, 'So this is what you're up to tonight then, Pete. I thought you were at your mate's. Lisa was right, you are a two-timing bastard.' She didn't seem surprised, or bothered, I have to say.

Pete leant over, stroked her hair and smiled. 'Megan, meet Rach, an old school friend. She's a private detective and we had to keep our meeting private because it's in connection with her work.'

'Is that true? You're a private eye?'

I nodded.

'Wow, how exciting. You must tell me all about it.' She looked round for a spare chair, but there weren't any.

'Megan, I'm going to my mate's later, that's why I didn't mention it. We really do have to talk privately now. Can I call you tomorrow?'

She looked disappointed but muttered something and moved off to a group standing by the bar, where she was soon laughing and joining in the conversation. I turned to Pete.

'What was going on there?' I said sharply

'I don't know why you're angry. We're not dating, are we? Unless I missed something? I mean, if you'd like to have an exclusive relationship, then that could easily be arranged. I really like you, Rach. I just didn't think you wanted to get involved.'

I gulped. He was right. Swiftly I managed to cover my tracks. 'I mean, don't use me to back up your lies. We did come out for pleasure not business, and I didn't hear you say you were going to your mate's later.'

'Calm down, Rach. Megan's got loads of friends. She just thinks she wants to go out with me full-time because of my money. I have to watch girls like her. They're nice company, but I can't let them get the wrong idea and think I'm at their beck and call. Now with the right woman, one I respected and one I could get passionate with, it'd be different.' He leant close and stroked my cheek.

He was slick, I gave him that, he was fanciable, but I couldn't trust him as far as I could throw him. I decided to stay an hour or so, then I was out of there. Maybe he meant what he said. Maybe he was so used to mixing with the pretty girls, the eye-candy, that he treated them how they were used to being treated. It was something I'd come back to and think about later.

I didn't want to seem childish and rude. I got a second coke on the true premise that I was driving, and we sat and chatted about inconsequential things. He was good company and made me laugh, flirtatious without being too in-my-face. Eventually I asked if he minded if I left, as I was a bit tired.

If he was annoyed, or amused, he showed no sign of it, and he behaved like a perfect gentleman, even insisting he leave with me. There was no sign of Megan when we left so he didn't need to pretend he was leaving to go to his mate's. Who knows, maybe he was going to see a friend later. I didn't know what to believe any more. He offered to drive me and I could pick up my car the next day, but I said I was fine, just tired. He walked me to my car, then pulled me close and gave me a heart-throbbing kiss, before walking off down the road. He was certainly dangerous, but whether that made him bad, I still couldn't decide.

I drove back to Steve's, mulling over the evening. I found Pete's charm really hard to resist, but I wasn't sure I could trust him. He was fun to be with and attentive, and if I wanted him, he'd be around more than Steve. But long-term? Would he drop me after he'd had his wicked way with me, as Gran would say, or when he was bored of me, or was he honestly ready to settle down? And Steve, did he want me long-term, or was I just someone comfortable to come home to after a long day at work, someone to have sex with when he wanted? Was he going to move on again when it suited his career, and if he did, would he ask me to go, and would I want to?

I couldn't park outside Steve's flat. The few parking spots were full. It was raining but I couldn't run for it in my heels so I just put my head down and walked as quickly as I could. That's how she took me unawares. One minute I was in daydream land, thinking of a warm room with a cup of tea and a biscuit or three, the next I was in a nightmare, a crazy woman standing in my path with a large knife in her hand.

'You just don't get it, do you? You're not even pretty, but you think you can have him. If you didn't keep ringing him up and taking him for cosy little drinks, he'd be back with me by now.'

I looked through my rain-splashed glasses at my tormentor. The path was narrow and ran between two small blocks of flats. I couldn't see any alternative but to turn and run. Unfortunately she wasn't hampered by heels, and mine had straps so I couldn't kick them off. I hadn't made it far down the alley when I felt her grab my hair and yank it backwards. I stumbled and fell. She stood over me, and waved the knife.

'You're going to get what's coming to you,

you bitch. I tried to warn you off, but you just won't learn.' I was wondering why she'd not stabbed me already. Maybe she wanted to give me a piece of her mind first. While she'd been talking I'd pulled off one of my shoes. Not much of a weapon, but it would have to do. When she bent down, I was ready. Who did she think she was, pulling my hair? No-one touches my hair. I was livid and threw my shoe at her, aiming for her eye. She put her hand up to her head for a moment and I kicked out with my other shoe at the hand with the knife. She dropped it.

I got up and charged at her like a rugby player and knocked her back on the ground. The knife was lying by the edge of the path, almost in the bushes. I lunged for it and just got to it first, throwing it deep into the bushes. I remembered Steve once telling me that you could never tell how things would end up if there was a weapon involved in a fight, so it was always better to get rid of any weapon rather than risk having it taken from you and used against you.

She obviously hadn't heard this advice because she dived into the bushes after the knife. I grabbed her ankles and hauled her back out. She kicked out and tried to go after the knife again. Her foot connected with my glasses and knocked them off. Brilliant. I was soaking wet, bruised from the fall and scratched from the bushes and now I could hardly see. I grabbed hold of her again. She couldn't have found the knife because I'd thrown it much further in. She turned her head and spat in my face. As if that was going to stop me. I'd had to hold my own against dirtier fighters than her when I was at school. It might have been years ago, but I remember being pushed in a flower bed by a lad intent on pushing nettle leaves down the back of my jumper for fun, and I knew packing up and crying wasn't an option. You had to win at any costs. Otherwise the nettles might even end up in your knickers.

I punched her. I know you might say that's not what a woman should do, but hell, I was mad. She'd made my life a misery and I'd had enough. She made this funny sort of noise and struggled, trying to get up. My knuckles hurt but I pulled her hair and punched her again. Then someone grabbed me from behind. I sagged. I couldn't fight two of them. I'd put all my effort into those punches and I was exhausted.

'You can stop now, Rach. It's over.'

'Steve?' I couldn't believe it was him. He never got home this early. I rolled to one side and he stepped over me, pulled Stella to her feet, twisted her arm up her back and then held both wrists behind her back in one practiced move. If he'd carried handcuffs in plain clothes, she'd be wearing them. I heard him make a call, but couldn't get up. I wanted to, but I seemed to be stuck in the mud. 'There's a knife, Steve. She was trying to kill me.'

'God, Rach. I've told you never to fight anyone with a weapon. You should just put as much distance as possible between you and them.'

I started crying. 'I did. I ran first, Steve, but I tripped. Then I kicked the knife out of her hand and threw it as far away as I could, so don't you dare tell me I did it wrong. I'd got it all sorted when you came. She didn't have a weapon any more and I wasn't going to let her get away again. It was so dark, I couldn't see her face properly to identify her again. I had to finish it so I can be safe.' I was still crying as a patrol car came. One of the constables handcuffed Stella and put her in the car while the other got a torch and searched through the bushes for the knife. He found it and bagged it. They drove Stella away. I heard Steve tell them he'd take my statement to save me going down to the station.

'I'd have made a citizen's arrest. I didn't need you. If I'd thumped her one more time I could have let go of her to look in my bag for my mobile and called 999.'

Steve pulled me to my feet. He held me at arm's length for a moment, then hugged me, even though I was covered in mud from head to toe. Now that's love, I thought. 'Come on, sweetheart. Let's get you inside.'

'Oh shit. My lovely shoes. I bet they're ruined. Where's the other one? And my glasses. Where are they?'

Steve picked up my shoe and handed it to me, and then plucked my glasses from a small bush. Amazingly they'd flown off and landed there instead of on the ground. When we got in the flat I walked straight into the bathroom. My hair was matted with mud, my face was scratched and dirty and my new blue top was caked in mud and ripped. I would just have to buy another one. I stripped off and stood in the shower, while Steve made a cup of tea. When I emerged again, feeling more human, he handed me it and said, 'I'd have come and joined you in the shower, Rach, but I thought you needed a cup of tea before you make your statement. I can't leave it till tomorrow. I'm sorry.'

'I wouldn't have had the energy anyway', I said wearily.

Comfy in my nightie, I let Steve use my laptop to type my statement while I towelled my hair dry.

'I'll email it to PC Jakes and he can put it on an official form for you to go in and sign tomorrow. The important thing is they have your version of events when they question her. Who is she anyway? Do you know her?'

'I presume she's Stella Cooper. Pete used to go out with her. I'd only just passed her name to PC Graham. Pete recognised her description in connection with a red Volvo, because she used to borrow one from her grandma sometimes. He thought she was a bit crazy but nothing like this. She must have been following him around and decided I was his new girlfriend.'

'Why should she think that?'

'Well I don't know' I said indignantly. 'She is loopy, after all. You don't think I've been standing on street corners necking with Pete, do you?'

'I hope not.'

I felt really guilty, but Steve was better off not knowing how close I'd come to getting involved with Pete. I sighed. 'Can I go to bed now? I think I've had enough for today.'

'Sure, Rach.'

'And Steve?'

'Yeah?'

'Thanks for coming along when you did and rescuing me. I might have managed on my own, but it wouldn't have been easy without my glasses.'

'You were really brave, and she probably deserved being thumped after what she put you through. If I'd come along any earlier then you wouldn't have been able to exercise your own form of self-defence. I hope I never end up on the end of one of your punches. She'll have a black eye at the least tomorrow, maybe even two.'

I crawled into bed and Steve got in not much after. He hugged me.

'Ouch! I don't know about that Stella but I'll be black and blue in the morning.'

'I'll leave you alone and let you sleep then. You can just snuggle up to my back if you want.'

'You haven't told me if you got anywhere with checking out Parker's fishing competition alibi.'

'Nothing definite either way yet. Weather wasn't good and everyone was buried under big umbrellas or hoods, and these fishing types keep their heads down anyway.'

I put all thoughts of murder far from my mind and lay there feeling glad my nightmares were over. I drifted into thoughts of when I'd first met Steve. I'd had too much to drink at a mate's party a couple of weeks into my first term at university, and had been in the kitchen trying to make coffee to sober up. I was spooning coffee into the kettle by mistake when this voice behind me said, 'I may be wrong, but I think you should only put water in there. I looked up into his eyes and giggled. I couldn't stop. Tears streamed down my face. I swear I really thought it was that funny. I must have looked a right sight, but he just grinned and said, 'Come on, you sit down and I'll sort that out for you. Are you always a walking disaster area?'

I remember nodding and then waking up hours later, snuggled up to his back. He must have felt me move, because he stirred and said, 'I'm Steve, remember? We do Psychology together. We met up at Jodie's party last night. Don't worry, nothing happened. I'd like to get to know you sober. Then, when I seduce you, you can appreciate it more.'

'I'm Rach. Pleased to meet you,' I mumbled, and that was that. We were a fixed item for the next two and a half years, and everyone thought there'd be wedding bells when we finished our courses, but of course Steve moved away.

16

On Monday morning Steve had gone to work when I got up. I didn't even hear him go. I must have been exhausted. I crawled gingerly out of bed. I ached everywhere and my body looked like I'd been in a paintball contest, only the purple and black wouldn't wash off. In the kitchen he'd left me a little note. 'Will call you later to see how you are. Love you. Sxx' That was the first time he'd left me a note in the morning, and he'd drawn a heart with an arrow through it. It was so sweet, I felt all mushy.

It took me a while to get used to moving around, but eventually I pulled myself together, got dressed, ate some toast and jam and walked over to the police station. I was glad I didn't have to bend to get in a car till I'd limbered up a bit. I was taken into a small interview room while PC Jakes printed out my statement. I could hear laughter from the corridor, and a voice saying, 'She's here then? Steve's mud-wrestling girlfriend?'

I was about to rush out all indignant and give someone a piece of my mind, when the constable appeared, with a grin on his face and said, 'You're quite a heroine, you know. You should be on the force. We're all just a bit sorry we missed the mud-wrestling. You must have a good right hook.'

I was mollified. 'One black eye or two?'

'Only one, but there's a massive bruise on her cheekbone. You should have gone for the other side of her face if you'd wanted a matching pair.'

'Has she confessed to everything?'

'Oh yes. No point in denying it any more. She's now hoping her ex- will come riding to the rescue.'

'She'll be waiting a long time. Did she confess to pouring the paint through my letter-box? Only I couldn't figure that out, when Pete told me he thought she must've been watching his house and started stalking me after she saw me go there to ask him..a a favour.' I broke off when I realised I'd nearly dropped Pete in it for checking out the number plate Mr Jenkins had noted down. 'I only went to his house after the paint incident.'

'She must have been following him as well as watching the house. She said she'd seen you having coffee with him in town and she thought you were out to steal him.'

'Blimey. That was weeks earlier. I hadn't seen him for years at that point. I just bumped into him by chance.'

'Well she thought you were flirting, I suppose.'

I hoped Steve wouldn't get to read her testimony, cos I hadn't got around to telling him about all my meetings with Pete, and more importantly, there was always a chance she'd seen me kissing him.

I signed the statement. 'What'll happen now?'

'She'll be up before a magistrate. Bound over to keep the peace, and a fine, I shouldn't wonder. She'll not be able to go near you either. What she should get is a prison term for going after you with the knife, but I expect her solicitor will say she was suffering from some sort of psychological trauma and get her off with a lesser charge, in exchange for going to a counsellor. I've no faith in judges these days.'

'Well, so long as she keeps away from me. She certainly needs some sort of help. As far as I'm concerned, she's crazy, and she's kept me out of my flat for far too long. Can I go now?'

'Yes, that's it. If you have to appear in court, you'll get a summons, but as she's admitted all the incidents, you may not have to.'

I thought I'd call round my flat; see if it still felt like home. I hadn't got around to taking Mr Jenkins that box of Thorntons though I could have done with a box myself to celebrate the fact that it was over. Mr Jenkins pretended he couldn't accept the chocs, but didn't take that much persuasion.

The flat seemed welcoming without the shadow of an ever-looming attacker. I thought maybe I should move back in pretty soon while Steve was still feeling sweet on me. Maybe then he'd propose when he missed me.

Thinking of weddings, I knew where I had to

go next. Luckily Gran was at Mum and Dad's too, so I could tell them all that I was safe now.

'See', I said triumphantly, 'I told you my job's not dangerous. My attacker had nothing to do with any of my cases. There are crazy jealous women pounding the streets of Hull.'

Dad snorted. Mum said, 'Well, Rachel, maybe you better be careful around this Pete. I didn't realise you and Steve weren't getting on. Last I heard, you were planning a wedding.'

'It's not that, Mum. Pete's just a friend.'

'Are you sure that's what Steve thinks, only you don't want him to think you're two-timing him, do you?'

What a nice old-fashioned turn of phrase my mum has. Of course Gran had to chime in with, 'If this Pete'll marry her it doesn't matter what Steve thinks. Pete must have plenty of money if he's got a big house in Sutton, like our Rachel says. It's high time she settled down and had a family with someone, whoever they are.'

'Look, everyone, no-one's asked me to marry them yet, so maybe you ought to hold your horses till they do. And don't get the wrong idea about Pete, Gran. He's got women swarming round him like bees round a honey-pot. He can have his pick of any.'

I left, feeling I'd enflamed the situation, rather than calmed it. They might not be stressing about my job now, but instead they were going into overdrive over getting me married off, and that was a subject I was more confused about than they were. There was nothing for it. I rang Sarah on my mobile and talked her into meeting me in town to browse the shops for an hour or so. She'd have the baby but hey, maybe I ought to see what it's like trailing a pushchair around.

I brought Sarah up-to-speed and she soon had me in fits, asking for more details and egging me on while I told her about my fight with mad Stella. I must admit, by the time I'd finished embellishing the story, I'd have even paid for tickets myself to watch.

We looked round a few shops and I managed to get the same turquoise top that I'd ripped. I was glad about that. I planned on inviting Steve out for a meal as a thank you for rescuing me if I could get him away from the police station. I could wear it then. We looked at the pretty things in Accessorise and wondered who got invited to places where you could carry along the beautiful embroidered and sequined bags they sold. I bought a feathery fan to surprise Steve with – a few gentle strokes with that and he'd soon be relaxed, I thought. We browsed in W H Smiths. I looked around for the latest edition of Glamour magazine. They often had coupons and it'd help while away the time till Steve came home or I got another case. I was bending down to pick up a copy from the rack as another woman reached for the pile.

When I straightened up I saw a familiar face. I couldn't place her at first. Then it came to me. It was Mrs Brooks. She looked a bit tired but not exactly as if she'd just lost her husband. In fact I was surprised to see her fingering the fashion magazines, and wasn't that a carrier bag from one of Hull's trendiest clothes shops? I shook my head but then thought we all have our own ways of grieving. I thought of giving her my condolences anyway, but realised she didn't know who I was. I'd just seen them walking along holding hands but they wouldn't have seen me.

Sarah bought a parenting magazine – I knew which I'd rather be reading – and said she'd better be heading home as Josh was beginning to get restless and niggle for his lunch.

That afternoon I answered Inspector Jordan's call and popped back into the police station to sign yet another statement, this time concerning my discovery of Mr Brooks's body. As he was escorting me out, a middle-aged lady was arriving and the DI introduced me to Mrs Brooks. Shaken, I offered her my condolences, then dragged a surprised DI Jordan out of the door with me. If he thought I was mad, give him his due, he didn't say anything.

'It's not her!'

'What do you mean, Rachel?'

'That's not Mrs Brooks.'

'It is. We went to her house to get her to identify the body. When she got to the house where the body was found, she spoke to Mrs Sanderson, the lady who lives next door.'

'Well, she's not the woman I thought was Mrs Brooks, not the one I saw him walking down the road holding hands with. I saw that woman this morning in W H Smiths. I must admit, she didn't seem to be mourning that hard, judging by the shopping she'd been buying.'

'Ah, now that's interesting. I wonder who she was? A lover perhaps? We haven't been getting anywhere with the youths. I don't think they had anything to gain by killing Mr Brooks and it looks like you might have just opened up a new line of enquiry for us, Rachel. Do you mind stepping back inside and giving us a description of the mystery woman?'

'I can try, but I'm not very good at recalling faces.'

I described the mystery woman as best as I could – dyed blonde hair, shoulder-length, a modern-dresser, not frumpy, and left them to it. I'd seen enough of Garden Village for a while, though I promised to drive round with a police officer if they couldn't turn up this woman's name by talking to Mrs Brooks and Mrs Sanderson.

The next day I remembered I'd not called Pete and told him about Stella's arrest. I can't think how it slipped my mind.

'Pete?'

'Hi Rach. Good to hear from you. Did you get home alright the other night?'

'Well, no, actually.'

I launched into the whole tale about the fight in the bushes and how his hunch about Stella had been right. When I'd finished, he sounded quite upset, unlike certain other people I could name, but there again, he'd not seen the black eyes I'd inflicted on Stella.

'Oh Rach. I am sorry, really I am, and to think it's all my fault for letting such a strange woman loose on you. I'm glad it's ended well and she's confessed. Did the police say what'll happen to her? Will she get put away?'

'The officer I spoke to thinks she'll get off with a fine and a caution – and Steve thinks she'll probably have a restraining order banning her from going anywhere near me.'

'She should be behind bars for what she's done to you.'

'I think she needs some sort of treatment. I only hope she gets it.'

'Well, we ought to celebrate the fact that there's no mystery person out to get you any more. How's about I take you out for a meal tonight? You must be sick of eating alone and I could do with the company.'

'Why? You've got plenty of girls lining up to go out with you.'

'Yeah, but they're all the same. Go on. Your copper who isn't yours doesn't look after you and I can get us a table at The Lodge.'

'Wow. That's so upmarket I don't even know anyone who's been there. OK then. I'll go, if only to come back and tell all my friends about it.'

'Pick you up at 7.30 then.'

'Can I meet you there please? Only with staying at Steve's, well it doesn't seem too polite you picking me up from his flat to take me out.'

'It wouldn't bother me, but if that's what you want. Get a taxi so you can have a drink though. I'll pay for it. I'll see you at the Lodge at 7.45.'

With that, he was gone. I'd done it again. Let him believe there was nothing between me and Steve, and agreed to go out. And to somewhere posh - when I had absolutely nothing suitable to wear. Worse still, I couldn't afford to go down the shops and buy anything either.

I had to make do with what I had. I got out a black chiffon skirt that goes with anything and a black silky strappy top that I'd not worn for ages. I was going to wear my flesh-coloured strapless bra under it but the fastening was broken, so I had to go for my black basque. It would give out the wrong signal if Pete saw it, but it was the only thing I had that I could wear under the top, and nothing else I had was as sophisticated as that black top.

Amazingly I was ready when the taxi came and it dropped me outside The Lodge on time. Its exterior was discreet, only a small sign by the door advertising the name. No menus in the window and the tables were upstairs so no-one could stare at you eating. I gave my name and walked precariously on my heels up the spiral staircase.

In the restaurant itself, everything was understated with subdued lighting and the walls a pale blue. There were few decorative touches but what there were – a picture here, a mirror there – were very classy. The tables were covered with crisp white tablecloths with pale blue napkins in silver rings that matched the candle-holders. It looked as expensive as I'd heard it was, and I felt out of my depth.

I couldn't see Pete at first but he rose from a table in the middle of the long room when he saw me, and held out my chair for me. A waiter arrived as if from nowhere and asked if I wanted an aperitif. I asked for a glass of wine because I didn't know what else to have. After I'd read the menu I asked Pete what he was eating and ordered something cheaper. It looked like the meal would cost what I normally spent on food for a couple of weeks and I didn't want to make the bill any more astronomical.

I was glad I knew which cutlery to use as there was loads. I managed the starter without making a mess but I was terrified. The trouble started when I'd almost finished my first glass of wine. Pete refilled my glass but I'd been too busy talking to realise. I tipped it right up, thinking there was only a little left, and it dribbled down my chin. I put down the glass and reached for the napkin, and knocked the full glass over the table. I mopped up as best as I could and the waiter arrived fairly quickly but even so, there was a large red stain spreading across the beautiful white cloth and he had to remove it and bring another. That meant another waiter had to come and help lift the dishes and everyone was staring.

Pete was full of apologies to the waiter, who was giving me daggers. I was grinning stupidly, but I was the only one who thought it remotely funny it seemed, so I told Pete I was really sorry, and he said, 'Don't worry, Rach. It doesn't matter. Maybe you better let me finish the wine though.' He smiled at the people he'd earlier pointed out as business acquaintances, and I couldn't help feeling I'd embarrassed him, though accidents can happen to anyone.

We finished the meal and seemed to be getting on alright again, till I got up to leave and my heel caught on the hem of my long skirt. As I stood up, the elasticated waistband pulled right down and showed off my black silk panties, stockings and suspenders on my basque to all and sundry, including Pete. Why had I worn them? Worse, my stiletto heel was twisted into the material of my skirt and Pete had to bend down and loosen it so that I could pull my skirt up. I can honestly say there can't have been a single person in the restaurant who didn't get an eyeful by the time he was finished.

I blushed bright red and I know they'll never let me in there again. They probably had me down as an escort girl. I'm sure their usual clientele don't wear stockings and suspenders. When we got outside I was so embarrassed that I suggested Pete get me a taxi straightaway. I muttered something about feeling tired and he didn't need asking a second time. He was smiling and very polite, but probably I'd ruined his reputation.

When I got home, I wished I could have told Steve. He'd have thought it was hilarious, but I could hardly tell him what I'd been wearing to see Pete. Anyway, the clothes were rinsed and in the washer and I was in my dressing-gown by the time he came home. He asked how my evening with Pete had gone and I said we'd just had a bite to eat to celebrate the fact that Stella wasn't going to be tormenting me any more, and I'd been home for quite a while, and that was all true.

DI Jordan rang me one day that week and asked if I could help them identify the mystery woman. I wasn't exactly snowed under, just tidying up my flat, catching up on washing and paperwork. I hadn't decided whether to move back into the flat or not, but thought it'd do no harm to get it nice again. Mrs Brooks was shocked at the thought of her husband seeing another woman, and didn't recognise the description as anyone she knew, but the poor woman hardly knew what day of the week it was.

Unfortunately, Mrs Sanderson was away on holiday. I thought she would have a shrewd idea who it might be. Anyway I dutifully drove around in the patrol car but didn't see any sign of the mystery woman. We could hardly go knocking on doors as the woman might not live on Garden Village estate. Maybe they'd have more luck hanging around the shops in town.

I did go so far as to suggest they go to the trendy shop she'd been in and see if they could supply credit card details, but as we didn't have a name, that was a step too far even for the boys in blue.

I got paid by the prospective buyers. They didn't see fit to tell me whether my report had helped them to decide to buy the house on Maple Avenue or whether it had put them off. It would have been nice to know, but they were paying, so if they didn't see fit to satisfy my curiosity, I could hardly complain.

One day when we bumped into each other in passing, I mentioned to Steve about moving back into my flat. He seemed a bit taken aback, but he could hardly say he was going to miss our sparkling conversations, the endless hours of steamy sex or even the beautifully cooked meals I'd prepared for him. I had been doing his washing and ironing though – maybe he was disturbed at the thought of having to do those for himself again.

'Can we talk about this later please, Rach, when I get back? I'll finish early.'

'How early's early?'

'I'll try for six so we can eat together for once.'

'OK. That'll be good.' I kept the note of disbelief out of my voice and mentally expected him in at around ten.

I nearly fell over in surprise when he let himself into the flat at twenty past six. I had to rush around playing the domestic goddess – alright then, putting a couple of pies in the oven and peeling vegetables. I made proper gravy at least, well I used a stock cube and thickened it with bisto and cornflour. None of that granule stuff. Steve laughed at my efforts in the kitchen. He used to scour my kitchen cupboards periodically and point out all the items which were out-of-date. I told him those dates were only guidelines and another unnecessary restriction by the nanny-state. Dry stuff like cornflour keeps a lot longer than those dates. The truth was, I could actually bake, but I'd got seriously out of the habit, living on my own.

I'd been keeping myself going on biscuits, planning to have a pizza if he'd not shown by eight, so I only peeled myself a small potato. I got the meal on the table without keeping Steve waiting long after he'd showered, and was feeling a proper little housewife. I even opened a bottle of wine.

'So, how's it been today?'

'No new leads, but we've tracked down the customer lists for photographic suppliers within a 40 mile radius of Hull and Bridlington. That covers all the people who placed orders for specialised items. There's no sign of Parker in the list, but he probably didn't use his own name. With the way he lit the photos, our photographic expert thinks that the murderer must be a photography buff, rather than someone using a top-of-the-range digital camera, but we still can't find Parker's camera.

'Of course, he could keep his camera where he takes his victims and he could have bought items in stock over the counter or have a digital camera. We've shown photos of Parker to the sales staff to see if they recognise him but so far, no joy. Still, unless we get some new leads, we have to follow up the photography trail as far as we can.'

'What about the internet? Could he have ordered that way?'

'Unlikely. Parker doesn't have a computer and by all accounts he's not computer-literate.'

It was the first chance I'd had to bring him up-to-date on the Garden Village murder and Mr

Brooks' missing mistress. I could tell he was pleased that I'd given the much-beleagered murder squad a lead. As for me, the wine was beginning to take hold. I was on my second glass by the time I'd finished my pie – it's thirsty work talking. My stockinged foot teased the front of Steve's jeans under the table and found its target.

In no time at all I knocked back the rest of my second glass. As I brought the chocolate mousse to the table, Steve pulled me down onto his lap. Things got a bit silly then. Steve put mousse on the end of my nose, I put it on the tips of his ears and with the wine, I was soon giggling helplessly, and in no time at all, we were half undressed. Suffice to say Steve had to help me to the shower to wash off the sticky remains and we went to sleep happy.

I woke in the morning feeling a little headachy but beautifully relaxed. Steve had gone. The bathroom was covered in wet clothes and his sheets were a tangled heap. I could imagine the horror on my mother's face if she knew her daughter behaved like this. Somehow we never got round to talking about my moving out of his flat, but it no longer seemed an attractive option.

17

By Saturday morning I was ready for a bit of mindless escapism, so I was feeling quite cheerful as I drove round to pick up Mum and Gran.

'Hello, Rachel. I tried to persuade your gran that she could get changed when she gets there, but she was having none of it.'

Gran looked like a wrinkly Spice Girl with attitude. She'd got on the red top and I'd forgotten how sparkly and tight it was. She wasn't wearing the black skirt. She'd borrowed a miniscule red velvet skirt with a slit up the side from a friend at bingo – and black fishnet tights. If that friend was older than eighteen, I'd be amazed. Then she was wearing mascara, eyeliner, bright red lipstick, and round blobs of rouge on her cheeks. She looked like an eight-year-old who's playing at being mummy.

'I could help you with your make-up if you wanted, Gran.'

'No need. I've done it myself. I've seen enough of those makeover programmes.'

Well, maybe the house makeovers where they put on plaster in thick dollops with a trowel, I thought, with a grin. Why wasn't I surprised?

There were roadworks on the motorway and with the delay, Gran decided she needed the loo so we had to stop at Ferrybridge services. I overheard some kids in the loo laughing their socks off at the funny old red witch and was glad Gran's hearing's not perfect. We got to Elland Road football ground and were herded like cattle into the 'holding area'. It was a good job Gran had a provisional audition slot. I'd heard that the ones coming to an open audition had to sing in groups of 20 by the pitch, and very few were picked out to go further.

Camera crews came round filming people waiting, singing and being outrageous for fill-in slots on the show. The unfortunate open audition folk had to leap around and cheer outside repeatedly on camera, even though they were knackered from sleeping out all night. Eventually Gran's name was called and she went through to give her performance. She was singing Tina Turner's 'Simply the Best', not because it suited her singing voice, but it was the only song she knew enough words of.

Five minutes later she burst out through the doors, positively stamping her feet. 'Would you believe it? That Simon, Louis and the girls weren't there. You have to get through another round before you get to audition in front of them. No-one tells you that. They're not even here today. It's not fair.'

'Never mind Mum. You did your best. Maybe you can try again next year.' My mum put her arm round Gran.

'Oh, I got through. It just means I have to

come over again next week on Wednesday, and I'll miss bingo. You think they'd sort it so you have all the auditions in one day. Can we get a cup of tea now? I'm parched after that singing.'

I exchanged looks with Mum. We were both speechless for at least half a minute. Mum recovered first.

'That's fantastic. Well done!'

'Yeah, great, Gran. I'll have to see if I can find time to bring you again.'

'If not, your dad can step in since he missed it this time. I'm not sure I want to miss bingo though.'

While Gran was queuing to arrange her next audition slot, Mum and I had a cup of tea with loads of sugar for the shock. 'I hope she doesn't make it through to the telly, Rachel. I'll die of embarrassment if the neighbours see her dressed like that. I didn't think she could sing.'

'She can't. They put through the really good and the really awful so it makes an interesting show.'

'Really? Oh I suppose they must. Maybe we could tone down the clothes and make-up before next week', Mum said desperately.

Gran came back for her tea. 'We get Simon Cowell next time at least. I expect I could miss bingo. It's not usually big prize money on Wednesdays.'

Mum and I were fairly subdued on the drive home. She was probably trying to think of ways to sabotage Gran's second audition to avoid humiliation in front of the neighbours. I was fairly safe as no-one was likely to know she was my gran, but I felt for Mum, living just round the corner.

Amazingly, Steve was home when I got in and I managed to cheer him up with the story of Gran's audition.

'I wish you could've seen her in that get-up, though it's embarrassing to be related to her'

'Your mum'll cope if she gets on the TV. It'll be something to pass down in your family history. Anyway, there must be hundreds like your gran. They can't put all the bad ones on the telly.'

'So, how's it going with you?'

'Well, I've been putting in the hours. I keep thinking I must just be missing something; that we've got the vital clue staring us in the face and if I could just make the right connection, I'd have the breakthrough I need. Some days I wonder if Parker's telling the truth, and he really did go fishing the weekend Emma disappeared. Just like your gran with the X Factor, it's a narrow line between success and failure, Rach. The Super's getting a bit impatient and the Chief Inspector's out of his depth, but if I could pick up on the lead that nails this high-profile case, it'd really help me in the promotion stakes.'

'I didn't realise you were that intent on climbing further up the ladder. Wouldn't that mean you moving to another force, like last time?' My heart was in my mouth.

'Oh no, I don't want to move, love. I wouldn't want to leave you again.'

Tears filled my eyes. 'You mean that? It's just, you've never said.'

'Well, I'd like to stay with you, that is, if you want me. I know you like your independence and you're obviously not ready to commit to moving in with me permanently, but I was hoping we'd have a future together, Rach.'

'I'm not that independent. Where did you get that idea? I thought you were the independent one.'

'Ever since I came back to Hull you've held me at arms' length, going out with this Pete, moving in with me when I insist but then moving back to your flat. What am I supposed to think?'

'Oh. Right. I can see it might look like that, but try looking at it from my side. You disappear to London promising it won't break us up, but eventually we're hardly in touch any more, then you turn up out of the blue and expect to carry on as if nothing happened. How am I supposed to know you're not planning on leaving again? I don't want to get hurt a second time.'

'Oh Rach, I'm sorry. I really am. I never intended to leave you. You see what it's like when work takes over. It was like that in London. I always meant to come back. I was a fool not to have made it clear.'

'Well I didn't want to come right out and tell you I wanted us to be together, in case you weren't going to stick around for good. I didn't understand how you could let it all fade away when you went to London, unless it was never serious.'

'What if I were to ask you to marry me? Would you want to get married?'

231

'You could try asking me properly sometime', I said, hardly daring to breathe.

'Maybe I will. But I'll have to be sure that's what you want first. We really need to spend more time together so that you can trust me when I say I won't leave you again. Let's get this case out of the way and see how things go, but do me a favour, please don't move back into your flat just yet.'

'OK'. My voice came out all squeaky.

'Let's get some sleep now. I have to go into work for a while tomorrow but I'll get away by mid-afternoon and we'll go out for a meal in the evening for a change.'

While he was in the shower I sat there thinking. I couldn't decide if he meant it, about getting married, or if he was joking. I couldn't decide if he wanted to ask me, or if he'd said it because he thought I wanted him to ask. I couldn't decide if he just wanted to keep me in his flat. 'Damn, why do we never complete serious conversations?'

Steve had gone when I got up. I woke with dreams of Gran singing at my wedding, though I seemed to be marrying Simon Cowell. I shook my head clear of the thought and made myself some breakfast. I remembered my conversation with Steve and wondered if we'd get out for that meal, and if he would propose sometime and what my answer would be.

I read the paper but felt unsettled, and decided to go out. Before I knew it, I was driving into the Garden Village estate. There was a 'Sold' sign on number 3, Maple Avenue, so it looked like my clients had decided to put in an offer after all. I hoped they'd be happy there. I trundled around the estate but there weren't many people on the streets. I wondered where Mr Brooks might have met his blonde. Neighbourhood Watch? Maybe. Or did he belong to any other groups?

I stopped outside his house and knocked. Okay, so it wasn't my job, but if I could help solve their murder case for them, then the police would stop pestering me, and I admit I was nosy enough to want to find out who the mysterious other woman really was.

Mrs Brooks was cautious till I told her I'd found her husband's body and this was the first chance I'd had to express my condolences. She asked me in for a cup of tea. We English are so civilised. I muttered something about her husband being a pillar of the community with his Neighbourhood Watch activities, and managed to discover he had an allotment (couldn't see the woman I met getting her hands dirty) and also belonged to a book group. She said she hadn't time for books. She preferred her TV soaps. 'More like real life', she said.

'Not like my life', I thought, but managed to discover his book group met at the local library. No doubt they could provide a list of names and addresses to the police – or to me when they opened the next day. I said my goodbyes and went back to Steve's for a snack lunch.

I was just wondering what to do with the rest of the day when the phone rang. It was a new case. Hurray! I still get thrilled when I get work. Might be something to do with the fact that I'll be able to pay my bills and eat. Hell, even living with Steve I have to pay the bills on my flat and there are always clothes and chocolate crying out to be bought. A Mr and Mrs Steele from Redruth in Cornwall were worried about their daughter Claire. She was in her first year at Hull University and usually rang them every couple of days.

When she'd not checked in for five days, they'd spoken to the police, but they said it was a bit too early to panic, and they hadn't really got the resources to check on every student who'd moved in with a boyfriend. Mr and Mrs Steele didn't know any of her friends' names yet, and there was no house phone, as they all had mobiles these days. They didn't want to come up from Cornwall and embarass their daughter if she had found a boyfriend and just dropped them out of her mind for a bit, but they wanted it checking. So they picked me out of good old yellow pages. (I keep meaning to go all twenty-first century and get on the web but never seem to have the time).

I took all the details and promised I'd call round to the house that afternoon. I could tell that made them feel a whole lot better. I drove round to the address of the student house and talked to the girls there. They all had nothing but good things to say about Claire, though they'd not seen her for a few days. It seemed our Claire had let her hair down once she'd settled in at university. And they thought she'd met some bloke at a concert. They couldn't remember exactly when they'd last seen her as she'd kept herself to herself and didn't eat with them.

I left my number and asked them to get Claire to ring her parents, or for them to contact me if they heard from her or found out anything about the bloke she was seeing. Then I rang her parents to let them know that it looked like she was just turning into a regular student. They insisted that their Claire wouldn't stop ringing them, stay out all night or take up with a lad without telling them, but I wasn't so sure.

I promised to check again if I'd not heard from Claire and asked them to ring me if they heard from her. I also made a note that if there was no news in a day or so, then I'd have to try to find out from the university if her lecturers had any idea if she was still turning up for lectures, seminars and tutorials, or when she last had. I didn't think that'd be easy as they wouldn't know one girl from another so near the start of term. Also, I'd been a student once. I remember missing lectures without a qualm when I had something more exciting in my life. Then I made out a case sheet with Mr and Mrs Steele's details and the agreed fee, and went to get ready for my 'hot date' with Steve.

18

It was blissful sitting in Steve's car, staring into the darkness that was the North Sea, punctuated only by pinpricks of light from passing ships. There're not too many views around Hull, unless you climb to the top of the Humber Bridge. The landscape's flat and unrelenting for miles until you get to the Wolds, so if you want a view, you go to the cliffs. Not that we were doing much in the way of admiring the view. Steve had turned up at around six – not mid-afternoon, but plenty of time for the promised evening meal out. I'd managed to drop his mobile out of Steve's pocket before we left the flat, we'd driven out of town and eaten at a restaurant in the country, and then I suggested a detour to look at the view. It had gone dark within a few minutes of our arrival. I planned to keep him away from the phone for as long as possible.

After five minutes of gazing into the dark, all our pent-up frustration took effect and things got pretty steamy. Buttons were unfastened, and zips unzipped, and I was licking my lips and getting really carried away when light dazzled in the rear-view mirror, as car headlights swept the cliff-top car park. 'Quick, make yourself decent.' Steve leapt into action, zipping his flies with one hand and starting the car with the other.

I was a bit slower – could be my hair got caught somewhere, so I was still trying to re-arrange my clothing as we left the car park by the far exit, but the police car had pulled to a stop in the entrance and didn't follow us.

'That was a close shave', Steve said, as he headed for the main road.

'Surely we weren't breaking the law?'

'Well you were almost 99 percent of the way there, and given another five or ten minutes we would both have been, if I'd had my way.'

Me, I was giggling fit to bust at being caught at it like teenagers, though a wee bit disappointed we had to leave. Still, Steve was laughing too, and I thought maybe we'd carry on where we left off when we got back to the flat. Of course when we got there, he was still going on about how the lads at the station would never let him live it down, and he reached for his mobile to see if his car had been recognised.

'Where's my phone? Oh Christ, I can't have left it in the restaurant, can I?'

'It's here. It must've slipped out of your pocket onto the settee.'

He gave me a look, but turned it on and I just knew that was my chance of a night of passion gone again. Sure enough. There was a message for him to call in.

'Inspector Rose speaking. Put me through to CID please.'

I could see him itching to find out what was going on.

'Oh no, not another one, and I was out at the coast myself tonight. Er, just eating a meal, Sir. OK. I'll be out there in fifteen minutes.' He ended the call and turned to me. 'Sorry, love, there's been another body found at Dane's Dyke. That makes four. We're going to have to catch up where we left off another time.' With that he was gone.

I thought about calling it a night and going to bed, but I didn't feel tired. I'd drunk enough coffee to keep me going till the early hours, so I checked my messages but there weren't any. Just then the phone rang. According to caller ID, it was Mum. I debated whether to answer, but decided it was less hassle if I did.

'I've been trying you all night. Have you been out? I said to your dad, "she'll be out working again." You want to be careful.'

'I've not been working, if you must know. Steve and I went out for a meal.'

'Oh, that's nice, Rachel. Anyway, I phoned to tell you, your gran's getting engaged.'

'Again? Doesn't she know she's seventy-nine?'

'I know. It's disgusting. She says it's true love this time. His name's Clive and he used to work on the fish docks. I expect he still smells of fish, even after he's been retired all this time. That's the third one this year. I can't keep up with her. Why haven't you rung to tell me you've set the date? I want to be a grandma. I'll be too old to enjoy your children soon.'

I'd heard it all before and I was tired and frustrated, so I snapped, 'the state of our sex life, you'll never be a grandma.' There was a stunned silence and I remembered who I was talking to. 'Oops! Sorry, Mum, I'm tired. I mean, maybe you ought to be saying this to Steve. Remember, he's not proposed yet.' I thought about our conversation the night before but decided that should remain classified information for the time being so just muttered something about ringing her in the morning, then hung up.

The next morning was Monday and the libraries were open. I dressed as smartly as possible – knee length black skirt, white blouse, black jacket and even tights and black low-heeled shoes – and went along to the branch Mrs Brooks had mentioned. I didn't mean to impersonate a police officer, but they must have just assumed that's what I was when I said I was investigating Mr Brooks' murder. The nice ladies on the counter had seen it in the paper and assured me it was no problem to supply me with the names and addresses of the other book group members, none at all. Unfortunately none of the librarians working that day actually went to the book group, so they couldn't tell me if Mr Brooks had any particular friends among the group, but after ruling out the few other men, that left eight women.

I couldn't decide what to do next, so I went back to Steve's flat for a cup of tea and some choc chip cookies. I was mulling over what I could say if I rang the women, when it occurred to me that I was going about it the wrong way round. If there was an attractive blonde woman in the group, it was the men who would remember her name, and they would probably be aware of her talking to Mr Brooks.

Sometimes we women don't give men enough credit for picking up on who fancies whom. It only took two calls to get the information I needed. Mr Brooks had been seeing Ann. John Atkinson was sure of it.

'Thanks very much for your help, Mr Atkinson', I said.

'I thought about calling your lot but I didn't want to add to his widow's distress by letting the cat out of the bag. Mind you, I suppose she's a suspect now, his widow?'

He was obviously hoping for confirmation of this juicy titbit so he could pass it round the book group's next meeting, but I remained non-committal. 'We're just following all lines of enquiry, Mr Atkinson. Looking at Mr Brooks' many friends and contacts, that's all. Unless you feel someone at the group could have been jealous of their relationship. How did you feel about it?'

At that, he was suddenly anxious to distance himself from showing any particular interest, and get off the phone. 'Not me, no, Ann isn't my type. Too modern. And to be honest, I think all the other men were aware how the wind blew and knew she was taken, as it were. If that's all, I have to go out shortly.'

I assured him it was, and rang off. Now, the next dilemma was, should I check this Ann was the person I saw holding hands with Mr Brooks, or should I just pass the name, along with those of the other book group members to my friend Inspector Jordan? Well, what do you think? I like to think I do a thorough job. Ann Ransom lived on James Reckitt Avenue, not that far from Garden Village, and just a couple of doors down from the shops, so it seemed reasonable to park almost outside her house and nip to the shop for a carton of milk. However there was no woman conveniently in the garden or standing by the window when I passed. Drat! I walked back slowly, weighing up my options, and had just decided to knock and ask if the Browns, a fictitious family, still lived there, when she came out of her house, got into a small white car and drove off. She was the woman I'd seen, I was sure of it.

Flushed with success I rang Inspector Jordan on my mobile – I thought blow the expense for once – and let him have the good news. He was very good about the library and didn't take me to task for making enquiries on my own. He just asked for me to call in at the station with the list of other names for him. In the meantime he'd go round to see Ann. I was starting to feel I spent nearly as much time at that police station as Steve did, but thought maybe I could get the desk sergeant to give his office a ring when I called in and I could take him for a sandwich.

No such luck. He was out following up a lead apparently. I left the list with the sergeant and wandered across Queens Gardens into the town centre. I couldn't resist peeking in a few shops to reward myself for providing DI Jordan with a new lead on his case. Maybe he could make me an honorary constable, I thought. I quite fancied the idea of having my own handcuffs.

I bought a couple of t-shirts as the weather was starting to warm up a bit and headed back to Steve's to try them on. Wouldn't you just know it? One fitted perfectly but the other was miles too big. When I looked at the label I realised someone had put a size fourteen back on a ten hanger. Now why would they do that? Why would they try on a ten and a fourteen, for crying out loud?

Then I had a brainwave. I could give Sarah the green one as part of her birthday present as she's got a proper bust, not like my flat chest. Problem solved. Nothing like a bit of lateral thinking for giving you an appetite, so I tore into my sandwich and had crisps and a Mars bar as well.

There had been no news from Claire's parents or her house-mates. I called round to see if they'd come up with a name for the lad she was seeing. You know what students are like, they might just not have got round to ringing me, but there was no-one in. But Wednesday was 'the big day' as far as Gran was concerned and I thought it would do no harm to wait a day. I even thought Claire might have just turned up, rung home and they'd forgotten to tell me.

I was round at Mum's early again, eager to see if she'd talked Gran into wearing something a bit more tasteful, but apparently those clothes were now designated 'lucky' so it looked like Mum and I would just have to grin and bear it and hope the judges didn't find her awful enough to put through to the next round.

We had a good run down the motorway to Leeds. Mum counted Eddie Stobart lorries and pointed out other points of interest like lorries for companies called 'Bonnie Tyler', belonging to a roofing contractor. She had a big bag of sweets for times when she couldn't think of anything to say. I think she wanted to avoid a repeat of the previous week when we'd had to listen to Gran practising her song on and off for a hundred miles.

This time we weren't herded into Elland Road but were in some sort of conference centre with plenty of rooms for people to wait. Simon Cowell was late, but I'd heard he often was, so I'd come prepared with food. I wasn't going to be wasting away because we couldn't get away for lunch when we'd planned to.

'Why didn't you bring tuna?' Gran complained.

'You wouldn't want greasy fingers, Gran' or clothes, I thought, but I didn't say that.

Gran is a very messy eater and if you visit her in the evening, you can tell what she had to eat for every meal that day. Mind you, why I should have wanted to keep her in perfect condition is beyond me, except I had a sneaking suspicion that if she looked like a bag lady she'd make an interesting person to put on TV as a failed auditionee, and I owed it to Mum to try and prevent that.

There were plenty of people eager to sing their hearts out and some of them weren't bad, so we were entertained while we waited, but I was glad when Gran was eventually called in to perform. I wanted to be clear of Leeds before the traffic started to build up around four o'clock.

Gran was ages. Eventually the door opened and she hobbled out, helped by Louis Walsh and a strong specimen who was presumably employed to eject those who begged and cried to be put through. Mum stood star-struck. She thinks Louis is marvellous. So it was up to me to go over and find out what had happened. I was praying Gran hadn't made a fool of herself. Louis passed her to me and said to Gran, 'It's been a real pleasure meeting you. Now just take care.' I couldn't tell if that was just show business talk or if he really meant it.

'Well?' Mum and I asked in unison.

'I didn't get through. I could tell Louis was weakening. Danni and Cheryl smiled nicely. Simon couldn't stop laughing and said I was most entertaining. But they all said "No". Louis said it would be too much for me to go further and there were some good candidates, but he hoped I'd enjoyed it apart from the fall.'

'What fall?' We sounded like the dames in a pantomime.

'I was dancing to the music, you know, getting in the groove, and I slipped. I'm alright. There's no need to fuss.'

'You could have broken your hip, Mum.

Whatever were you thinking of?'

'You have no idea what it's like to be a performer, Anne. You can't just stand there like a lemon and sing.'

'Well, I think we'd better get you checked over.'

'It's only my ankle. My hip's fine. Though it is starting to hurt more now and I can't really put my weight on it.'

'Oh no. I knew no good would come of this X Factor business, a broken ankle!'

'It's probably only a sprain', I said, trying to calm things down. Let's get off home and we'll see how it is then. I'll see if there's anyone can give us some ice to put on it.'

There were no food or drink places to be found anywhere in the centre, so we drew a blank looking for ice. I thought it was best if we headed for the motorway and stopped at the services. Gran looked a bit of a sight but I was past caring. She wouldn't stay in the car so we propped her on one of those chairs that massages you if you put money in the slot. I'm a bit suspicious of them, I have to confess. You never know if they're going to turn into bucking broncos. A disinterested girl behind the counter said she had ice but she only had a plastic beaker to put it in.

Mum had a carrier bag in her handbag. She has sewing thread, safety pins, plasters, indigestion tablets, in short anything you could need, although rarely do. No wonder she needs a bag twice the size of everyone else's. She couldn't resist saying, 'I knew this would come in useful one day.'

Gran put her leg up on my back seat and put the bag full of ice on it. I'd tied it in a knot but doubted it wouldn't leak water all over my seat. 'Mum, you make sure to take that off her when the ice's melted. I don't want my back seat all soaked.'

'You don't have to talk over me like I'm an invalid,' moaned Gran. 'You should be grateful to me. I forgot to tell you the good news, though. I'm going to be on the TV! I might not have got through but Simon said he'd never seen anything like my erotic dancing.'

There was a silence so deep you'd hear a spider creeping along its web to eat a fly, followed by two shrill voices, 'Erotic?!'

I was all for dumping Gran by the side of the road except you can't stop on motorways. Mum just kept muttering under her breath, the gist of which seemed to be, 'The neighbours. What will the neighbours say?' As the M62 gave way to the A63 I breathed a sigh of relief. I'm not a keen motorway driver and as the pace calmed down and I knew I could stop if I wanted, I felt less pressurised. When we came into Hull down the wide dual carriageway, centre island filled with beautiful flower beds, I thought like I always did, that there was nowhere quite like it, and I was coming home figuratively as well as literally.

Amazingly the back seat was still dry. Gran had thrown the bag over the back of the front seat when the ice had melted though, so Mum had got a bit splattered, but that was the least of her troubles, in the light of the impending damage to her reputation. She insisted we call at casualty to get Gran's ankle x-rayed. I think it was just a delaying tactic so she didn't have to get home and tell Dad that his mother-in-law would be doing erotic dancing on the telly wearing sparkly red with make-up to match.

I was past the point of being cross, tired, anything really, by the time Gran was eventually wheeled off for an X-ray. Mum turned to me. 'Oh my God, Rach. What will we do?'

'I thought you took that really well.'

'Well, I couldn't spoil her excitement while she was in pain.'

'I would have, if I lived round the corner from Gran.'

'Don't remind me. She's thrilled to bits, Rachel, but I think we should go on holiday when the programme's shown.'

'Or the morning after.' There was a sharp intake of breath as Mum realised even I agreed with her that it would be horrendous and she hadn't imagined the day's excitement. 'No, Mum. It'll be alright. They probably won't put her on. Think how many people were there, and how many are at all the other towns. And they do have to show quite a few of the decent ones; the ones who've got through.' I didn't believe what I was saying myself. I knew Gran would be on TV. She looked outrageous enough without the erotic dancing, the fall, and of course her total inability to sing. I just wanted to make Mum feel a bit better for a while.

When we got out of the hospital, I felt like I'd spent the entire day waiting, and not getting anything. I dropped Gran off at her house. They'd strapped up her ankle but the swelling had already gone down a bit and she could hobble on it. She was adamant she didn't want taking to Mum's. 'I want a cup of tea in my own house and to put my feet up after you two exhausting me all day.'

I looked at Mum in silence.

'I'm glad she said she wanted to go home. It's going to be hard enough breaking the news to your dad without being unable to choose the right moment. Gran would've come straight out with it.'

'Mm. Let me know what he says, Mum'.

She looked like someone on borrowed time as I drove off. It was rush-hour now and heaving. I wanted to get home and have a cup of tea myself, not sit in more traffic. I turned onto the main road and came to the roadworks. There were temporary traffic lights and I just got through as they turned to amber, but there was another light a few yards further and that turned red. The driver in front braked and I pulled up too. Almost immediately there was a thud on my rear end. I couldn't believe it after the day I'd had. I got out to survey the damage and was amazed to find there wasn't a scratch on the car. The bloke behind was full of apologies.

'Sorry, dear, I was trying to beat the lights.' He attempted a smile. 'So it's OK then?' I had to admit the bumpers on my beautiful new car had plenty of 'give' in them. It cheered me up, I can tell you. I jumped back in and was ready to set off when the lights turned to green again. Bless Ford motors, I thought. Fancy finally making a bumper that works instead of breaks. I dived in the bath with my favourite bubble bath and listened to Corinne Bailey Rae soothe away the day's stresses, before summoning up the energy to cook. It seemed hours since we'd eaten. I scoffed four or five biscuits while I was waiting.

I fished out my mobile to text Steve and found I'd missed a call from a girl called Charlotte, who said she lived in Claire's house and had some news for me. It seemed she'd been away on some sort of geography field trip for a couple of days when I'd visited the house.

When I tried Charlotte's number in the morning I got a message telling me it was unavailable. I decided she'd probably run out of battery on her phone, like I'm always doing. I made a note of the number on a scrap of paper and stuffed it in my handbag so I could keep trying, and then I headed out to the shops. I'd helped Steve eat most of the contents of his fridge and cupboards, and even the freezer only had things in it that were either suspiciously ancient-looking, or stuff I couldn't imagine anyone would want to eat.

When I got back, I was unpacking happily when a pot of yoghurt slipped from my grasp and landed with a splat. How can such a small carton make such a large mess? Not just on the floor, but up the bottom of the cupboard units and the front of the fridge. I cleared up as best as I could, then made a cup of tea, trying to decide if I could still smell strawberries. I drifted off into the past, remembering when I'd spilt an orange yoghurt in my schoolbag and it had reeked of sour milk and orange for weeks till I'd persuaded Mum to fork out for a new one.

Armed with this memory I got some very hot water and cleaned everything down a second time. By the time I'd finished I needed another cup of tea and it was time for a spot of lunch. After I'd demolished some of the new yummy things I'd bought, I settled down with my invoice copies and the big hardback book I use for my accounts. The bloke who lives next door to Mum, otherwise known as my accountant, had been pestering me to get everything up-to-date so he could help me with my tax return. I don't earn enough to be registered for VAT thankfully.

I tried Charlotte again when I'd finished. The phone rang and rang but no-one answered. I was just drying my hair after a shower, ready to drive round again, when Charlotte called me. She'd been out clubbing and had had a hangover half the day so had only just got round to ringing me.

It seemed Claire's boyfriend was not particularly good looking, tall with brown hair and no distinguishable features. Charlotte said the two were inseparable, happy as anything, but she couldn't tell me his name or what he was studying, and he'd hardly said a word to her when she'd bumped into the pair in the street. She did know where he lived though, as she'd seen the pair go into a student house off Pearson Road with a bright yellow door and she told me the street, even though she didn't know the number.

It sounded like Claire was just too preoccupied with this lad to ring her mum, and I thought I'd at least be able to ring and put Mrs Steele's mind at rest after I'd called round, so I nipped round there straightaway. I found the house easily enough and knocked.

The door was answered by a tall lad in a t-shirt and jeans.

'Hi. I'm looking for Claire Steele. I think she's going out with someone in this house. It wouldn't be you, would it?'

'Sorry, who are you?'

'My name's Rachel Hodges. Her parents live in Cornwall and they've not heard from her for almost a week, and when she first came to Hull, she rang them every couple of days. You know how parents worry, so they asked me to see if she was OK. Her housemates haven't seen her for a day or two, but they told me she was going out with a lad who lived at the house on this street with a yellow door.' I decided to imply I was a family friend, rather than telling him I was a private detective. I didn't want him to tell Claire her parents were getting neurotic and hounding her.

'She's going out with Richard. They're away at the moment. They've gone off to the coast for a couple of days. I could ask her to ring when she gets back, if you like.'

'That'd be good, thanks. I'll give you my number. I don't suppose I could come in and look around?'

'Sorry. I'm in a rush. I'm just going out and there's no-one else in.' Unsurprisingly he seemed a bit uneasy at a stranger wanting to gain access to the house. I looked up at the house but there were no lights on, so I just thanked him and drove home. I couldn't say why I wanted to go in and look round. I didn't have a feeling that Claire was in the house. I'm just naturally nosy I guess.

When I got back to Steve's, the phone was ringing.

'Rachel?'

'Yes.'

'DI Jordan here. I thought you'd like to hear the developments resulting from your good detective work.'

'Oh yes?'

'Forensics have matched a hair taken from Mr Brooks' body to Ann Ransom, the lady you identified as walking down the street holding hands with him. She denies killing him. She said she left the house first, as was usual, so that they weren't seen together, but I'm sure she's our murderer. At first she said she'd only known him from her book group meetings but then she admitted they were having an affair, after we told her what the other members had said. Anyway I'm convinced enough to have sent officers to search her house. I don't expect to find the weapon. She'd be mad to hold onto it, but you never know.'

'Well, I'm glad to have been of help, Inspector. I must admit she didn't look like a grieving lover when I caught sight of her in town the other day. Do let me know the outcome, if you can.'

'No problem. Maybe you ought to consider joining the force?'

'Steve'd never forgive me.'

He laughed and we said our goodbyes. I toyed with the idea of becoming a policewoman, but I've never been able to see myself working the kind of hours Steve puts in, and I like the freedom of answering to no-one except my clients.

My thoughts were interrupted by the phone ringing again. It was Mum. 'Have you heard from your gran, Rachel? She's not been in touch with me since we got back from Leeds. I've called round a few times to see if she needs any help with her ankle being strapped up, but she's never in.'

'I've not heard from her, but if she's never in, then she can't need your help, Mum. Quit worrying.'

'But where can she be?'

'I thought you said she'd got engaged. Won't her fiancé be looking after her?'

'No. Didn't I tell you? She broke it off the next day. She said he was only after her pension.'

'Don't worry. She'll have someone else dancing attendance on her. Someone she's mesmerised with her tales of being famous and on the telly. You know Gran, Mum. She can't half spin a tale.'

'I suppose you're right. How are you? Have you any news about an engagement yet?'

My wedding plans, or lack of them, were not a high priority at that moment. In fact I'd forgotten all about the cosy time we'd spent huddled over Bride magazine, drawing up guest lists. 'Steve's far too busy at the moment, Mum. You've seen the news. They're saying the police aren't doing enough to ensure girls can walk the streets of Hull safely.'

'I suppose it'll wait, but you're not getting any younger and the churches get booked up such a long time in advance.'

'Mm. Anything else, Mum, only I was going to get Steve's tea on?' No point in telling her just yet that I'd changed my mind and wouldn't be going for a church wedding when I get married. I've not got a religious bone in my body, and I don't think Steve has either, and I'm not the sort to get married in church when I don't go on Sundays. I'd rather opt for Sewerby Hall if she wouldn't settle for a quiet registry office 'do'.

'No. You go then love. I mustn't stop you cooking.'

Poor Mum. If only she knew. I was only going to slam a couple of pieces of bread-crumbed chicken in the oven, I doubted she'd call it "cooking", but they did taste good.

19

It was turning seven when I heard Steve's key in the door. He'd been at work getting on for twenty-four hours.

'Hi. You look exhausted. How's it going?'

'It's not. We're going round in circles now. We've had to let Parker go. We've already identified this latest victim as Kirsty Edgill and Parker was coming to the end of an eighteen months' sentence for rape when she went missing. We're not giving up on him, in case she'd been living on the streets for a while and then he picked her up, but it seems unlikely.'

'Oh, Steve.'

'And do you remember, he dredged up that shaky fishing alibi for Emma, the previous victim? Well, he could have been telling the truth. Some bloke has just come forward to say he saw a silver car leaving the competition car park about a quarter of an hour after she was picked up, and he seems reasonably convinced the driver was Parker. He couldn't have been in Hull to pick Emma up, take her and leave her tied up somewhere and then drive all the way back to the car park at Hornsea Mere in that short a time.'

'No, he couldn't. So what do you do now?'

'To be honest we're in a right mess. We've hardly any new leads to follow up, even with this latest murder, and now if we've been off on a wild-goose chase with Parker, potentially other facts that didn't fit with the idea of him as murderer might have been overlooked. We will have followed up all other serious leads as much as manpower allowed, but it's the little things that we wouldn't have had time for.'

'Oh dear, that doesn't sound good.'

'After the last murder we'd reached the stage detectives hate – knowing we'd probably need another murder to give us that elusive clue. It's horrible, Rach, but I know I'm not the only one who was thinking like that. And of course now we've got our wish, but not only has it not given us anything solid to follow up, but it looks like it's ruled out our only real suspect and just left us with more contacts to interview.'

'Oh, Steve, have something to eat and I'll rub your shoulders. You look so tense.'

'I can't face anything to eat and my head's still full of statements, trying to go back over them and find that something we've missed. I'm not sure I'd be able to relax, even with one of your massages.'

If Steve was off his food, and not even jokingly mentioning sex in relation to one of my massages, I knew he was really low and needed help.

'Look, I'm not a policewoman, but maybe if you run things by me, lay out what you've got, then I might pick up on something. You know, a woman's instinct or whatever. And if nothing else, telling me might get you to look at the cases from more of a distance.'

'Are you sure? It seems awful, hardly seeing you, then coming in and bringing work home with me.'

'Just as long as you give me a sanitised version. I don't have to see crime scene photos and I'd rather not hear anything gruesome that isn't necessary. And I have had a bit of success in the detection field recently.'

I filled him in on the latest happenings on the Garden Village estate.

'That's brilliant, Rach. It'll free up a few more people for our case.'

'Right, well, while you're telling me, you can eat. I'll draw up a little list of the main facts and then I'll ask questions. You need some food inside you or you'll be no good to any girl this maniac might target next.'

I slammed the chicken pieces in the oven while Steve had a shower and changed into a t-shirt and jeans. Quick but nourishing food, followed by ice-cream for a bit of a treat. Then I sat on the settee and let him stretch out across my lap, his head on a cushion, and I opened a pad of A4, resting it on his chest.

'OK then. I know you've been following up leads on the items found on the bodies but I can't help you much with the practical stuff. Let's list the victims and where they were found, and what we know about them. See if I can find any new link between them when they were alive, or any reason why the killer would target them or how he might have met them. He must have known all the victims, surely, or else someone would have noticed a struggle between strangers. It seems hard to believe that four girls all seem to have disappeared without anyone noticing, but I remember cases in the news where toddlers disappear and no-one sees them go, so if the girls were willing, it's going to be even more likely.'

'Right. It's worth a try. We never did link Parker properly to the first or third victim. He drives a small silver car, and one was seen near the cliffs when the first body was dumped, but so do thousands of other people. All we had was the witness identification in the second case where we linked him to the victim via the museum, the fact that he was keen on amateur photography, and his rape record, and that seemed enough even without the eye witness who said she'd seen him with Nicola. Like I said though, we were waiting for an incontrovertible piece of proof, because none of us were convinced the witness's eyesight was good enough for the ID to stand up in court.'

'Let's start at the beginning anyway, love.'

'Right. The first body we found, back when you took up being a private detective again, was Susan Hardy. You remember the Chief Inspector suspected Peter Taylor, the father of the little boy she was an au-pair for?'

'Yes, till the next body was found. Anyway, apart from being young and blonde - all the victims were, weren't they?'

'Yes, all between eighteen and twenty-two, all with long blonde hair.'

'Right, other than that, what's significant about her? She was a long way from home, but she wasn't living on her own, was she?'

'No. She stayed in at the Taylor's house most evenings, either with them or in her room. She didn't have many friends.'

'And the friends she had, did they mention a boyfriend?'

'They didn't know anyone, but said she'd started dressing up a bit more, wearing make-up, that sort of thing. Only thing is, she hardly went anywhere on her own, so they couldn't help us narrow down any places she might have met someone.'

'So she didn't go to clubs then. Did she join any groups to make friends, go to classes, that sort of thing?'

'Not so far as anyone knows. She hardly ever went out in the evenings. She got a bit secretive just before she went missing, but the Taylors weren't that concerned at first. We later found out that she'd taken some of her clothes, but she had said she was going away for the weekend with a friend. They thought it must be a girl. They didn't know of a boyfriend, although she'd been acting a bit different, like I said.'

'Well, she could have met a bloke in a café, or even the park where she took the child.'

'We had a uniformed officer hang around the nearest park and talk to the mums with kids, but drew a blank.'

'Did she have a computer?'

'No.'

'No internet romance then, not unless she spent time in an internet café.'

'Hull's not exactly brimming with them and we showed her photo round, but no-one remembers seeing her.'

'OK. Who was the next victim to be found?'

'Nicola Kennedy. She'd been dead a lot longer though. For some reason he left Susan's body out in the open, so it was found quickly. All the other bodies that have turned up since Susan's were killed before she was. He may have been prevented from taking her body to the sort of woody areas where he buried the others, or maybe he was fed up with waiting for recognition of his crimes. As you can imagine the psychologists are having a field day with that one.'

'Well, don't tell me their theories. I'll try and think up my own when we've covered all the bodies. This Nicola – she was found in woods then? I think you said near a picnic site in woods?'

'Yeah. Near Danes Dyke. You know, between Bridlington and Flamborough.'

'Well, he must have buried her at night. A lot of people pass that way in the daytime and stop at the picnic area to stretch their legs or to walk dogs.'

'You're right. It's quite a busy place. She worked at Wilberforce House, selling entry tickets and small souvenirs.'

'Oh, yeah? I haven't been there since we went on a school trip. I remember the museum attendant shouting at the boys for trying to take the wig off the life-size model of William Wilberforce.'

'Well, Parker made stationery deliveries there. That was our link. She lived with her parents still. She was only eighteen. Again, she had a couple of friends but didn't go to clubs. She went to cookery nightclass, but it was an all female class.'

'Have you looked into the other classes held the same night? They might have all gathered round the one coffee machine in the interval. She could have got talking to someone.'

'We thought of that. We've interviewed every male who went to classes at the school on Wednesdays. No-one of interest turned up, though we can't keep them all under surveillance.'

'What about at work? Maybe one of her colleagues? Or maybe someone she worked with could have introduced her to Susan, and they went somewhere together.'

'We've grilled all her colleagues quite intensively.'

'Where did she live?'

'East Hull, not far from your parents' house.'

'And Susan, where did she and the Taylors live?'

'In Cottingham.'

'Mmm. Tell me about body number three then. She was found at Dane's Dyke as well, wasn't she?'

'Emma Chamberlain, aged twenty-one, worked as a dental receptionist at a practice on Beverley High Road. She lived near Pearson Park, again with her parents.'

'So, they were all quiet homely girls then, maybe a bit on the innocent side. They probably went willingly with someone who flattered them. Did she go out much?'

'No.'

'So you think they were targeted? Apart from Parker, I presume there were no other real suspects on the sex offenders' list?'

'That's right. The Chief Inspector thinks if the killer wasn't Parker, then it's someone who hasn't offended before, because we went through that list with a fine tooth comb. He thinks it'll be someone who didn't have a lot of luck with girls, probably socially inept and probably not too intelligent.'

'Could be a computer geek. They're often socially inept, but not unintelligent.'

'Yeah, but he reckons because the girls didn't go out much in the evening, he can't have worked nine-to-five in an office. Either he had a job which took him out and about or he couldn't hold down a job at all.'

'So when does the Chief Inspector reckon the girls could have met him then? They all worked. Unless he met them at their jobs. He could still be an office worker and met them in his lunch hour. I'm not convinced by his theory. Just because they didn't go to nightclubs, doesn't mean they never went out in the evening.'

'Mmm. Could be your mate Pete. He works when he chooses and he's a computer geek, isn't he?'

'It's hardly him, Steve. He's not what I'd call a geek and he always has girls flocking round him. Don't you think I'd notice if someone was really a slime-ball?'

'Only joking, Rach, but even slime-balls can come across as just innocent and naïve.'

'True, and he must have some considerable intelligence to have carried out four murders and got away with it. I think the Chief Inspector's way off beam with the 'not too intelligent' tag.

'It wouldn't be the first time he's been way off beam in this investigation. Remember how he pursued Peter Taylor before we had Parker in the frame, when it was obvious to anyone with half a brain cell that it couldn't be him?'

'I've never met him, but I must admit he doesn't seem that brilliant. Makes you wonder how he got to his elevated position.'

'Don't get me started on that, Rach!'

'Alright then, to get back to the girl who worked in the dentist's. Emma, wasn't it?'

'Yes, and before you ask, we've closely examined her few colleagues and found no suspects or likely links with the other two girls. '

'What about the patients?'

'Around a thousand. We filtered out the females and any males under eighteen and over fifty-five, but there are still a couple of hundred. We got a PC looking into their alibis and background whenever he'd got time, but it became a low priority for us, I'm afraid, once we couldn't find Parker's name amongst them.'

'Did the other two girls go to her dentist's perhaps?'

'No. We did check that.'

'They might have met somewhere else. Have you thought that the girls might go to the same hairdressers, if they don't go to the same clubs?'

'It's an idea, but a bit of a long shot, Rach. I think we've almost decided the girls didn't know each other. In fact, it's beginning to look like he just picked them up somewhere, maybe even off the street.'

'They don't seem that sort of girl to me. I admit it's difficult though. They all lived and worked in different places too. Who was the latest victim? You did say she's been identified already?'

'Yes she has. She was Kirsty Edgill. She's been missing the longest. We'd taken statements when she was reported missing by her parents because she still lived at home. When Susan's body was discovered, she'd not been reported as missing at that point, so we looked through all the recent missing persons to see if the body was one of them. When Kirsty's body turned up, we already had a list of young blonde girls and it was easy to identify her because she'd been in a car accident when she was

264

young and had metal pins in her leg.'

'Tell me about her then.'

'She worked at Lloyd's bank opposite the university and lived in Willerby.'

'Right, and I suppose the colleagues check out?'

'It's too early to know that, Rach. She's only just been identified, remember. But she doesn't appear to have any links to any of the other three girls as far as her parents know. And as for hobbies, she belonged to a swimming club, and we're only just starting to look into the other members and the instructors. Once again, she seems to have disappeared out of the blue in the middle of the day. That, and the fact that in every case it's thought a few clothes were missing, is the only link between them. Like I said, Rach, maybe we'll get another lead from having had this other murder, but, going on first impressions, there's nothing. You never know when you'll get a break though.'

'Where did you say Kirsty worked?'

'In a bank.'

'Didn't you mention the university?'

'Yes, the University branch, just over the road.'

I sat stock-still, wheels turning in my head.

'That could be it. The link could be the university, Steve! Susan lived in Cottingham, where there are a lot of halls of residence. Kirsty worked at the University branch of Lloyd's Bank. Emma worked at a dentists on Beverley High Road, and I'll bet it was the end near Cottingham Road where the university is.'

'Could be, Rach. Hey, you could be on to something. He could be a student. Why hadn't we made the connection?'

'Because you've only just found Kirsty, who has the strongest link to the university. Not sure about him being a student though. He has to have a car to move the bodies, and not many have the money these days with the student loan debt they carry around. He could be a lecturer though, or someone working in the library or a laboratory. There's a lot of people connected directly or indirectly with the university. Don't know whether it'll help to have all those extra suspects. Oh, but Steve, what about Nicola? She didn't work or live nearby. Damn, that throws the theory out of the window.'

'Not necessarily, Rach. You've given me an idea. The killer could be something to do with the history department, and have been to the museum to do research into the abolition of slavery.'

'Mmm. Yes. It's definitely worth looking into, and if he is connected to the history department, that will narrow things down tremendously.'

Steve reached for his shoes. I knew he had to go. I didn't blame him. Even I was excited about the lead. I just hoped I wasn't sending him back to work on a wild-goose chase.

As he rushed out again, I knew it was down to me this time that I was left on my own again, but I wanted the bastard caught too, and not just so I'd see Steve more, but because I didn't want any other girl to end up like the four he'd killed already.

I was just opening a book and a bar of chocolate when I remembered the fact that Claire was a student, a missing student and by then it must have been almost ten days since she'd rung her mum and dad. An icy draught shivered down my spine. I grabbed the phone and hit the buttons for Charlotte's mobile. While I waited, I thought about Claire. I still couldn't believe she hadn't got a mobile. Even though her parents thought they would give her a brain tumour and wouldn't buy her one, I felt sure she'd get one herself, but her house-mates said she'd told them she didn't need one and couldn't afford one anyway.

The number rang and rang but Charlotte didn't answer. I couldn't let it lie. I grabbed my coat, pushed my feet into my trainers and drove round there straightaway. The house was in darkness. I cursed, but there was nothing I could do about it. I scribbled a note in the brightest thing I had – lipstick, asking her housemates to ring me immediately and pushed it through the door, then drove back to Steve's. I tried to settle to the book, but in the end I ate the whole bar of chocolate, had two glasses of wine and went to bed.

20

The next day I called at Claire's house. Charlotte was in. Claire still hadn't turned up and they hadn't heard from her. I didn't want to frighten them for no good reason but they weren't stupid.

'Look, you don't think Claire going missing has anything to do with those murdered girls, do you? We missed the reports on TV but the Students' Union put up notices about them, saying girls shouldn't go out alone after dark, and we wondered about Claire. She couldn't be in danger, surely?' asked one of the girls.

'Whoever it is, he's not killed any students, and Claire was wrapped up in that boyfriend of hers.' Charlotte tried to sound reassuring, and I must admit that I hadn't imagined there was any connection between the murders and Claire's disappearance until Steve and I thought of the university as a possible link. It may sound like we were overlooking the obvious, but the university is off to one side of Hull and the students and the rest of the city don't really mix. Also it really did look as if she'd gone off with her boyfriend. But you do start

268

to wonder.

Charlotte said she'd go to Claire's boyfriend's house with me as she needed to return the padded jacket she'd borrowed from Claire for her geography trip. She'd left hers at home in Manchester because she thought winter was long gone, but then she had to go on that field trip to the middle of freezing nowhere.

We knocked on the door and a different lad answered. I explained again that we were back round to look for Claire, and was she or Richard in?

'I'm Richard. I don't know any girl called Claire though. Who did you talk to when you came round last time?'

'He didn't give me his name. He's about your height, on the slim side with fairly long brown hair.'

'That sounds like Simon. He's a PhD student in his final year. You're out of luck. He moved out yesterday, and I can't say I'm sorry to see him go. He gave me the creeps.'

'May I ask why?'

'We only found out recently, but he was in some trouble for taking photos of girls in the shower at his last house and they kicked him out. If we'd known that, when he'd come to ask for a room at Christmas, we'd not have let him have it, but the previous bloke had chucked in his course and we needed the rent money. Anyway, Simon seemed OK at the time. He always paid on time and was no trouble, but he just made me a bit uncomfortable.'

'Did he have a girlfriend?'

'He had quite a few. Never really spoke to any of them. They all seemed the shy type. All looked a bit similar really. Smallish and slim, and all of them blonde. I said to Chris that he must get them mail-order. Mind you, none of them lasted that long. They'd be round here all the time for a couple of weeks and he'd be taking them out in his car for rides in the countryside and then he must have started staying round at theirs because he was away overnight a lot. Then suddenly he'd be back here for good on his own. Till the next one.'

I started to feel really uneasy.

'So you haven't got a girlfriend called Claire?'

'No. I'm not seeing anyone at the moment. I don't know why Simon thought I was.'

I had my suspicions but I had to ask, 'What about your house-mates? Could any of them be going out with Claire?'

'Steve's been going out with Emma for ages, Andy's just broken up with Marie and Kieran's been seeing a girl called Sally for a few weeks. No Claires now or in the recent past that I know of.'

'Thanks. What about Simon? Could he have a girlfriend called Claire?'

'He has been going out with another blonde recently, but I don't know her name. In fact, I presumed he'd moved out to shack up with her, though God knows how he does it, lucky sod.'

'When did you last see her?'

'A week, maybe ten days ago. Not sure, really. I could ask the others for you when they surface.'

'Has he been staying away overnight the last couple of weeks?'

'Yeah. Not seen that much of him. Like I said, that's why I thought he'd moved in with her.'

'Can you tell me what subject his PhD's in?'

'History. He's writing about slavery.'

'So he'll have visited Wilberforce House to do research?'

'I expect so, don't you? We didn't talk much. Sorry, but where's this leading? I don't really know who you are, though I recognise your friend from round the union.'

By this time, I felt chilled. Not only was he a history student, but now it seemed Claire's boyfriend was a photographer. Simon might just be a silly lad who'd been through a spell of getting his kicks from taking photos because he couldn't get a girl, and now he'd suddenly developed the knack with women, but what would you think?

'I'm a private detective. I'm trying to find Claire. She's been missing over a week now and her parents are worried.'

'Oh, I'm sorry. Wish I could help but I haven't a clue where she lives.'

'I live with her and he's not moved in with us', Charlotte said.

'What exactly did he say when he left?'

'Not a lot. He loaded up the car and said he'd drop the keys back at the landlord's this morning. He said he was moving in with his girlfriend. It was a bit sudden, but he's paid till the end of term and didn't ask for any money back.'

I told Charlotte not to worry and she should hold onto Claire's coat for the time being, and I dropped her off at home. She looked worried sick and I didn't blame her, but I tried to play it down. I wished I'd not let her come with me to the house, but I hoped she'd be able to identify the boyfriend for me. At least she didn't know about the link to Wilberforce House. After I left her, I drove straight back round to Simon's house and asked Richard if he had a key for Simon's room. He hadn't. I went and sat in the car and rang Steve. I filled him in on my conversation with Richard.

'He must have done a bunk after I called round to see him last night, Steve. He could be anywhere now. I must have spooked him. He could be your murderer. I should have chased things up harder but I thought Claire was just being the usual student, away from her parents and spending all her time with a boy she'd met. Now I feel dreadful. He must have Claire and it's all my fault.'

'Rach, if you hadn't gone round there, then we wouldn't know he existed. Don't worry, it's not your fault at all. He still might turn out to have nothing to do with the murders, and even if he does, he would have already taken Claire somewhere before you got involved. Now that's not down to you, is it? At least now we've got a firm lead. We'll take it from here.'

Give him his due; he knows when to act on a hunch, mine or his. Uniformed officers came round to the house straight away, got the phone number of

272

the landlord and got him out with the key to Simon's room. Contrary to popular opinion, the police don't break down doors unless it's absolutely essential, and certainly not to save the five minutes it took them to arrive. They searched Simon's room but it was almost entirely empty of everything except the usual student room furniture, the odd smelly sock kicked under the bed and a poster of a rock band on the wall.

Steve turned up not much later. He'd rung the contact number for the reference that Simon had given the landlord, but it was unobtainable. And he'd run Simon's name through the computer. If it was his real name, Simon Johnson didn't have a criminal record.

'We'll track down his parents, Rach. They must know something, even though he probably lived in Hull all year round since he's a PhD student. You go on home. I'll ring you if we find out anything, I promise.'

Later, much later that night, Steve filled me in on the rest of their day. He'd interviewed Richard, and other officers had woken up the other lads in the house, but they couldn't tell him much more than Richard had told me, except Simon had said he was from Oxford. The student registry provided the last home address Simon had given them, but that was in South Wales, and it turned out to be a non-existent address. None of the lads knew the registration number of his car, but they knew it was a silver Nissan Micra. Steve's team had contacted the DVLA at Swansea, but there wasn't one of those registered to a Simon Johnson, so either it wasn't his real name, or he wasn't the registered owner.

The history department gave Steve the number for Simon's PhD supervisor. They'd only managed to track him down late in the evening. He'd seen Simon the previous Thursday as arranged for their latest session, but he knew little of Simon's background, except that he'd got his MA from Durham University, and as he had to show his certificate when he'd registered over two years previously, then it seemed that Simon Johnson was his real name. It wasn't likely he'd be able to fake a degree certificate, but they'd get on to Durham and check.

I knew that they'd leave no stone unturned to find out where Simon came from and where he might have gone, but it didn't seem to me like they'd got very far.

'Forensics are going over the house with a fine tooth-comb. They're looking for anything with Simon's DNA obviously, but to be honest it's more likely they'll only come up with his fingerprints. He seems to have cleaned his room before he left but male students aren't renowned for their cleanliness so his prints should be somewhere. He may have cleaned his room quite well, but he could hardly scour the kitchen and bathroom without it looking obvious that he was up to something.'

'Would there be skin cells in the sock?' I asked hopefully. I couldn't bear the thought that he'd just walked out of there without leaving a trace of himself behind.

'We'll try, but it could belong to a previous occupant of the room. Anyway, we have nothing to match fingerprints or DNA to, if he hasn't got a criminal record. There's been nothing found on any of the murder victims, not so much as a stray hair. We're just covering all the bases in case, before any evidence is lost or contaminated. We've got a team searching Claire's room in case he gave her anything or touched something, but I must admit the girls don't think he ever went to their house, unless it was when they were all out.'

The next day Steve checked in with me mid-morning to say a Simon Johnson was awarded an MA in History at Durham, and the local Durham police would be interviewing lecturers there to check it was the same student. They'd also be contacting and interviewing anyone who knew him there, looking into the home address he gave at the time, as well as interviewing anyone at Hull University who knew him. Although the DVLA showed no silver Nissan registered to a Simon Johnson, there were other car models registered to men called Simon Johnson, but it was a common name and they could all be red herrings. They would all need checking out though. The car could be their main lead to tracking him down. Unless he'd conveniently taken Claire to his parent's house, it didn't really matter how quickly they found out where his family home was, unless the car was owned by one of them.

There was one other lead. A search of the communal rooms turned up one of Simon's books with a photo as a bookmark. Obviously he'd cleared out his room in such a hurry that he'd forgotten the book. The photo was of a narrow stream leading into a wide river, which looked like the Humber. It was a long shot, but maybe it was taken at the place where he took his girls.

Steve sounded tired. He had come home the previous night, but only because there was only so much they could do at that time of night. Despite the urgency of needing to find Claire as soon as possible, you still couldn't really drag university lecturers out of their beds to answer questions in the early hours. Of course they'd contacted Claire's parents. A police inspector had visited them in Devon and gently probed for any further information, but had only succeeded in worrying them sick.

I felt awful that I'd failed them, even though, as Steve said, it looked like Simon had taken her away before I was called in. The truth is, I was haunted by the fact that I'd spoken to him and not realised who he was. I'd done nothing but send him underground, and I was finding it difficult to cope with that thought. Steve said that Claire's disappearance and this Simon might yet prove to be unconnected with the murders. She could be fine, tucked up in some love nest with Simon, but I couldn't accept that as even a remote possibility.

I went round to see Sarah in the morning and after warning her she couldn't breathe a word to anyone yet, told her everything.

'You can't blame yourself, Rach. I agree with Steve. You did all you could. If you hadn't gone round to this Simon's house, then the police would have known nothing about him. I know you, you'll keep beating yourself up about it, and it feels worse because you can't go off trying to track him down yourself, but you just can't do anything except feed Steve and look after him, and listen to him, and that's it.'

'Thanks Sarah. You're right of course. I'll try to take a back seat and wait. It's just hard that's all. Maybe if I had some other work, but the phone's stopped ringing.'

'Did you hear what happened to that awful Stella? Will she go to jail?'

'I've not heard any more. She's pleaded guilty so I don't think I'll have to go to court and I hope that's the last I'll hear of her.'

'And Pete, your other boyfriend, how's he?'

'He's not my boyfriend. I've not heard from him since we went to the Lodge, and I'm not likely to, either.'

'You went to the Lodge? Wow, Rach. You never said. What's it like?'

'I made a right fool of myself. I don't think I'll be invited anywhere upmarket again. In fact I think Pete might have realised I'm not his kind of woman after all.'

'What did you do?'

By the time I'd finished explaining, Sarah was laughing, and I was too. I could see the funny side of it now.

'You are a case, Rach. Pete's not worth a look-in with you if he takes himself too seriously.

Least Steve's more on your level, if you know what I mean. You've had a fair few laughs together when you've made a fool of yourself. He loves you as you are.'

I thought she was probably right. If it'd been me and Steve in the Lodge, we'd have had a hard time keeping our faces straight, and would have cracked up as soon as we'd got outside.

'Yeah. Remember when he took me on that picnic and I thought I was being all posh, taking a tablecloth, only I spread it out on a cowpat without realising it was there? Then I found I hadn't picked up the bag from the flat and I'd left the sandwiches and sausage rolls in the fridge. All we had were some biscuits. We ate them with a drink and then he said jokingly I was only good for one thing and he led me back to the car to prove his point.'

'That's what I mean. You and Steve have always had fun. Just cos he's busy right now, I shouldn't worry that you're drifting apart. You'll be OK. Now then, I almost forgot. I've got my new catalogue. Do you want to have a look?'

We lost ourselves in the new Autumn and Winter fashions, even though Summer had barely started, and by the time I left, I felt much better.

I managed to stay upbeat till late afternoon and then I started to worry that there'd not been any news.

I tried to convince myself that the police could have found Simon and Claire and that she was safe, but ringing me to put me out of my misery was the last thing on their minds. Trouble was, I knew

278

Steve would have spared two minutes to make a call if there was anything to tell me.

When I'd worried myself sick again over Claire, the phone did ring, but it was DI Jordan. Wrong policeman, wrong case. Still, it was good news of a sort. It seemed the search of Ann Ransom's house had turned up a knife block missing one knife. The other knives had the same profile as that indicated by the pathologist, and the size missing also fit the wound. She said the knife had gone missing weeks earlier and one of the yobs who came onto the estate to deal drugs could have taken it. However, there'd been no break-in reported at her house and it was strong circumstantial evidence.

And then he revealed the clincher. They'd found a pair of shoes that she must have worn when she killed Mr Brooks. They'd been cleaned and polished but forensics had discovered minute traces of blood in the gap between sole and upper, and that was all that it took. There was no way she could have got his blood on her shoes unless she was the murderer. She'd already said he was fine when she left the house that night, so she would have to admit she'd been lying if she now wanted to try to pretend he'd been injured when she left him, and that was how she'd got the blood on her shoes.

Eventually she'd confessed. She'd told him she didn't want to see him any more. She'd said she'd slept with her husband again and was going to try to patch things up. He wouldn't accept it. He told her he loved her too much, and she was scared he'd tell her husband about the affair, so she'd made some excuse to make him wait in the house for her and she'd nipped home for the knife.

'She seemed a real tough sort, so I'm glad she confessed', DI Jordan said. 'We had to pull people off the serial murders at a bad time so it'll be good to have them freed up to go back and help out on the more important case.'

'Thanks for ringing me. I really appreciate it.'

It was the early hours when Steve came in. To be honest I wouldn't have been surprised if he'd worked through the night, but as he said, it was only a short walk from the station and he couldn't keep his eyes open. Even if he only got three or four hours sleep, he'd be less likely to miss something important.

He said their main hope lay in someone seeing the police appeal on that night's news for sightings of Claire or information about signs of life in out-of-the-way buildings. I'd missed the piece on the news. Also, they'd circulated the photo Simon had taken around local police stations and even post offices around the banks of the Humber to see if a local bobby or postman recognised the view. All the officers who could be spared were out looking for Claire. I still couldn't help but feel I could have done more.

I hugged him and he let me undress him and push him gently into the shower where I soaped him down, rinsed him and dried him as if he were my child. There wasn't a sexual thought in either of our heads, and yet the moments felt more intimate than almost any we'd shared. I knew how exhausted he was. And I knew he'd keep giving everything he could until Claire was found. I understood now why he worked such long hours sometimes. This case was personal for me, and it always got personal with Steve. I really loved him in that moment, more than I'd ever done before.

We lay in bed and just held each other tight for a while, then I snuggled up to his back and stroked it until I heard his breathing change and knew he was asleep.

21

I woke at seven and Steve was gone. There was nothing to eat. I hoped there'd been an odd slice of bread left for him, but I couldn't be sure. Still, he had the canteen at work. I walked down to the marketplace and was having a cup of tea and a teacake in my favourite café when my mobile rang. It was Mum.

'Any news, love? I saw about your missing girl on the news. I suppose they think she's been killed as well by this maniac, but it'll turn out okay, I'm sure. I know the police shouldn't talk about cases at home, but I just thought…' her voice trailed off. I think she knew I'd have told her if I could, but as it was, there wasn't even anything to tell.

'No Mum. I'll let you know if I hear anything.' I'd told her the previous day on the phone that Claire was the missing student I'd been looking for and about how I'd met Simon and of course also that I felt so guilty for letting him slip through the net.

'Oh, Rachel. Don't fret. You did all you could. They'll find him soon, and Claire too, safe and sound, just you see.'

'I hope so, Mum. How's Gran? Has she turned up?'

'She's fine. Her ankle's nearly back to normal. She's made of stronger stuff than me. She's been having a great time, getting all her men friends to fetch and carry for her. That's where she was when I couldn't track her down. One had taken her to his bungalow because he was jealous of all these other men turning up with flowers and cream cakes.'

'I'm glad to know someone's OK, but I'd better go, Mum. You never know, Steve might be trying to ring me right now.'

The phone stayed silent while I did a supermarket shop. I couldn't have been concentrating that hard though, as I got home without bread or milk, or petrol. So when Steve rang and asked if I wanted to take a ride out for lunch, I had to use Steve's own car to pick him up.

'Well, this is nice. How did you manage it, Steve?'

'I've hardly eaten anything apart from canteen food for days, I needed some sane conversation' (he raised a weary grin at that) 'and I thought you could come with me and have a pub lunch while I called in at shops and post offices off the beaten track between Hull and Dane's Dyke.'

'So you think the photo of the Humber's just a red herring?'

'No, but we've got every Tom, Dick and Harry looking round there and I wanted to do something hands-on, so I thought I'd cover another possible area. We've already been round everywhere near Dane's Dyke, so I thought I'd try places off the Bridlington Road.'

'Fair enough. I'm in your car 'cos mine's almost out of petrol. I didn't want to waste your time stopping to fill up.'

'That's OK. I'd prefer to drive anyway, and there aren't any unmarked cars left in the car pool.'

The road to Bridlington runs north-east from Hull. Dane's Dyke is a few miles on the far side of Brid. We ended up stopping here, there and everywhere, as I guessed we would, eating sandwiches as we drove, rather than going in a pub. Still, he cheered up away from the station, and I hope I made him smile a little. We drew a blank everywhere though. We worked our way south-east from the Brid road to Hornsea to stop on the front to go to the loo. The sun was shining and I thought back to Judith Parry and how I'd love to kick off my shoes and go for a paddle, even though it was cold. Steve caught my eye and must've been thinking the same. 'Sorry there's no time for a paddle, love, but I think I'd better head back. It's been a bit of a waste of time apart from being with you.'

'No it hasn't. You've eliminated some chunks of countryside.'

I didn't get to hear his reply, because his phone went, and I knew there must have been a significant development. 'That's great. I'm out at Hornsea. I can be there in fifteen or twenty minutes.'

He finished the call and turned to me. 'A local postman recognised the view. It's of a creek near Sunk Island. There's a house there with lots of outbuildings. The postman didn't think there was anyone living there, but he gets junk mail to deliver, and as he said, it's not his place to say it's only junk and that he won't bother driving up the lane with it. He always has to turn round at a gate overlooking the creek and he recognised the view. He's sure it's the same as on the photo found in Simon Johnson's book. Anyway, my sergeant Matt has just rung to say there's a silver Nissan Micra parked out of sight in the yard, and so it's looking good. If I drive us there, can you take my car home please, love?'

'Of course. Oh I do hope she's OK.'

'So do I, sweetheart.'

Steve attached his removable blue light to the Alfa's roof, climbed back in and set off at great speed, light flashing and horn blaring when he met slow traffic. The ride would ordinarily have been a real thrill, but I had an overwhelming feeling that I should be at home. This was much too dangerous for me. Still, I did have Steve to look after me, and he'd taken one of those police driving courses not long ago.

'It's only about fifteen minutes by car from Sunk Island to where the third body was found on the beach. Maybe he drove the other bodies a long way from his bolthole and where he probably did the killing, but didn't have time to drive the thirty-odd miles up to Dane's Dyke to dump the last one. There's a team heading out to secure the area, break open the doors and search, but if we hurry, we won't be far behind.'

I certainly hoped he was right and Susan's body was the last one, and not Claire.

I couldn't remember ever having been to Sunk Island though its name had stuck in my mind from when I'd heard it as a child. The name conjured up a place where Enid Blyton's adventures would be set. It was south of the road that goes east from Hull to Spurn Point, and had once been an island, along with the equally interestingly named Cherry Cob Sands. Rising seawater (yes, it happened before the days of global warming too) in the thirteenth century had led to early settlements being abandoned and these two islands being left as sandbanks in the Humber estuary. The land was reclaimed four hundred years later and it made a vast area, miles and miles of prime farmland.

Despite its proximity to Hull, it was still a desolate, windswept, totally flat landscape, with straight narrow lanes, often single-track, seemingly leading nowhere. There were just odd farmhouses dotted about. It seemed that little had changed since the seventeenth century.

After the quickest twenty minute drive I can ever remember, Steve swung the car into a narrow driveway and parked behind a police patrol car. He told me to stay in the car for a moment and strode into the yard. I thought it best to obey.

A few moments later, Steve's sergeant, Matt came up to the car and said there were no women police constables available, and Steve had asked if I wouldn't mind staying until one arrived, in case they found Claire alive. 'OK', I squeaked. I was astonished to hear myself say that. I was sick and shaking. What was I thinking of? I know - Claire.

It later transpired that the house belonged to Simon's late uncle, but we didn't know that at the time. It was also his uncle's car, which is why the police hadn't been able to track Simon down from the registration number. The uncle was the only relative Simon had left, and he'd died recently. Much later, questions would be asked as to whether his death had been of natural causes.

After about ten minutes, three more police cars arrived and the occupants spread out to search the house and outbuildings. It didn't take long before there was a shout from the doorway of one of the outhouses. Most of the others left the house to investigate. A while later Steve came over to his car and gestured for me to open the window. 'There's no-one there Rach, but we're close. Someone's been here and recently too, by the look of it. There are some chains and a blood-stained knife in one of the outhouses.' Another police car arrived, complete with two female officers for good measure. I was more than a little freaked and knew not to stay when I was no longer needed.

'I'll go home and wait to hear from you', I volunteered, and for the first time that day, a smile flashed across Steve's face.

'Good idea, love. But thanks for everything you've done, and for playing it by the book this time and staying in the car.' This was rare praise from Steve, though it did remind me of nearly being burnt to a crisp in that warehouse by the River Hull, a reminder I could well have done without. I can't help it if trouble follows me around, as Steve keeps telling me.

Before I could drive off, Steve took the blue light off his Alfa and Matt came out. 'It has to be him, sir.'

'What've you found? Any sign of Claire?' They talked as if I wasn't there.

'No, but there's a chance she may be still alive, if he was the one who took her. In a locked desk drawer in the house there are newspaper clippings of his victims, and also a ring binder. In it there are plastic inserts and in each there's a sealed plastic bag and a computer-printed label bearing a girl's name. Each of the bags contains something that we're fairly sure must have been taken from a victim. There's a necklace, some hair clips, a watch, a ring, a bracelet and a notebook. The worst thing is, there are six sets of bags, and we've only found four bodies.'

As he talked, I started shivering. I felt sick. Sick and cold.

'So that must mean he's killed Claire?' I couldn't help but ask, my voice catching as I spoke. 'And one other girl.'

'Not necessarily. There were only first names, but there was no Claire. There was a Becky and a Michelle though. It looks like there are two bodies somewhere that we've not found yet and Claire might still be alive. He may keep them for quite a while before he kills them.'

'But she wasn't in the house?' Steve spoke

briskly.

'No, Sir. There are some clothes and shoes in the lounge. They could be hers. It looks like he's had a bonfire in the garden and there are scraps of charred material there. He could have burned the clothing of his previous victims, but either didn't get around to Claire, or kept hers for her to wear again.'

'Mmm..' They turned away but I could still hear Steve say, 'It doesn't look good, but the car's still here. If he was out disposing of her body, surely he'd be in his car?'

I wanted to go home. This was way out of my league. It looked like Steve agreed with me, because he turned back and said, 'Rach, I know it's hard, but leave this to us now, like we agreed. Try and put it out of your mind and I promise I'll let you know if we find Claire or there's any other news.' He kissed me on the cheek and I closed the window and started the car.

The narrow lane ended at the estuary as the postman had said. It was right on the banks of the Humber and you could see clear back to Salt End Oil refinery on the outskirts of Hull, but it seemed like where we were, was a totally different world. I had to turn the car around and then I drove quickly away from the house. When the house was out of sight, I allowed myself to stop, dug out a map, and found a route I could take back to Hull. When I set off again though, I found the roads were confusing, and I kept meeting signposts that pointed to places I thought I'd passed, or which should have been in the opposite direction. The map was useless. I was just beginning to despair of ever getting remotely near civilisation when I came across a village shop cum post office – well that sort of shop, but without the attached village, just four houses.

After what I'd been through, I was shaking and thought chocolate might help. Who am I kidding? It always helps, and in my case chocolate may not be better than sex, but it's often all I can get, so I eat a lot of it. And of course I couldn't go in to ask the way without buying something, now could I?

Getting back in the car, my phone fell out of my handbag – again. It's a wonder the thing works, and the reason why I love it. Despite all my ill-treatment, it remains a faithful friend. I remembered I'd got no credit and for some reason I'd turned it off. I'm a bit illogical like that. I forget that you can receive calls without credit. I went back in the shop and bought some credit and turned it on. I just love how you can do that. Magic. No messages. Well, after the last hour or so, I needed the rest of the day off.

I tucked the phone in my jeans pocket and set off along the route indicated by the lady in the shop. It sounded complicated and I wanted to get to the B road before I forgot. I took one of the narrow bends a little too quickly and had to slam the brakes on. Good job I did or I'd have driven right past the phone box without giving it more than a glance. As it was, the car nearly hit it. The first thing I thought was, 'I wonder which division Hull City have just got promoted to, and if they'll ever to get to play Chelsea, Arsenal or Manchester United?' because it had 'Tigers for the Premiership' graffiti'd on it in orange paint.

The second thing I thought was, I'd found Claire and she was alive. I was fairly sure I recognised her from the photos her housemates had shown me, but even if I hadn't, it was a fair bet it was her, standing dirty and half-naked, screaming as she struggled with a youth who was blocking her exit from the phone box. During the few seconds it took all this to register, she went quiet and I realised the lad, presumably Simon, was strangling her. I didn't have time to think. I grabbed my old umbrella off the back seat and leapt from the car. He was so busy, he never noticed me till I hit him. I was a bit scared I might have killed him as I could only think to hit him on the head and that brolly's short, thick and heavy. I know that for sure. I used to lug it around in my shopping bag till I got a nice light aluminium-framed one. Thankfully it'd ended up in Steve's car because he didn't have a brolly and I hated rain dripping down the back of my neck.

Simon collapsed against the phone box but he was groaning, so I knew he wasn't dead. I put my arm around Claire to support her. She seemed to be wrapped in some sort of curtain, but apart from that, was wearing nothing. Her feet were bare and bleeding. It might have been early summer but she was shivering as well as gasping for air. I asked, 'Have you rung the police?'

She nodded. 'Right, let's just get away.'

I almost carried her over to the passenger door of Steve's car. She could hardly walk and it

291

took an agonising time. I'd opened the passenger door to help her in when I was grabbed from behind. I heard Claire gasp in agony as Simon kicked her to the ground.

He dragged me round to the driver's side, his arm bent around my throat, grabbed the keys and then lugged me to the rear of the car. I was struggling and kicking but he was too strong for me. I screamed but he punched me in the stomach and that took my breath away. He lifted me off the ground and threw me into the open boot. My shoulder slammed into a wheel arch. It hurt like mad. He must have come prepared because before I could scream again he pulled out a roll of tape from his pocket and in one smooth action he tore off a strip and stuck it across my mouth. I struggled to get upright, anything to escape, but he expertly bound my arms behind my back and then my legs together. He slammed the boot lid down and it went dark.

It was all over in seconds. He slammed the passenger door then the driver's door and the car was moving. I prayed the 999 call had been routed to Steve and he was driving down the road towards the phone box, and then maybe he'd see his car with a man driving it, block the road and rescue me. But the Sunk Island house must have been further from the phone box than I realised, or maybe they were still tracing the source of the call, because we didn't stop. We seemed to drive for ages but it could have been as little as ten minutes or as many as twenty. I couldn't tell any longer. I'd thought I should try to memorise the left and right-hand turns, but it was so disorientating being in the boot, thrown from side to side with no way of holding on to anything, that I hadn't a clue which direction we might be taking. It felt like we were driving really fast, but surely Simon wouldn't have wanted to attract attention to the car. It was just that without a seatbelt I fared little better than those carrier bags of shopping I put neatly in my boot at the supermarket, then find all higgledy-piggledy when I get home.

To tell the truth, I was terrified. Then I calmed down as I remembered Claire on the ground by the phone box. She'd be able to tell the police that Simon had taken off in a maroon car with a wild-haired woman wearing glasses who'd hit him, and Steve'd realise it had to be me in his car. Then they'd put out a call for the car and it wouldn't take long for them to find it. That thought comforted me until the car lurched onto a rough track and after a short distance, drew to a halt. What if he killed me before Claire was found, or before Steve heard about the car and realised it was his, or before they found it? I didn't know what I should or could do when Simon opened the boot. I was bruised and didn't feel very strong, but I had to try to fight him if he lifted me out. I dreaded to think what he had in store for me.

I heard the car door open and braced myself to kick out at him as hard as I could as he opened the boot, but he didn't open the boot. Instead I heard another door open. Then I heard a loud slap followed by whimpering. It had to be Claire. He must have put her inside the car and brought her with us. Suddenly it went quiet. 'There, you bitch. Now I'm taking my latest girlfriend for a drive. I've had it with blondes. Maybe this girl'll appreciate me more since she's not as pretty.'

With that, the door slammed and we set off again. I was devastated. What had he just done to Claire? Was she dead? One thing was for certain, she hadn't been left at the phone box as I'd thought, so there was no way the police would know I was involved. They wouldn't know that Simon had taken off in Steve's car. How stupid of me not to have rung Steve. I know I was in a hurry to get Claire away from there, but I could have kicked myself if my legs hadn't been bound. I'd just thought that her phone call to the police was enough.

I blinked back the tears. I had to remain angry. It was the only way to stay focused and one step ahead of Simon. If he planned to have me as his girlfriend maybe he wasn't planning on killing me yet, but on taking me some place else. The police wouldn't have a clue what had happened, so I had to get out of this myself. If Claire had managed to escape, then so could I. 'Think, Rach', I told myself. 'So I'm not pretty, eh? I'll beat the crap out of him, first chance I get, for saying that.'

22

Back at Sunk Island, Steve had his hands full coordinating a more detailed search of the outbuildings and the grounds. Some of his men were ordered to look for any signs of recently-disturbed earth, and yet others were drafted in to search the surrounding area for any sign of Simon. The Nissan's bonnet had been slightly warm when the first officers arrived, which indicated that Simon had not long returned to the cottage. At first they resigned themselves to the idea that he must have been out burying Claire's body, but then the news arrived that she had rung 999 and was alive, or had been up until five minutes earlier. She must have run across the fields and he'd taken off after her on foot, rather than taking the car.

It took ten minutes longer to locate the source of the call. Steve and Matt had raced along to the phone box, only to find it empty. Some of the forensics team at the cottage were diverted to go over the phone box and its immediate vicinity. Steve got back in the unmarked police car and slammed his hand angrily against the steering-wheel. He couldn't believe they'd just missed Claire. They'd come so close to rescuing her, and she'd obviously been through hell to escape.

There were a few small bloodstains which were quickly established as not from a life-threatening wound, and the forensic people found partial smudged toe-prints so seemed to believe the blood came from wounds on the feet, consistent with walking barefoot, rather than drops of blood that had been walked through.

Although police cars flooded the area, it seemed that Claire and Simon had vanished into thin air. Steve's boss was convinced Simon was hiding out in some barn or other with Claire. He'd ordered that a wide area be cordoned off as soon as he'd heard the phone box was empty. Steve had to go along with this, and men spread out far and wide searching all buildings and possible hiding places within a fifteen minute walking distance of the phone box. However Steve couldn't shake off a niggling worry that Simon might have had access to another car, though it seemed highly unlikely.

Reluctantly he returned to the station and made his report on the day's events so far to the Chief Inspector, who was going to make another appeal for sightings on the local TV evening news a few hours later. Then he instructed someone to go through the outstanding missing persons' cases to see if there was a Michelle or a Becky. He rang Rach at his flat to let her know that Claire had called from the phone box after she'd left, but there was no reply. He thought she was probably round at her mum's, telling her what she'd been up to, and put it to the back of his mind.

He grabbed a cup of tea and a scone from the canteen and headed back up to the incident room. The forensics team could only find a short trail of bloodstains leading away from the phone box, so they were assuming Claire had presumably been picked up and carried away or stopped bleeding.

They'd found a selection of articles around the phone box. There was the inevitable used condom - they had no sample of Simon's to compare the semen traces with, but didn't think he would have taken the time to ejaculate whilst wrenching Claire away from the phone box. He must have known that the police would be on their way. They also found used cigarette butts, crisp wrappers, scraps of newspapers and an old, broken, though rolled-up, umbrella. Steve didn't think any of them related to Claire or Simon, but forensics would still try to take prints and match them to any on their database. The umbrella niggled at Steve. The description sounded like one Rach had. It was black with outlines of tiny white cats and dogs, saying 'it's raining cats and dogs'. Had Rach been at the phone box? He shook his head. He had Rach on the brain. She was always getting herself into scrapes, but she'd left for home a long while before the phone call from Claire.

There was no news from the search parties and hopes of finding Claire quickly dwindled as time passed. His spirits sank even further when both a Michelle and a Becky proved to be among the missing persons list. Michelle Hunter had gone missing five months previously. She'd not been considered a possible murder victim as her parents had recently split up and her dad had moved to Spain. Her mum had been worried enough to report her missing, because she'd not said she was going, but when her passport was found to be gone as well, she'd not taken it any further but had returned to her new boyfriend, glad that the quiet girl who never went out was finally out from under her feet, and they could have the house to themselves. A couple of female officers were sent to call at Michelle's mother's house to break the sad news that her daughter might be dead. He hoped they found her body soon, or else the family would suffer until they did.

The charred remnants of Michelle's passport were later identified in the bottom of an old dustbin, in the yard of the house at Sunk Island, hidden under the burnt-out carcasses of small animals and birds and both Michelle and Becky's remains were found buried beneath some trees a short distance from the house.

As the afternoon wore on, Steve's boss put his head round the door and asked him to step into a four o'clock conference to discuss events and decide where to go next. First, as a side-issue, they decided not to say anything to the press about Becky Fletcher, whose name matched the sixth victim. She was an orphan and had disappeared from a children's home. A little younger than Simon's other victims at only sixteen, she had been missing for nine months. She was on the missing persons' list but the authorities hadn't spent too long looking for her as they'd heard from friends that she'd been seen with an older lad and they thought she'd disappeared onto the streets of Leeds or Bradford.

Steve got another cup of tea and tried his home number again before going into the meeting. Rach still didn't answer and this time he was sufficiently bothered that he tried her mobile. It rang and rang but no-one answered. What was she playing at? Didn't she have it with her? He tried her mum's number, but it seemed Rach hadn't been there all day. Worry growing, he tried Sarah, but she hadn't seen her either. He knew he shouldn't waste resources, particularly when they were under such pressure, but he rang the duty desk and asked Sergeant Jeff Knight to send someone to call by his flat to check for his car, then he rushed into the meeting.

'You're late, Steve.'

'Sorry, sir. Just following up a lead.'

'And that might be?'

'Well, I'm not sure it's relevant, sir, but since we can't find any trace of Claire or Simon, I was wondering if they had got hold of a car after all, and my girlfriend Rach appears to be missing.'

'Surely she left the cottage as soon as the female officers arrived? That was a long time before Claire's 999 call? She should have been back in Hull by then.'

'I know but she's not answering the phone at

home or her mobile, and her mum and best friend haven't heard from her.'

'Probably gone shopping, Steve.'

'I'd normally agree, but there's another thing bugging me, sir. The old brolly found at the scene is like one Rach has.'

Just then Jeff rang through from the desk to say that Steve's car wasn't in the flat car park or anywhere in the nearby streets. Steve tried Rach's mobile again straight away. It still rang without a reply.

'Sir, my car's missing and she's still not answering. I'm really worried now.'

'OK, Steve. Put out an alert for, Rachel, is it? And let's get details of your car circulated. If her mobile's still turned on, get a trace on it.'

He'd just put the wheels in motion when Matt and his team returned from the Sunk Island area. They were exhausted and had been relieved by a smaller number of fresh officers who would continue to look for anything in the now-expanded search area. Matt was really down.

'Looks like they've disappeared into thin air.'

Steve told him that Rach and his car were missing, and about the brolly.

'Oh shit, sir. I hope she's OK.'

'I can't sit here doing nothing. I'll be in radio contact. I'm going out that way to look around myself. Let me know the minute we get a trace on Rach's phone, Matt.'

He'd just got into an unmarked car and was

about to leave when Matt ran into the yard, waving him to stop.

'Have they traced her phone yet, Matt?'

'No, not yet, but they've found Claire. She's safe and sound, though bruised and battered. She was lying in a ditch off a farm track, about ten minutes drive from the phone box where she disappeared. It's just off the Withernsea road. She was naked apart from a curtain, and Steve, your instinct was right. A girl answering Rach's description hit Simon over the head and rescued Claire. Only he came round as they were getting into what must be your car, and Simon tied up your Rach and put her in the boot. After they'd driven for a while, Claire was slung out into the ditch and Simon drove off, telling her he'd got a new girlfriend.'

'Oh no.' A despairing groan left Steve's lips. Much as he'd suspected Rach was involved, he hadn't let himself really believe it up until that point. And he now knew she was at Simon's mercy. Before, if he'd let himself think anything at all, he'd just thought Simon had taken the car and maybe dumped her. Now he knew why she wasn't answering her phone. Thank God it was still turned on. He daren't ring it again though, in case Simon heard it and got rid of it, and then there'd be no signal to trace. 'Where exactly was Claire dumped, and how long ago?'

Two minutes later, armed with answers to his questions, Steve raced out of the police yard, blue light flashing and siren blazing. He'd start where Claire was found and just keep on looking. He'd not give up till he had Rach back safe in his arms. She was a magnet for trouble, but he loved her.

When Steve first tried my mobile, I was lying in the boot of his car and I felt my phone vibrate against my hip. Good job it was on 'silent'. I'd set it like that when we were haring off to Sunk Island, not wanting any possible call to disturb the police search when we got there. At least Simon couldn't hear it ringing. I tried to fish the phone out of my pocket so I could answer it. It might be Steve. It was so hard to move my arms enough to get my fingers to my pocket. I wished I'd got looser jeans on. I finally managed to get a finger to the phone when it stopped ringing. 'Bugger.' I tried to remain upbeat but it was hard.

I was in the boot of Steve's car and it wasn't a hatchback. I reminded myself that it was good I'd stuck the phone in my pocket when I'd put credit on it, instead of putting it back in my handbag as usual, because Simon must've taken the bag. He hadn't thrown it in the boot after me. He'd probably ditched it somewhere. I told myself someone would find it and report it, but I wasn't convincing myself. No doubt he'd left it somewhere miles from anywhere. Maybe even with Claire's body. I shuddered and tried to put the thought from my mind. It was no good though. I'd rescued Claire for nothing. She was dead after all. She had to be. Simon wouldn't just have left her lying around.

I distracted myself by trying to remember what was in my handbag. I hoped someone found it. Besides my flat keys and Steve's, both our car keys and my credit card, all of which are hell to replace, there was money of course and then more personal things that I just couldn't bear to lose. You know the kind of thing, girls – notes from Steve, photos, cinema ticket stubs and also my strawberry lipgloss, which Boots saw fit not to make any more. The pot was virtually empty, but I held onto it in case I could match it with any I tracked down anywhere else. I gave myself a reality check in the middle of my daydream. If I didn't get out of this alive, it wouldn't matter how hard things were to replace, because I wouldn't need them again.

At least I had the phone. Maybe I could make a call myself. We were moving fast so I doubted if Simon would hear me if I spoke quietly. Of course, there was one major drawback to that – I had tape across my mouth – but I had to try something. First I gradually eased the phone out of my pocket with my fingertips. Then I rubbed the tape over my mouth against the rough carpet and felt a pull on my skin as the edges started to come unstuck.

The phone started vibrating again. I could see the time lit up – 4.13, but it had shifted away from my fingers and as the car drove round a corner, it slid out of sight across the floor of the boot. Helpless, I could hear the slight noise it made as it vibrated against a firm object – probably the wheel arch. If I could just press the green button with my nose, I'd answer the call and whoever it was might be able to hear sounds at my end, even if I couldn't talk.

As I turned my head, the glow of the phone caught my eye. I lunged for it with my face. I failed miserably, only succeeding in banging my head as it stopped again. If it rang again, I was going to be ready, I told myself. I was all cramped up with my nose near the button, when I heard the car slow and the engine cut out. Terrified he'd find the phone and turn it off or break it, I headed it into the corner of the boot, moments before the lid was lifted. The light hurt my eyes. Although I'd seen the time, I was somehow amazed that it was still afternoon. It'd felt like I'd been cramped up in there for hours.

Simon loomed over me. 'I'll not be long. I need to buy a new camera and a present for you. You behave yourself and when I come back we'll go somewhere quiet where we can get to know each other.' He checked the tape round my arms and legs and put more across my mouth. You've been trying to get this off, haven't you? Bad girl. I better make sure you can't get up to anything.'

To my horror he took off my glasses and taped my eyes shut before slamming the boot lid. I realised now, that although I had thought it dark in the boot before, there must have been pinpricks of light, as well as the glow from my mobile, because now it was truly pitch black. It reminded me of a school trip to some caves in Derbyshire when they'd turned out all the lights for a few moments, so we could imagine what it must have been like in there at night when our ancestors had taken shelter.

The only consolation I could draw was that he'd let some fresh air into the boot whilst the lid had been open and that he was planning on returning. That at least meant I would get a chance to escape. I prayed the phone would ring again. I might have had my eyes taped but I could bang about as much as I wanted, trying to find it, while Simon was away from the car, and maybe I could press the button to answer it and send some sort of signal. I set about trying to feel for the phone, whilst dredging my memory for the morse code for SOS. I figured I had half an hour, tops, before Simon came back to the car, because the shops would be closing soon.

After grovelling around for a while, my fingers closed around the phone. I had the idea of trying to send a text while I was waiting for a call. I could actually say something even though I couldn't talk. It was easy to find the large menu key. I pressed it, and then pressed the small top left button to select messages, then again for texts then again for create message. I was so used to doing that, it was second nature to me. My fingers went down to the bottom row – that was for punctuation etcetera. I moved up to the next row and pressed the left hand button four times – 's'. I knew that key started with p, so went up a row, to the right hand button and pressed the key three times for 'o' – I knew there were three letters on most buttons and pqrs with four was an exception. Then I went back to 's'. So far so good. I had my SOS message.

I really had to think now. I pressed the top

left button again. I thought that was 'options', and then again for 'send'. Then I was stuck. You got a chance to search the alphabetical list of contacts next. I pressed the top left button again. It felt right. I hadn't a clue where Steve would come in the list, but he sure as hell wasn't at the top. I pressed the 's' key four times, knowing that brought up the 'S's'. I was concentrating really hard but my mind went a blank then as I tried to remember how many people I knew starting with 'S'. Sarah and Steve? Could that be all? I pressed the big down key to go down past Sarah to Steve and then top left to select, then the top left key again to send. Then I pressed the top right key a couple of times. You always have to do that to get back to your message so you can send it to someone else. I had hoped my obsession with sending text messages could help me, but I'd got totally muddled by that point so I hit the right hand key in the second row that clears you back to the start and began again.

I went through it all again but this time went down two names under 'S' in my address book in case there was someone in the list before Steve, and hopefully sent the message again. I was going to try one more name when I heard the car door slam and the engine start up. As Simon reversed quickly, I lost hold of the phone. Well, I'd done the best I could. I only hoped I'd managed to send at least one message, and that whoever got it, they would realise it wasn't a joke, and contact the police. Otherwise I was on my own. The message failed to get through to Sarah's home number, which I'd listed as 'Sarah home', as well as to Sarah's mobile, next in the list, because it was turned off. She was shattered at the time and had finally got baby Josh off to sleep and didn't want to be disturbed. Just as well I didn't know, because it was the only hope I could cling to. I'd had a black moment when I was convinced I was going to die, but finding the phone and concentrating on sending the text had kept me going.

I had to believe I'd see Steve again. I'd realised his was the first face I wanted to see, his hug I needed. I'd been a fool to waste time flirting with the idea of a future with Pete.

About five minutes before Simon drove Steve's car with Rach in the boot, out of a quiet cliff top car park on the outskirts of Bridlington, Steve got a call on the radio to say the phone had been traced. His instinct had been to head north from where Claire had been dumped, so he was only about fifteen minutes away from Bridlington and its seafront.

'We've got all patrol units in the area looking for your car, Steve. We'll find it soon, don't worry', Matt tried his best to reassure.

Steve drove as fast as he dared without endangering anyone else. He checked in by radio as he reached Bridlington, and was told, as he expected, that the signal from Rach's phone showed his car to be heading east from Bridlington. He sped around the outskirts of Brid in the direction of Dane's Dyke, calling back to Matt to ask for the North Yorkshire police to send a car down there straight away.

Matt came back on the line. 'A car'll meet you there. Steve. I've got bad news though. We've lost the signal near Sewerby. Let's hope he's at Dane's Dyke.'

A little over ten minutes later, Steve pulled off the main road onto the narrow lane leading to Dane's Dyke. He hoped his instinct was right. After all, there'd been no police presence there for a week or so. But when he pulled into the car park it was empty. A minute later, a patrol car approached from the overspill car park down the side track, and a constable lowered his window. No sign I'm afraid, sir.'

'OK. Thanks. Could you hang around here for a while, please, in case we got here first? They've lost the signal.'

'No problem. You drift in and out of signal range all the time around here. It'll probably pop up again soon.' The constable seemed to know what he was talking about. Steve had been worrying that Simon had found the phone and destroyed it, but consoled himself that it could just be the nearness to the cliffs and the lack of transmitters that had caused the signal to fail.

He set off back to the main road and debated which way to turn. As the signal had been lost near Sewerby, he thought he'd backtrack and try near the Hall. Five minutes or so later, he was pulling into the near-empty car park there, as Matt's voice came through on the radio. Steve was cursing under his breath at drawing a blank again, as he listened to

308

Matt's report. 'The chief inspector's back from the TV appeal, Steve. It's gone out on local radio too. So far all that's happened is we've got hordes of reporters back outside the station, demanding progress and preparing sensational headlines for tomorrow's Hull Daily Mail.'

'The mobile signal's not come back yet?'

'Sorry, no.'

Steve looked at the map before leaving the car park and driving back out to the east again. The signal had been lost at Sewerby but his car wasn't there. Either the car had continued heading east or north. If it'd gone back into Bridlington it would have come back into range again, and south was the sweep of the bay that was the North Sea. He picked east, because north was inland where there were villages and he thought fewer places for a car to go undiscovered. To the east was Flamborough Head, with lots of tiny roads and other than the village of Flamborough itself, very few houses.

'Steve?'

'Yeah.' Steve's hopes rose.

'They've called out the police helicopter from Humberside Airport. It'll be in the area in about fifteen minutes.'

'Thanks. I think he'll have taken her out Flamborough way. Unless he's fooled us all by ditching the phone in the sea at Sewerby and then heading back the way he came.'

'Someone would've seen your car by now, Steve. There aren't that many maroon Alfas on the road.'

Steve knew how easy it was not to see a car right under your nose if it was parked in an underground or supermarket car park but he hoped Matt was right. He had a feeling time was running out for Rach.

23

I was hoping someone was looking for me as a result of my text. I'd found the phone again but the car had driven over some badly rutted ground and it had jolted out of my hand. It felt like we were heading for the middle of nowhere. I hadn't a clue where we were. I did wonder if Steve had gone home for tea and noticed his car was missing. I knew you could track someone down if their phone was on, but of course that only happened if they knew you were missing in the first place. I had no idea that Claire had been found alive and had told of my abduction, nor that a full-scale search was on for me. Before I could reach out for the phone again, the car stopped.

I heard the boot lid open. Despite the tape over my eyes, it seemed to grow a bit brighter. I prayed he'd give me my glasses back. I'm almost as blind as a bat without them and I felt so vulnerable.

'Out you come, darling. You'll look as gorgeous as a model in a moment and I'm going to take some lovely photos of you for my collection. Are you OK? This camera's not quite as good as my other, but it was the best I could get at short notice.'

He lifted me out and propped me against the side of Steve's car. My legs nearly gave way, but then I managed to stand unaided. He untaped my eyes. It was so bright I squinted, even though there wasn't full sun. Somehow I wasn't surprised to see we were on a clifftop. The sea sparkled, waves building. I could just hear the sound of them crashing onto rocks below, above the constant noise of gulls as they landed and took off from ledges out of sight on the cliff face. It was a beautiful place. We were high above a couple of coves, worn by the erosion of the soft white chalk.

The car was parked next to a large wooden shack and I couldn't see what was on the other side as the windows were boarded up. It looked like it might be a café, probably derelict, or at least locked up until the Summer rush. Maybe it opened at weekends after Easter, but it was mid-afternoon on a weekday, so I didn't think anyone would be along to rescue me.

My skin hurt where the tape had been. I don't know about looking like a model, I must have looked a right sight with a red stripe across my face. I didn't want to die, but there wasn't a soul in sight. It was all down to me, then, I thought with my stubborn Yorkshire determination.

As if he read my mind, Simon broke into my thoughts, 'Now don't bother shouting or screaming. There's no-one around for miles. We're at the far edge of a big empty car park, miles away from any houses.' With that he pulled the tape from my mouth. 'Good girl. I can see we're going to get on well. Now I'll help you get changed while the redness of your skin fades'.

'Can I have my glasses back, please?'

'No, I don't think so. You look better without. They're nice and safe in the glove compartment. I'll look after them for you.'

The chilling realisation hit me that he would keep them safe – they'd be the souvenir he kept of my murder. He didn't yet know that his little binder with its pathetic remnants of pretty girls' lives had been discovered. Well, I wasn't about to become his next victim. At least I wasn't trapped in an isolated cottage. I might be far from civilisation, but I wasn't imprisoned within four walls, and the first chance I got, I'd make a break for it.

He brought out a cheap carrier bag and opened it. Inside I could see garish red nylon. I remembered the tarty underwear in the photos left at the murder scenes. I knew my best chance was to play along with him in the hope he let his guard down and I could try to escape, so I kept my mouth shut and waited.

At that moment Steve was driving through Flamborough village and turning right after the church towards South Landing. With still no signal on Rach's mobile he was getting desperate. There were lots of small roads in the area but no wooded areas. Maybe Simon had thrown Rach's phone away. Maybe he'd taken her somewhere already and was hurting her. If Simon'd hurt her, Steve vowed he'd make him regret it every moment for the rest of his life, and if he had his way, it'd be a very short life.

Steve drove faster; far faster than he should have done. He almost missed the sign to turn right and nearly lost control and skidded into the ditch. Reluctantly he forced himself to slow down, at least when cornering. It didn't take long before he pulled into the small car park on the left of the road and scanned it, looking for his maroon Alfa. There were quite a few cars but as at Dane's Dyke and Sewerby, his was not amongst them. There was a small track heading further on down through a wooded area. It said 'No Unauthorised Vehicles', and Steve's hopes rose as he thought Simon might well assume he'd pass undiscovered if he ignored the sign. After driving down to the end though, he had to admit this wasn't the place. He looked at his mobile again. No signal. Rach had to be out here somewhere.

He headed back to Flamborough. Flamborough Head itself juts out into the North Sea, with accessible bays to the north, east and south. You have to go back through Flamborough village to get to each of the bays. There's no short cut or coastal road between them. He'd drawn a blank on the south-facing bay so he stopped at the first junction he reached in the village and read the sign. He could never remember which bay was which until he got there. He'd only been a few times and each time he'd been with Rach. He could picture her in his head, frightened in the boot of his car. He wiped that image away and replaced it with one where she was smiling. He thought of her giggling as they'd played putting at Sewerby a few short weeks previously. He'd never forgive himself if anything happened to her. He'd driven her out to Sunk Island. It was his fault Simon had got her.

That train of thought was getting him nowhere though. He pulled himself together, blinked to clear the image and followed the sign to the lighthouse and Flamborough Head itself. Maybe this would be the place he'd find Rach. It was a wider, straighter road so he drove fast again, indeed almost suicidally so, he realised, when he reached a sharp right-hand bend. He just managed to regain control of the high-powered police car as it came out of the bend and put his foot down again on the straight. He passed the old original rough stone lighthouse and then a few minutes later he saw the coastguard station on his left and the entrance to the car park. There was an attendant on duty and Steve lost his temper when he stepped in front of the car and flagged him down.

'Look, this is a matter of life and death. Get out of my sodding way!'

'There's no need to take that tone of voice. You need a ticket to get past this point.'

'This is a police car for God's sake. Are you blind?'

'I'll still need to see proof before you get through. People'll say anything to avoid paying. You're not in uniform. You might have stolen it.'

Steve had met his sort on many occasions and somehow stopped himself from getting out and flattening the bloke. He fished his warrant card out of his pocket.

'That's fine, Inspector. If I can be of any help at all…'

Steve didn't reply. He was already driving through the barrier and up past the lighthouse into the car park. But there was no sign of his car. He turned and drove round behind the pub into its car park, already cursing his own stupidity. 'Damn!' This place was far too public. He should have realised that the lighthouse attracted too many visitors even this early in the year. He'd forgotten the coastguard station and pub were there too.

He swung the car around and accelerated back towards Flamborough. He passed a track to a golf course. He wasted valuable minutes investigating. That was way too public as well. There was even a caravan site down there.

He prayed he'd find Rach at the North Landing or he'd have run out of ideas. He knew there were other cars on their way, and the helicopter would be overhead soon, but he couldn't help feeling it was down to him, and him alone, to rescue her.

About the time Steve was starting his tour of the bays of Flamborough Head, Simon was removing my jumper and unbuttoning my blouse. I so wished it was Steve doing the helping. I didn't struggle and even tried to smile as Simon undressed me, although the touch of his fingers made my flesh

316

creep. I tried to imagine I was just acting a part. If I got out of this, I told myself, maybe I'd take up amateur dramatics. I could see myself playing some femme fatale. Mind you, I'd never remember the lines, and knowing me, I'd probably trip up over someone's foot and turn it into a farce. That's how I kept myself going through the indignity of being undressed by a murderer. It was so hard not to let my revulsion show, but I owed it to those other girls not to end up like them. I had to be the one who brought it to an end.

'I've never worn red underwear before'. My voice sounded a bit shaky. I'd have to overcome that, if I was to get him talking.

'It really suits you. Makes you look sexy.'

Cheap was more like it. 'Well, thanks for buying me it. I can keep it, can't I?' I had to let him think that I didn't know that he'd killed, and that I was the next victim.

'Course you can. I'm going to get some great photos. Now, that's it. This car's a beauty. It'll make a perfect backdrop to drape you over.' He bent me backwards over the car bonnet. The metal was cold. He stared at my breasts. 'Perfect. And you're turned on. That makes a change.'

The stupid tarty bra had holes in the middle of the cups. I was actually freezing and that was why my nipples were erect, but let him think what he wanted. He was strong, I'd give him that, despite his lanky appearance. He'd held my wrists in an iron grip whilst he'd untied my arms and clumsily put the bra on.

I was desperate to make a break for it and when he turned away with my clothes and shoes, I nearly tried to follow but my legs were still bound together and it was impossible to bend forward off the bonnet. I hoped I'd get a better chance. When he came back he smiled and pulled my nipples. He held up the matching tacky crotchless panties and said, 'You'll look great in a minute', before bending to undo my ankles so he could remove my jeans.

He must have been so intent on thinking what he'd like to do with me, that he forgot the consequences. Instead of keeping my legs taped together whilst he pulled my jeans down, then taping my bare legs again before sliding the jeans over my feet, he just undid the tape and my legs were free. With one foot firmly on the ground I brought my other knee up under his chin and kicked out as hard as I could, hoping for his balls. He yelped. 'You fucking bitch'.

I was off across that field not knowing where I was heading but hoping I could get there before him. The circulation wasn't good in my legs but terror gave me strength. It dawned on me that he might just get in the car and I'd be done for, but no, I could hear him running after me. I had to run close by the cliff to get past the hut, but suddenly I came to a steep drop. I risked a glance over my shoulder. He was still a few strides behind me. I must have inflicted some pain. Good. I swerved to the right and kept on going. He was gaining on me and I knew I couldn't outrun him in bare feet on slippery grass.

Steve pulled into the car park at North Landing. It was big but he saw at a glance that his car wasn't there. There was a large café and again it was far too public. He thumped the steering wheel in frustration. Had his instincts let him down? He'd felt sure Simon would make for the coast and Flamborough seemed the most obvious choice if the signal had disappeared at Sewerby. There wasn't much in the way of seclusion though. He'd remembered the area as being far more isolated than it actually was. He was putting the car in reverse as a voice came on the radio.

'What's your position, Inspector Rose? We're at South Landing and there's no sign of your car.'

'Shit', he muttered to himself. He'd been so bent on his one-man rescue crusade that he'd completely forgotten about anyone else. He should have been calling in with updates on his search and whereabouts. He decided to spare them the news that they'd wasted their visit to the South Landing. 'I've been to the Head and drawn a blank. I've just pulled into North Landing and it's the same here. Sorry for not checking in earlier. We'll have to have a re-think.'

'Just a minute. The helicopter's overhead and I missed that, Sir. What did you say?'

Steve repeated his words as he consulted the ordnance survey map again. He could cut north to Bempton from Flamborough. There was a lane to the cliffs there. Simon did seem to be attracted to coastal spots. That was all Steve was going on. But was his hunch about the coast wrong? If Simon knew he was being hunted down, it really made sense for him to go inland instead. But he might not know about the phone signal that had led them as far as Sewerby. 'I'm heading to Bempton, to the cliffs. The road crosses Dane's Dyke again. There's no car park but maybe he's parked on the road and taken her into trees near there. Could you drive back into Sewerby and head up to Bempton on the other road please? Let's hope the helicopter comes up with something. We could be running out of time.'

The wind whipped my hair into my eyes but I ran on regardless, going on the memory of what I'd been looking at a moment before. Then my left foot slid away from me and I was falling. I grabbed at the wet grass as the cliff crumbled away and somehow clung onto the very edge with my knee locked against a thicker clump of weeds. The erosion on the East Coast is famous. Metres and metres of ground have given way to the steady onslaught of the sea and whole houses have disappeared. I daren't move in case I slid further. That was it. I was a sitting duck for Simon. I turned my head slowly. He was probably waiting to see if I fell, not daring to reach for me in case I pulled him over. I'd do it too. It was kill or be killed now.

He was smiling because I was trapped, but I

could see the anger in his eyes, and I didn't think he was planning to recapture me to take photos, at least not of me alive. He was going to kill me and very soon. He paused for a second or two and then took a stride towards me. As he did, a huge chunk of cliff collapsed. The soil beneath it must have been damp and crumbling. Simon's mouth opened in surprise or shock as he tried, and failed, to grab a handhold on solid ground. The ground beneath him slid away, taking him out of my sight.

Where was he? I risked a glance down towards the cove and could just make out a blur of blue clothing, spreadeagled on the rocks. I never heard him cry out, but if he had, the wind would have carried it away. I found it hard to see without my glasses but I squinted and he didn't seem to be moving. It was a hell of a way down and it looked like he was dead. I couldn't have saved him, even if I'd wanted to. I didn't feel any elation, just an immense sense of relief.

I stayed where I was for several long minutes, then leant over to my right, pulling my left leg very, very slowly up onto the cliff. Gradually I inched away from the cliff edge, spreading my body and therefore my weight, as if I was in danger of being sucked into quicksand, which I was in a way. When I'd moved a couple of feet from the edge, I risked rolling over and over until I was, I hoped, a safe distance from danger. I got to my knees and took gulps of air, finally giving way to emotion and bursting into tears. Then I stood and walked back to the car, keeping as far from the cliff as possible.

I went straight to the glove compartment and my glasses. I was absolutely desperate for the loo, so I grabbed a couple of tissues and went behind the hut. I hadn't been since I was on the front at Hornsea with Steve, which must have been hours, but seemed like days ago. Steve teases me no end about it, but I keep saying one day I'm going to compile a directory of public loos, and other easy-access ones like in supermarket entrances, and it'd sell like hot cakes. No woman would be without one in her glove compartment. Sarah agrees with me, Mum and Gran too. I'd be an overnight best-selling author and make millions!

Feeling much better, I went back to the car and got my phone from the boot. There was no signal. Never mind, I told myself. I was safe now. I'd just pull myself together and drive to the nearest house, wherever it was. I still hadn't a clue where I was. The cliffs looked like those near Flamborough, but there was no car park, no road and nothing I recognised as any of the bays I'd visited. Where else were there cliffs like this? The chalk disappeared near Filey, but there were cliffs just to the south of Scarborough, but nothing like these coves, as far as I knew. Could we be north of Scarborough? Could we have driven that far?

I looked for my blouse and jumper, but they weren't there. They hadn't been in the boot and they weren't in the front. Now that the adrenaline and the heat from running had worn off, I was shivering. I looked under the car and all around. No sign of them. 'Bloody great'. I could only assume the bastard had thrown them over the cliff, knowing I wouldn't need them again once he'd photographed and killed me. He'd have stripped me of the underclothes, and then taken my naked body to dump it somewhere else I supposed.

I got in the driver's seat and decided there was nothing for it but to go as I was. There wasn't so much as a rug in Steve's boot. There was some chocolate left though and I ate it, hoping the sugar boost would help. I thanked heaven I still had my jeans on. I could put the heater on and it wouldn't be so bad. I went to turn on the ignition and got a shock. No keys. Of course, he'd have pocketed them. I suppose I'd been lucky he hadn't locked the car, but where did that leave me? Damn and double damn!

What next? I could set off to walk as I was, no doubt dying of hypothermia if I didn't get lost as night fell or I could scramble down and get the keys, maybe even pick up my clothes on the way, if that's where he'd tossed them, warm up by the car heater and then drive to civilisation .

I could see there was a path leading down the cliff to the cove. It started somewhere on the far side of the hut. It wouldn't be easy going down barefoot, but there again it would have been difficult in stilettos. I thought of my lovely shoes thrown somewhere at the bottom of the cliff and I made my choice. In about an hour it'd be dark but I could be down the cliff and back up in that time.

I set off carefully but it was chilly out of the sun and I speeded up the nearer I got to the beach. As I picked my way across the large boulders at the bottom, towards where Simon's body lay, my foot slipped on the slippery seaweed and I fell.

Steve hadn't set off immediately. He was trying to decide where to go next. He spoke to Matt at the station, 'Have you any ideas, or shall we go with Bempton, Matt?'

'Seems as good an idea as any, boss', came the reply, so he set off back to Flamborough, to pick up the Bempton road, the B1229. He'd only gone a few hundred yards when Matt was back on the radio.

'Steve! The helicopter's spotted your car. It's at Thornwick Bay.'

'Where's that?' Steve'd never heard of it, but he wasn't local and hadn't visited every part of this coastline.

'Only about a third of a mile from North Landing. If you drive slowly towards Flamborough, there's a track, not even a lane, off to the right. In summer there's a sign out and the owner collects a fair few bob in car parking fees. Used to be a café there once, but it's been derelict a long while. Your car's parked up behind it, at the very end of the track.'

'I'm on my way. Any sign of Rach?'

'The helicopter thinks there's someone in the car but it's stationary. They'll keep an eye on it and follow it if it sets off. They can't land on the clifftop there as it's all uneven and full of ruts and holes, but you're very close. They're going to drop someone down on a winch to the beach.'

'Why?'

'Steve, I'm afraid it looks like there's a body down there. I didn't want to tell you, but I had to, before you got there. Be careful, and Steve, don't do anything stupid, will you?'

Steve's blood ran cold. He didn't answer Matt. He had a lump in his throat but couldn't give way to tears. There'd be time for that soon enough. He took a deep breath and knew what he had to do. He was going to kill Simon.

He raced off, then thought better of it. He couldn't risk missing the turning. As it was, he overshot the opening slightly, but soon he'd turned off the road onto the track towards the cliffs. The track was dreadful. Even though he was in a hurry, he accepted that he couldn't go more than five miles an hour over most of it. Deep craters pock-marked the area and he had to steer round them, the car sliding in and out of the deep ruts.

He saw the hut at the far end of the track, and behind it, his car. It looked empty. He got out and saw Rach's phone on the seat, a purple chocolate wrapper, but nothing else. He tried the boot, but that was empty too. The view was spectacular but that didn't register with him as he walked to the edge of the cliff, fearful of what he'd see - and there she was, lying dead on the rocks below. She was too far away to see clearly but he'd recognise her unruly hair anywhere. He felt so incredibly sad. He didn't think he'd ever feel happy again.

And then she moved. 'Rach! Rach!' he shouted, but the wind whipped away his words. She was alive and that was all that mattered. He looked around for the start of the path and ran towards it.

In the morning I'd have a massive bruise on my knee where I'd smacked it against a boulder when I tripped, but luckily that was all that was hurt. I struggled on across the bottom of the cliff, oblivious of everything (including a noisy police helicopter, so I was informed later – but the wind was howling and that's my excuse!), till I reached Simon. He'd fallen with his legs hanging down backwards over a large boulder. I couldn't see any blood, but I couldn't see him breathing either. I had to stretch out, almost my full length to reach his pocket, arching my body over his head so I didn't touch him. That's why Steve thought I was lying down there dead, we realised later.

As I got the key from his pocket, his legs moved and I screamed. He was alive after all. I expected him to reach up and grab me like in some grisly horror film, but he didn't. His head and upper torso didn't move. His legs moved again and this time I could see they were being washed gently in and out by the tide, where his feet hung between the rocks. I pulled myself back upright and turned back to the path, to be faced with the most wonderful sight I could ever have imagined. Steve. He was running hell for leather down the steep path, shouting my name, or so I realised when he was near enough for the wind not to take his words away.

I hobbled off the rocks and onto the path and fell into his arms. God, I love a happy ending, don't you?

After he'd held me tight for ages, he loosened his grip, holding me at arm's length.

'What the hell are you wearing? You must be freezing, love. And your poor feet.'

I looked down. My bare feet were red and all shades of black, no doubt a mix of dirt and bruises. I was wearing the tacky red bra with the holes in it, and my jeans. Steve wasn't wearing a jacket but insisted on taking off his shirt and fastening it gently around me. Then he picked me up and carried me up the path.

'It's steep, Steve. Let me walk. I'm too heavy for you to carry all the way up there. I'm OK. I rescued myself. I only went down there for your car keys because I didn't know how far it was to walk to the nearest house and it was getting dark. Where are we anyway and how did you know where to find me? And what the hell did that Simon do with my clothes?'

Steve stopped me from talking by pausing to kiss me. 'First things first. Let's get you up to the top and into my nice warm police car. Then I'll tell you everything I know, and you can do the same. Is that a deal?'

'Suppose so.' I had to admit it was probably a good idea, but now I was safe I was dying to know all the answers. The police helicopter was still hovering overhead. They wouldn't have to risk winching anyone down now. The body could be recovered up the cliff path, or if necessary attached by the police to a stretcher and winched into the helicopter. The tide was going out so they'd probably wait for a police doctor to go out and certify him dead, and for forensics to take photographs, though they'd have my witness statement. A chill thought struck me.

'Steve. I didn't kill him. I know I would have done if I'd been forced into it, but I didn't. He slipped when he was chasing me. I swear. They won't think I did, will they?'

He kissed me again. 'Hush, Rach. No-one's going to accuse you of anything, though I'm glad for your sake that you didn't have to kill him.'

We were soon back at the car. It may have been a steep path but Steve was determined to do his share of rescuing me and he's got the strongest leg muscles of any man I know. There were other cars in the car park. As I'd thought, some officers were on their way to secure the area around the body, and the others seemed to be waiting for orders. I was suddenly conscious of the fact that I was wearing next-to-nothing under Steve's shirt, which was a fine muslin-type cotton and didn't do much for my modesty.

'Do you think someone could find my clothes, please, Steve? I think he must have thrown them over the side of the cliff. I couldn't see them on my way down, but maybe they didn't go too far.'

Steve sent someone to look. No-one had a

rug or anything similar, but I was soon in the warm police car, wearing someone's jacket. I wanted to go home, but I wanted my clothes too. I decided to wait five minutes then beg to leave the place. It was beautiful, but at that moment I was having a hard time taking in the beauty. I couldn't see past the horror of what had happened there. Someone found my blouse and jumper partway down the cliff.

'Can I take off this tacky bra, Steve? It won't spoil any chain of evidence or anything, will it?'

'No, you're OK. Just wait a tick while I get an evidence bag to put it in.'

He ushered the other officers away to give me some privacy to change. My own bra was still missing but I felt better without the slutty bra, just in a blouse and jumper. I handed Steve back his shirt. I felt almost human again. Then it struck me.

'My shoes, Steve! My beautiful red stilettos! You've got to find them!'

'Calm down, Rach. It's getting dark now. They're bringing lights to finish up on the beach before they move the body, but I think your shoes will have to wait till morning. I'll leave strict instructions that they are to be tracked down at first light and returned to my heroine, though.' We had to leave Steve's car on the clifftop. It would be taken back to the police garage on a transporter and forensically searched, but with Simon dead, Steve thought they wouldn't keep it too long. So we drove back to his flat in the police car. 'I've spent hours today in this car, most of them bad, but driving you home in it more than makes up for all the rest. Your statement will wait till tomorrow and my shift ended hours ago so I'll call in and tell the Chief Inspector I'm calling it a day.' Then he turned off his mobile. 'I'm not turning that back on till tomorrow. I'm all yours now.'

I started to tell him all that had happened to me from the moment I'd left the cottage at Sunk Island but I was shattered and nodded off somewhere along the way. As a result, the journey back to his flat didn't seem to take long, and soon Steve was helping me out of the car. I felt naked without my bag. Thankfully Simon had thrown it out of the car when he left Claire, so I didn't have the trauma of losing its contents. Steve put his arm round my shoulders, led me into his flat and guided me to the settee.

'Do you want a shower first or would you rather eat?'

'Eat. I'm starving.'

'That's what I thought.' He'd gone through the drive-through MacDonald's for food on the way home and I hadn't even noticed. He put a plate and a mug down in front of me, and we ate, so hungry we didn't talk again until the plates were empty. Then Steve looked up and grinned. 'Do you know something? If you weren't such a chocaholic and stopped at that shop, you wouldn't have been given directions to take you past the phone box in time to stop Simon killing Claire.'

'Claire. Oh God, I'd forgotten about her. Is she OK?'

'She's fine, considering what she's been through. I know it took us a while to track you down, but it was because you were a more exciting proposition that Simon left Claire bound and gagged in that field. He would have finished strangling her if it hadn't been for you.'

'A while! It was an eternity.' I woke from my trance and hit him with a cushion.

'Maybe I should tie you up to stop you hitting me.'

I hit him harder. I was horrified. 'That's a dreadful thing to say. It makes me think of all the girls he tied up with chains.'

'Sorry sweetheart. Cop humour. I don't need ropes.' He pulled me gently into his arms and kissed me. I started to relax. 'I've my own handcuffs'.

He leant back, as if to duck the cushion, but I pulled him towards me. I might have been a bit bruised and battered, but I needed holding close and as Steve soon discovered, I was more than ready for him. We decided to share a shower. Well, that's not strictly true. There was no deciding involved. Steve undressed me (because I was tired, you understand) and then he had to hold me up and soap me and rinse me, so it made sense for him to get in too. We were almost past the point of no return when a phone rang.

'Not your bloody mobile again, Steve.'

'No. It's yours for once. I turned mine off, remember. Now, finally, yours has decided it's going to have a signal.'

'It might be Sarah. I sent her an SOS text message, or at least I think I did. She'll be worried.'

'OK. Let me get it for you. You need to get dry and into bed.' He looked at the caller ID and answered, 'Hello.... No, this is Steve, her boyfriend... Sorry, no, she can't. She's going to be tied up for a while. All night, in fact. Yeah, I'll tell her Pete rang.' He ended the call, turned off the phone and tossed it on the settee. 'Now, where were we?'